D0640610

Schooling Carmen

By Kathleen Cross

SCHOOLING CARMEN
SKIN DEEP

Don't miss the next book by your favorite author.
Sign up now for AuthorTracker by visiting
www.AuthorTracker.com.

Schooling Carmen

Kathleen Cross

AVON

An Imprint of HarperCollins*Publishers*

SCHOOLING CARMEN. Copyright © 2004 by Kathleen Cross. All rights reserved. Printed in the United States of America. No part of this book may be used or reproduced in any manner whatsoever without written permission except in the case of brief quotations embodied in critical articles and reviews. For information address HarperCollins Publishers Inc., 10 East 53rd Street, New York, NY 10022.

Designed by Elizabeth M. Glover

ISBN 0-7394-4661-4

On October 2, 2002, Todd Barr,
my fiancé, best friend, confidant,
counselor, and the love of my life,
answered a call for help from a friend
sucked out to sea by a violent riptide.

Without hesitation, Todd ran into the waves.

Though his friend's life was saved, Todd was
pulled under by what officials called
"the strongest rip currents of the season."

He did not survive.

I am left to drown now
in this ocean of dreams, memories,
poems, lyrics, inside jokes, movie quotes,
and *cartoon owl impersonations* ☺
that can never be physically resurrected
or adequately shared with anyone in this life.

This book is dedicated to the memory of you,
my soul mate, and the only human being
I can honestly say really knew me.

You are my Layla, Todd.
I am trying hard to bless the watchman,
and I will not rest until I find you again.

—Love forever, Blue
28♥28♥28♥28♥28

Acknowledgments

To all of you who called or prayed or just sent good thoughts my way, please know that you are the biggest part of the reason this book *is*. Thank you all. You know who you are.

There are many whose contribution to this effort consisted of some specific needs being filled—mostly unasked, always without expectation of anything being received in return. I honor those people here:

My daughters, Khalia, Melody, and Akira, without whom I would not have survived one very trying year. Thank you, Akira, for the countless hours you spent listening to the original drafts of this book, Melody, for always urging me to write when it seemed the most impossible thing to do, and Khalia, for knowing exactly how to love a mother in mourning.

My family, Mike, Linda, Eugene, Todd, Candy, Kerry, Uncle Greg, and Mom. Despite my tendency to be the hermit of the family, you all never stopped pulling for me.

Shilloy Sanchez, who, unasked, single-handedly spearheaded the tour for my first novel, *Skin Deep*—I never got a chance to thank you adequately; I'm not even sure putting it in print here represents my sincere appreciation for what you did back then.

Rita Ewing, author of *Homecourt Advantage*. Thank you for my very first literary review.

The first prereaders of *Schooling Carmen*. Todd Barr, Laura Coleman, Laura Ramos, Lauren London, and Shilloy Sanchez. It's been a long stretch of time since those first few chapters were typed and previewed by you all—thank you for caring how Carmen's story took shape and for your feedback—a special thanks to Laura Ramos for the Spanish lessons. Lauren—I used your last name in this book, did you notice? Faith Holmes—thanks for your help at the finish line.

Oscar Barnes. Who knew a phone call and a challenge would lead to so much? You are one of the main reasons I finished this book.

Billy, Cora Jean and Melanie Barr. If there is anyone who doubts the power of love, encouragement, and prayer—*talk to one of them.*

Joyce Germaine Watts. I will always appreciate you for constantly expanding the way I see the world and my role in it. Carmen learned many things you taught me.

Phyllis Hart. Your support I can't even begin to describe, but I think you know. You've always believed in me.

The network of amazing booksellers, book clubs, and organizations that support the reading and writing of good books. Tia Shabazz (Black Writers Alliance), Pamela Walker Williams (the Good Book Club and the Summit at Sea), Kimberly Hines (It's Like Butta Baby), Shonell Bacon (Nubian Chronicles), Emma Rodgers (Black Images), Zahra's Books, RAW SISTAZ, Page Turners, Sistah Friends, and far too many more to mention here (see www.kathleencross.com).

The many authors who have influenced, encouraged, or inspired me to write: Haydar Ali, Asha Bandele, Tiffany DeBartolo, Dannion Brinkley, Octavia Butler, Evelyn Coleman, Eric Dickey, Rita Ewing, Thomas Green, Howard Colby Ives, Barbara Kingsolver, Dawn Knight, Nathan McCall, Victor McGlothin, Trisha Thomas, Pat D'George Walker . . . I'd better stop; this list could fill an entire book.

My agent, Denise Stinson. Has anyone ever told you you are really good at fussing at folks over the phone?☺ Your encouragement, patience, advice, expertise, and support are more appreciated than you could know.

My editor, Carrie Feron. In the dictionary next to the word "patience," your picture must be there. Thanks for giving Carmen and me the time we needed to complete our journey.

To T. J. and Amanda Barr, I pray you understand the incredible human being your father was. He loved you more than you will ever know—he is the main reason I am an author. I will always be grateful to him.

⇛ 1 ⇚

Never-Never Land

Carmen DuPrè lifted her Diet Coke up into the darkness and sent a silent wish to whomever there might be in the universe with the power to dole out desperately needed favors. *Can I get some damn mercy down here?*

Seated on a discarded student desk in a darkened storage room, she swallowed her drink in long, slow sips, sending icy relief to her worn-out vocal cords. *Two and a half hours locked in an auditorium crowded with out-of-control ninth graders. Am I a counselor or a damn baby-sitter?*

She leaned back against the cool cement wall, basking in the brief escape she'd found from the sights, sounds, and smells she was forced to endure day in and day out in her job as a guidance counselor at an overcrowded, understaffed, academically pitiful, mostly Latino high school on the outer edge of East Los Angeles.

Carmen hated her job. She hated the irritating racket of Spanish rock and gangster rap music blaring from the parade of brightly painted lowriders as they screeched into the parking lot each morning to let out their smoking, cursing passengers. She hated the wafting odors of the burritos, churritos, taquitos and every other kind of food ending with "ito" the cafeteria served up day in and day out. She hated the way every damn thing she said had to be repeated in Spanish for some parent or student who Carmen wished would just buckle down and learn the damn language of the United States. She hated the graffiti that covered the lockers, doors, walls, and windows of Overland High—grafitti that seemed to magically reappear no matter how many times it was painted over by the custodians. But most of all she hated the bigwigs in the district office for having assigned her—Carmen DuPrè—to the damn hellhole in the first place.

If only her daddy were still alive. Carmen would never have had to step foot on Overland's campus if Wilfred DuPrè had not left his daughter alone in the district to fend for herself. With his twenty-two years in local politics and his popularity with both the school board and the teachers' union, Will DuPrè would have made sure his daughter began her career at a school somewhere on the Westside. The Leadership Academy, or perhaps Beverly Hills High. But Dr. DuPrè had been dead nearly three years, and though the folks in personnel knew good and damn well Carmen was his daughter, somehow they'd sent her to what just about everyone in the district referred to as "the war zone."

The only reasonable conclusion Carmen could come up with for her exile to the Eastside was that some bitch in central administration was jealous of her. What other explanation could there be for Carmen ending up at Overland? By her own measure she was overqualified for the place. She'd earned her bachelor's degree in English from Spelman, though that didn't seem to impress the powers-that-be making hiring decisions, nor did the fact that she had both a teaching credential and a counseling certification. Nearly half the teachers at Overland were hired on "emergency status," with no teaching credential or experience. Carmen didn't appreciate being treated like she was one of *those*. Before Overland she'd spent two very trying years teaching third grade math, and it seemed only reasonable to her that with actual classroom experience under her belt, she should have at least had an automatic "in" at a school in the Valley. Instead she had been assigned to a campus that was perpetually on the list of the ten worst schools in the city, a school the staff had sarcastically dubbed "Never-Never Land."

"Never-Never" certainly seemed an appropriate name for the place. A big, fat "never" was exactly what Carmen experienced on a daily basis in her job. She never heard so much as a whisper of support from her coworkers, who constantly reminded Carmen how lucky she was not to have to stand in front of a classroom all day. She never got a chance to get her name and photograph in the education section of the newspaper like those Westside counselors did when more than twenty percent of their seniors were accepted into colleges and universities. In the year and a half since she'd begun the job at Overland, she'd never had one student—not even among the honors classes—that she believed had the potential to apply, let alone be accepted, at an Ivy League school. And worst of all, she never got a chance to brag to anyone in her family about anything that had to do with her lackluster job. What made matters worse was that Carmen was forced to listen to story after story from the rest of the overachieving DuPrè family about the glamorous and lucrative aspects of their careers.

Carmen's brother, Maxwell, was an entertainment lawyer; her older sister, Della, sold high-end real estate; Lindsey, the youngest of the four, was a software designer; and DuPrè cousins all across the country held positions that ranged from airplane pilot to obstetrician. And then there was Carmen.

It wasn't that she hadn't tried other occupations before settling for a job in education. She'd taken her English degree and her sassy attitude to Boeing, Weyerhaeuser, Amgen and a dozen other corporations in Southern California. She'd even tried to get her foot in the door at a few of the movie studios in Hollywood, but none of them was willing to give her a job with a starting salary she could accept. She finally decided that a job as a high school guidance counselor might be the best alternative for her for the time being. If she worked hard, was nice to the right people, and dropped her father's name in the right places, she just knew she could make her way up the administrative ranks to one day become the superintendent of the whole school system. The current superintendent earned a quarter of a million dollars a year, along with some hefty perks that included an on-call driver and a fat expense account.

Carmen was confident she would someday fit in with the rest of the successful DuPrès, but for now her job was a constant source of humiliation at family gatherings. No matter how she tried to package herself to the rest of them, she could never find a way to shine, and when she was in the company of her family, she would quietly slink off into a corner when they began bragging about their prestigious careers.

Guidance counseling at Overland High was certainly far from prestigious. According to her job description, Carmen was being paid to help prepare students for college, but more often than not she found her day filled with discipline referrals, suspensions, expulsions, and transfers. She had just transferred another pregnant girl to the nearby alternative high school that very morning—just a few minutes before the assistant principal gruffly informed Carmen she was expected to help with winter term registration. After shouting the English version of registration instructions to a crowd of sweaty, noisy, and clearly disinterested ninth graders, Carmen had at last managed to make her escape to the dark, eight-by-twelve storage room for a much needed cold drink and a break from the morning madness. A break Carmen hoped could last at least another ten minutes.

"Excuse please." A sliver of light at the door spread into a ten-inch-wide beam as one of the school janitors poked his head into Carmen's refuge. "Miss DuPrè?"

Carmen closed her eyes and silently wished him away. She

had no desire to hear whatever message it was Ricardo had come to relay. Someone in the main office had probably sent him with a so-called urgent demand that had come straight from Principal Schuyler's mouth. Schuyler's office manager, Anita; Anita's receptionist, Rosa; and even the office assistant, whatever her name was, were all known for using Ricardo to run their little errands for them.

When Ricardo's eyes settled on Carmen, he smiled sincerely at her, his gold-rimmed front tooth glistening in the dim light. "Excuse, miss. I have message for you from Rosa. She say I tell you is muy importante."

"Yeah, Ricardo. Isn't it always?"

Ricardo gazed serenely at Carmen, nodding his head in agreement with her question. "Si. Yes. Is always emergency, yes?"

She took note of the look of admiration on Ricardo's face and decided not to give him too much eye contact. She had made that mistake before with one of the Hispanic teachers on campus, and the man asked her out on a date. As if she could ever consider bringing a Mexican home to meet Mavis DuPrè. Hah. That would be the day. Mavis would surely oust her right out of the DuPrè family.

"What's the emergency this time, Ricardo?" Carmen asked in her driest tone.

"Rosa say you have important messages. Emergency. She say come to her desk, por favor"—he quickly translated—"please."

"Sure," Carmen replied tersely. She felt a twinge of guilt at taking her irritation out on the man. He didn't ask to be the designated gofer. She softened her tone and added, "Tell Rosa I'll stop by her desk before lunch."

Ricardo backed apologetically out of the door, pulling it gently until the beam of light narrowed into a tiny sliver.

Carmen sighed heavily. *Emergency?* No doubt Dr. Lee had called again. Carmen had scheduled, canceled, and rescheduled with her gynecologist three times in the last month and a half, and the doctor had been leaving messages for Carmen every other day for a week. *The woman acts like she doesn't have any other patients besides me.*

Carmen took another swig of Diet Coke and evicted the thought of Dr. Lee from her mind—that was an avoidable bridge she'd cross only when she absolutely had to—and she didn't have to do anything at the moment but hold on to her hideout for as long as possible. Closing her eyes and pressing her back to the coolness of the cement wall, she savored the peace and quiet she'd found. She knew it wouldn't be long before her solitude would be shattered again. It was inevitable. If Gordon Iverson, the obnoxious though amusing varsity basketball coach, didn't find her, Eugene Timms, the semihandsome but clueless chair of the math department, would.

From the day Carmen stepped foot on the Overland campus, she had become the much sought after prize in a furiously fought attention-getting contest between the two men. Although other men on campus had shown a timid interest in her, Iverson and Timms were ahead of the pack, jockeying for position on Carmen's calendar. And since Gordon had season tickets for the Lakers—*courtside*—and Eugene was the deputy superintendent's nephew, so far the two men were neck-and-neck in the competition.

And, boy, was it a competition. Since the beginning of the

school year Gordon and Eugene had been making Olympian efforts to outdo each other. They brought Carmen little cards and gifts at least once a week, leaving them rather conspicuously on top of her locker in the staff lounge. They had both sent flowers to her home. Gordon had even gone as far as to sneak the keys to Carmen's Lexus one morning, and when she got in her car at the end of the day, she found that he had taken it to the gas station for a fill-up during his lunch break— and left a single red rose on the dash.

Though Carmen didn't really care too deeply for either of the men, she saw no reason to put a stop to any of it—at least not right away. Now and then a little voice invaded her conscience—a faint whisper of a voice that tried to convince her she should be ashamed of herself for using them—but she'd simply chase that voice away by telling herself the two deserved whatever using they got. Why should she feel sorry for them when she knew exactly why they were hanging around?

Carmen was what folks—usually men—liked to refer to as drop-dead gorgeous. Her parents must have known she was going to turn out to be beautiful, because they'd had the foresight to name her after that Carmen in the old Dorothy Dandridge musical. And, when it came to looks, Carmen DuPrè might even have had Dorothy outdone. Green-eyed and honey-complexioned, with long legs, an ample bosom, and a narrow waist, she was the kind of beautiful that made men whisper "dayyum" under their breath when she walked by. Men with a hunger for beautiful women went after Carmen with a vengeance, and, as far as she was concerned, if one of those ravenous wolves got his little paws stepped on in the process, shame on 'im.

Carmen's sister Della believed Carmen's four years at Spelman had made her "beyond conceited." To hear Della tell it, those years of being fought over by the "Morehouse maniacs" had turned her sister into a self-serving beauty queen; but Carmen would simply respond to Della's analysis with a flippant *"College did not make me conceited, Dell. It made me convinced."* By the end of Carmen's sophomore year, when she snagged "Morehouse's most wanted," a six-foot-six ebony god named Randall Winston, nobody could tell her she wasn't *all that* and then some.

Randall was fashion-model gorgeous, incredibly intelligent, and impossible not to worship. When they began dating, Carmen was sure she had finally accomplished something her mother would be proud of. She just knew Mavis would be offering a slew of *thank-yous* to Jesus, Mary, and all the patron saints she whispered to for sending a prize like Randall her daughter's way. But when Carmen brought her man home that first Christmas, his skin tone was the only thing about him Mavis seemed to be able to focus on. Though Carmen's father took an instant liking to Randall, Mavis treated him with cool disdain. It didn't make one bit of difference to Mavis that Randall was articulate, charming, and ambitious; she rejected him on pigment and hair texture alone, which Carmen considered beyond ridiculous.

"You better not marry that blue black man, Carmen," her mother had warned, *"The last thing I want is a crowd of little nappy-headed grandchildren in our family photographs."* Mavis laughed when she said it, but Carmen knew she wasn't kidding.

Figuring out how to please Mavis remained an unsolved mystery to Carmen, but the one thing she knew for certain was that to Mavis, appearance was everything. As far back as Carmen could remember, there was only one thing about her Mavis had ever found worthy of praise—her looks.

"I do believe this daughter of ours must be the most beautiful child on earth, Wilfred," Mavis would boast as she fingered Carmen's curly locks. "Carmen Marie, you have the prettiest hair," Mavis would croon as she watched Carmen brush her hair each morning. "Carmen, honey, come in here and show Mrs. Gibson the tiara you won in the Jack and Jill beauty pageant."

The last thing Carmen wanted to do was be on Mavis's bad side, but Randall Winston was the man of her dreams, and she had no intention of ever losing him. Without telling her family, she moved into Randall's Atlanta apartment at the end of her junior year at Spelman and managed to keep their living arrangements secret. After graduation Carmen accepted a position teaching third grade math at a local Atlanta public school while Randall finished his law degree at Emory. But when the two lovebirds moved to a nest back in Los Angeles, Carmen realized there was no way to hide the fact that she and Randall were living together. She had no choice but to sit her parents down and tell them the truth. Her father calmly voiced his disappointment, but Mavis loudly swore she would never forgive or forget.

"What kind of women moves in with a man who doesn't have enough decency to marry her first?" Mavis shouted furiously. "You are a disgrace to this family Carmen Du—"

Mavis clutched the string of pearls around her neck and glared at her daughter. "No. You will be Carmen *Marie* in this house from now on. You will *never* hear me call you a DuPrè again as long as I live."

Wilfred DuPrè wasn't having that.

"DuPrè is *my name*, Mavis," Wilfred shouted at his wife. "Don't you tell my daughter it doesn't belong to her. Don't you dare."

Wilfred died in a tragic car accident two days after that argument. At the funeral, when all the DuPrè children crowded around their weeping mother, Carmen stood alone outside their tight mourning circle with tears streaming from her eyes. If Randall hadn't felt sorry for her and gently led her to a seat nearby, Carmen might have stood there until the church closed, and Mavis wouldn't have noticed.

The year following her father's death, Carmen was struck by another unexpected tragedy—Randall suddenly and heartlessly dumped her. Though he offered her a weak attempt at an apology, he had given her no logical reason for the breakup. How the man managed to sweet talk her into making love to him the morning the movers came, she still hadn't been able to make sense of. He held her tenderly in his arms, stroked her hair, and whispered her name. Then changed the locks and got a restraining order against Carmen when she found it difficult at first to stay away.

Nearly two years had passed since their breakup, and she didn't get the urge to drive by his house anymore. She felt stupid about the windows she'd broken and the tires she'd pounded nails into. She was sorry she threw bleach on his front lawn, and she really regretted spray painting, "A LYING MOTHERFUCKER LIVES HERE" in fluorescent orange on his garage door.

Mavis surprised everyone in the family by not mentioning a word of it—ever. When Carmen got dumped by Randall, she was sure her mother would take advantage of the opportunity to rub some I-told-you-so salt in her wounds, but Mavis never mentioned Randall's name again. Instead she adopted a strange habit of trying to hook Carmen up with any and all of her friends' single sons.

"You're not getting any younger you know, Carmen," Mavis would suddenly spout in the middle of a conversation—right before she went through her list of son-in-law prospects. *"Trudy Wilson's son Lamont is single, you know. Or how about Misty and Frank Gravenburg's son Joshua? Now, there's a man running his own company. He'll make a great husband, and he's so handsome too."*

Carmen didn't pay attention to Mavis and her matchmaking, and the last thing she wanted was a handsome husband. After the vicious way Randall had shattered her heart, she had no intention of ever hooking up with another exceptionally good-looking man. All she had to do was see a gorgeous man coming, and she could feel all the little hairs on the back of her neck stand straight up. Date a handsome man? Not a chance. When it came down to it, Carmen wasn't interested in competing with some fine man for attention, and she certainly wasn't trying to jump through any hoops to show how "grateful" she was supposed to be for being "chosen" by one.

Since Randall, Carmen had been content to stick with the

average crowd; that way she always knew where she stood—way up high on a pedestal—where she belonged. Which explained why she even bothered to give a couple of low-budget high school teachers like Gordon Iverson and Eugene Timms the time of day.

Sitting alone in the dark in her little hideout, Carmen wondered which of the two would find her first. The thought had barely materialized when she heard a soft knock and a whisper outside the door.

"Psst. Carmen?"

Eugene. Damn. I knew he couldn't leave me be.

"Are you in there, sweetheart?"

He knows better than to call me sweetheart. She tilted her Diet Coke to her lips and let its sweet coolness flow over her tongue.

Timms entered the room slowly, inching his way toward the small desk where Carmen, in navy slacks and a red silk blouse, was comfortably perched.

"There you are, sweetheart. I thought I might find you here."

"Eugene," Carmen responded saltily, "how many times have I asked you not to call me sweetheart?"

She hated to be mean to the man after he had been such a gentleman with her. Each of their dates he brought her flowers, and he never complained when she refused to go any further than a good-night peck. With his flawless pecan-toned skin, decent cheekbones, and beautiful dark eyes, Eugene actually was bordering on handsome. He might have had a chance at being a ladies' man if he had even a slight clue how to be smooth. But the unfortunate reality was, Eugene had been camped out in nerdsville far too long to ever turn into any kind of Casanova. Overall he was pretty harmless, but he seemed to always do something to get on Carmen's last nerve, like refusing to remember not to call her sweetheart.

"I'm so sorry, swee—" Eugene stifled a nervous laugh and straddled Carmen's outstretched legs. Taking the Coke from her hand and setting it on a bookshelf nearby, he wrapped both arms around her and kissed her forehead. "I mean . . . I'm sorry, Carmen, you have asked me not to call you that."

Carmen breathed in the scent of spicy aftershave. "Eugene," she complained as he kissed her left cheek. "Not at school. You know I don't like that."

Eugene planted a quick peck on Carmen's lips, then backed quickly away from her. "Sorry. This better?" He stood with his hands held behind his back. His gray plaid shirt was buttoned clear up to his neck and tucked neatly into a pair of black vintage polyester slacks, which were belted at his thick waist with a brown faux-crocodile belt. Along with the wire-rimmed glasses and pouting bottom lip, it all made him look like a little boy in trouble with his mommy. It was making Carmen nauseous.

"Are you going to need me to give you a ride home after work again today?" His wide-eyed expression said he hoped so.

"I damn sure better not," she snapped. "That mechanic is *supposed* to deliver my car this afternoon." Carmen's reply came out much harsher than she'd intended. She didn't have any real reason to be so curt with Eugene; at times he just seemed to bring out the bitch in her.

Eugene muttered quietly, "We st-still on for tonight?" His eyes begged Carmen to confirm.

"Mmn hmnh." She managed to soften her tone. "We're still on. But I can't be out too late." She pointed a sculpted fingernail at her out-of-reach Coke can, wordlessly demanding he return it to her. He quickly obeyed, glad for the chance to stand nearer.

Eugene watched her lift the can to her lips, his eyes glinting with what looked like envy—as if he wished it were he, not the sweet brown liquid, that had the honor of quenching Carmen's thirst.

"It—it's just a little dinner party. My uncle is having some administrator-types over to celebrate the construction of the new district offices."

"Sounds like a blast," Carmen muttered dryly. She took another swig of Coke.

"The contractor will be there, and some school board members. Word is the superintendent is going to show up."

Carmen nearly choked on her mouthful of Coke. *The superintendent?* She had been hoping for a private audience with Dr. Browning since she'd heard about a counseling position opening up at the district's Talented and Gifted Academy. Carmen wanted that position—bad. She was sick of Overland High. Sick of working with a bunch of kids who were perfectly content to be heading down a path to nowhere and even more content to depend on Carmen to help get them there. Carmen fantasized daily about being in that position as head college counselor for gifted students. Never mind this hellhole full of barely literate hooligans. That TAG school was filled with kids whose parents wanted better for them, and their ninety-nine percent graduation rate and ninety-five percent college-going rate proved just that. If Carmen got that job, she could actually sit across the counseling table from some kids who had a real chance to be accepted at a university. And wouldn't Mavis be pleased if Carmen could find a way to get promoted?

Eugene interrupted her thoughts with a loud sigh. "Um, well, Carmen, I guess a meeting with a bunch of district folks is not quite what you had in mind for this evening. We don't have to go to my uncle's if you don't want to. Would you rather go to a movie?"

She smiled softly at him. So what if he wasn't a ladies' man? At least he knew Carmen's value. Though she didn't see anything spectacular when she looked at Eugene, he had a nice enough smile, beautiful eyes, and a clean-shaven face that made him appear to be a few years younger than the thirty-six years he was. He was a stocky man, just under six feet tall, barrel-chested, with a thickness that made him look healthy and masculine without looking fat.

Carmen smiled coyly, staring seductively into his eyes, which were fixed on hers expectantly. She doubted Eugene had any idea how excited she was by the evening he'd arranged—*an opportunity to be in the same room with the district superintendent?*

She raised one eyebrow at him teasingly, her face lit softly by the glow of fluorescent light from the slightly opened door behind him. She reached forward and, grabbing the buckle on his belt, gently pulled him toward her.

"I'm really looking forward to spending this evening with you, Eugene. That dinner party sounds nice. I was thinking of wearing that burgundy pantsuit you like so much."

A broad smile stretched across Eugene's face. His eyes settled for a split second on Carmen's cleavage, which was peeking from the topmost button of her blouse. "I do," he said, trying not to speak to her bosom. He looked up at her face. "I do like that pantsuit. That burgundy makes your eyes shine like emeralds. I'll—I'll pick you up at seven?"

A sudden glow of light across the room illuminated a teenaged face peeking in the doorway. "Excuse me, Miss D," the girl whispered nervously. "Th-there's a Pedro somebody on line three for you. And—and Jessie Diaz's mom is here to see you."

Carmen let out an impatient sigh. "What does Mrs. Diaz want?"

The student shrugged. "She said she *has* to see you, and she'll wait all day."

"Unh," Carmen grunted. "Tell her I'll be with her shortly. And the call?"

"Line three." The student hurried away, leaving the door open behind her.

Carmen walked briskly past Eugene without a goodbye, hurried down the hallway, and stopped outside the door to the counseling room. Taking hold of the doorknob, she muttered under her breath, "What the hell does that woman want now?"

Mrs. Diaz had already left three irate messages requesting a schedule change for her ninth grade son—a ridiculous request to put him in an algebra class, which, Carmen had already explained, was impossible. *Algebra? What planet is that woman from?* Carmen thought. *They don't pay me enough to deal with this shit.* She needed an unscheduled conference with an irate parent like she needed a chili con carne burrito. Carmen took an extra deep breath, pushed open the door, and readied herself for the coming war.

≋ 2 ≋

Too Far Gone?

Mrs. Diaz was seated in one of the hard wooden chairs in the partitioned-off area of the counseling room that was Carmen's "office." Jessie, her son, was slumped lazily in a chair beside her. The two were obviously waiting for Carmen, but when she stepped through the door she did not acknowledge their presence. Instead she stopped at the nearest desk and picked up the call waiting for her on line three.

"Hello." Carmen waited for a response. "Hel-LO," she repeated with loud impatience. She could make out a man speaking in Spanish to someone else on the other end, but no one was acknowledging her presence on the phone, and she was going to give them one more chance. "I said *hel-LO!*"

"Hello Ms. DuPrè? This is Pedro Camacho at *At Your Service*. I understand you have been trying to reach us regarding dissatisfaction with the service you received on your 1998 Lexus?" The voice was deep and assertive, and the words were accent-free and clearly enunciated. It struck Carmen as unusual that the Mexican on the other end managed to switch from obviously native Spanish to the perfect English he was speaking now. But she didn't give a damn how well the guy had been trained to speak to customers; she didn't appreciate yet another peon employee being passed off on her—no matter how well he had mastered English.

"Look Pay-dro . . . I said I wanted to speak to the *owner*. I have been leaving messages for him for three days, and frankly I am not interested in speaking to any other person at your establishment. I really just want my car back, and I want it back *today*. As a matter of fact, I expect the owner of At Your Service to deliver my car to me his damn self if he wants to receive payment for some repairs I did not authorize."

Carmen heard the man take in a deep breath. In a most polite phone voice, he said, "Of course, ma'am. The owner will bring your car to you right away."

"I'll be expecting him here *before* noon," Carmen barked. She did not appreciate the fact that the repairs she had requested were never even attempted, and some other work she had never asked for had been done without her approval. She planned to give the owner a piece of her mind when he got there.

"Before noon, Ms. DuPrè. I will make sure he knows, ma'am."

Carmen didn't bother to say goodbye, but slammed the phone to its cradle and turned to face Mrs. Diaz and her boy.

She had talked to the woman on the phone once or twice, and had pictured Mrs. Diaz to be overweight and unattractive. She was neither. Slim and youthful, with no makeup and a casual, almost tomboyish appearance, the ponytailed, sweat suit–clad Hispanic woman looked more like she should be the boy's older sister than his mother, and from the expression on her face, she looked as if she had come to fight.

Straightening to all of her five feet and seven inches, Carmen walked briskly across the room toward her cubicle. She stopped to shake Mrs. Diaz's hand stiffly before sitting down across from her at the ancient wooden table Carmen had been given to use as a desk. Trying to look official, Carmen shuffled a couple of file folders around on the table, opened the top drawer of the file cabinet that doubled as a desk drawer, and took out a pen and pad of paper. She figured a smile would be a wasted gesture, so she stared blankly at Mrs. Diaz and blandly asked her what the problem seemed to be.

Mrs. Diaz didn't smile either. She glanced at her son, who was slumped lazily into the wooden chair beside hers. "My son needs to be in algebra." The woman looked calmly at Carmen, daring her to disagree. "At the beginning of the year you put him in some other kind of thing. What's it called, mijo?" She poked her son's shoulder, but he didn't respond. "Discovering Math. Something like that."

"Math Discovery," Carmen corrected her abruptly. "That's our basic skills review for students who aren't quite ready for college-preparatory mathematics."

"Well, he's been in the class for a whole semester, and the

work ain't getting no harder. It's too easy for him, miss. My son ain't no dummy."

Carmen began rifling through the stack of files on the table. Jessie's file would be close to the top since he had been kicked out of his computer keyboarding class by an extremely irate teacher just a few days before.

"I'm *sure* your son is very smart, Mrs. Diaz." Carmen tried not to sound too patronizing, but she didn't believe a word of what she'd just said about the boy, and it was obvious Jessie didn't believe it either. He grunted—the first sound he'd managed to make thus far—and slumped lower in his chair.

Mrs. Diaz stared directly at Carmen, keeping the fire behind her eyes down to a warm smolder. "Look. I'm not saying Jessie is no angel. But he is a smart boy." She looked over at her son. He didn't appear to be paying any attention to the two adults. He was focusing intently on the hundreds of little graffiti messages that had been carved into the wooden tabletop over the years.

Mrs. Diaz looked back into Carmen's eyes and announced firmly, "You think I don't know. I know he needs to be in algebra. He can't go to college unless you put him in algebra."

Carmen let out an exasperated breath. *Is this woman serious?* She couldn't really expect her son to go to college. The boy would be lucky to graduate, let alone ever step foot on a college campus. Carmen was expected to counsel boys like him every day. Counseling in a case like this meant little more than helping the student be realistic about his obvious limitations. Carmen would just have to do her best to help the woman accept reality.

She sat up straighter in her chair, her voice taking on an authoritative tone. "Mrs. Diaz, Jessie is failing the Discovery class he's in now, and that's basic mathematics. *We* don't think putting him in *algebra* is a good idea."

"You don't know my son. He knows math. He's a smart boy, miss. My son is going to college. He wants to learn computers. Ask him. Did you ever ask him?"

Carmen sighed dramatically. There were nearly six hundred ninth graders at Overland; what on earth would make this woman think Carmen had the time to ask every single one of them what fairy-tale college they wanted to never get into? Overland's test scores were in the bottom ten percent in the nation. With the exception of a handful of honors students who *might* have a chance at a noncompetitive college, any kid graduating from Overland would be lucky to be eligible for a factory job when he got out of school. "Your son *is* on track for graduation," Carmen offered unenthusiastically. "You should be proud."

"Why don't you ask him?" Mrs. Diaz repeated coolly.

Carmen turned her attention to Jessie. She studied the young man then. She really looked at him for a few quiet seconds. He could have been any nameless Chicano boy Carmen drove by every day on Los Angeles's inner-city streets. A baby-faced precriminal scowling at life from a man-sized body, giving Lexus-driving women like herself good cause to check the door locks. *Why can't this woman see that her son is already too far gone? Doesn't she see his khaki pants five sizes too big? Does she think the crisply ironed pleats gathered and belted at his waist are just a fashion statement? And that handmade tattoo, m-a-l-o, spelled in blue ink across his knuckles?* Carmen shook her head sadly, a gesture the mother calmly ignored.

"Ask him, lady. Ask him what he wants to do," she challenged, trying to suppress the anger in her voice.

Carmen decided to do just that. "Well, Jessie. Do you want to go to college?" The boy didn't flinch. "Do you want to work with computers?" A shoulder shrug, and with the mention of computers, a new motion from him—his index finger began tapping softly against the tabletop— but still no words from the boy. Carmen glanced at her watch impatiently. It was time to put an end to this nonsense. She'd be at this all day if she didn't just get it over with and put this woman in her place.

"Mrs. Diaz," Carmen began sharply, "are you aware that I had to remove Jessie from his computer keyboarding class just last week, at the teacher's request? Miss Bradshaw said he was disrespectful to her *and* he was abusing the equipment, and frankly, Mrs. Diaz, our computer equipment is *not* easy to come by. If your son were really interested in a career in computers, it seems to me he would pay more respect to the ones he has access to." She exhaled loudly and waited—expecting the woman to apologize for wasting her time.

It was Jessie who spoke instead. Without raising his head he muttered quietly, "Respect is mutual."

"Excuse me?" Carmen wasn't ready for the words the boy chose. She doubted he even knew the definition of the word "mutual." She raised a sarcastic eyebrow and waited for him to explain what he meant.

"Honors? *They* get web design," the boy grumbled huskily. "*We* get keyboarding." He grinned slightly, then went back to tapping softly on the tabletop with the index finger of his right hand. "I showed her," he grunted.

"You showed her?" The impatience and disbelief in Carmen's voice boiled over into a sarcastic whine. "You showed her what, young man? You loaded an obscene webpage onto a school computer. *That* doesn't sound like such a bright move, Mr. Diaz."

Carmen was tired of them both. Meetings like this one were the reason she desperately wanted that TAG counseling position. Why did these people have to make her life so freaking miserable? Why didn't they just get up from her office, settle for the math class the boy was already failing, and leave her and her now warm Diet Coke alone?

"He designed it, you know." Mrs. Diaz was staring at Carmen angrily.

"Excuse me?"

"He didn't just *load* a webpage. He *designed* it. Tell her, mijo. Tell her what you told me this morning."

Jessie didn't respond.

"He taught himself how at the library. HTL, or something like that. What is it, mijo?"

Jessie's head bobbed ever so slightly, indicating he found something humorous in what his mom said. "HT*M*L, Ma." He looked at his mother briefly and smiled, then looked down at the tabletop again. He mumbled softly, "It's like graffiti."

Carmen shot a stern look in the boy's direction. "Graffiti?" Her tone said she didn't have much patience left for Jessie or his mother. "Is that what you think the school's property is here for? Jessie Diaz, you loaded a page on the school's computer that read . . ." Carmen pulled a sheet of paper out of Jessie's file folder. "And this is a direct quote, 'Miss Bradshaw is a pinchy gringa cabrona.' I may not speak Spanish, but I know whatever *that* means—it's not good."

Jessie let go a quiet chuckle, and his mother promptly smacked the back of his head. "Dile lo què me dijiste, Jessie. Tell her what you told me," she said sternly.

"I designed it. I used HTML." He looked Carmen in the eye for the first time, and she was sure his fourteen-year-old face was saying without words, *You stupid bitch, you don't get it, do you?*

"What do you know about HTML, young man?"

Jessie was enjoying it now. He knew something important that she hadn't a clue about, and she could see how much it brought him to life.

"It's like tagging, you know? Like I know what the letters mean . . . but not everybody knows. The letters make the computer do what I say. It's like a code. I made the page black and I made the words blink in different colors. I don't think she liked it, the teacher." Jessie beamed at his mother, obviously proud of what he had done.

"*Tell her* what Miss Bradshaw told you, mijo." Mrs. Diaz poked her son again, and it seemed to deflate the boy suddenly. All his energy just seemed to dissipate, and he slumped in his chair and went back to tapping softly on the table. Carmen could barely make out the words he finally mumbled into his folded arms.

"She said design class is only for honors. She said I would never get in because I had to get her recommendation and she would never give it to me. So I programmed a page just for her."

Carmen was finally appropriately awestruck. "You taught yourself how to do that?" Jessie didn't look up at her, but his head bobbed affirmatively a couple of times.

Carmen took a minute to let the boy's words sink in. He had taught himself something that was a part of the honors-level curriculum. The kind of intelligence and talent needed to do what Jessie had done, Carmen did not notice at Overland too often.

"I can talk to her," Carmen finally said in a quiet tone. "I'll see about you bypassing that keyboarding class and getting into web design. But you'll have to apologize for the words you used, young man. In writing. Agreed?"

Another head bob.

"What about the algebra?" Mrs. Diaz was at it again. "He is going to college, miss. He has to have it."

Oh, please, Carmen thought. Playing around on a computer was one thing, succeeding in college-prep math was quite another. She wished the woman would get a clue. If her son was failing basic math, how in the hell did she expect him to succeed in an algebra class that would be an entire semester ahead of him? *Give me a break.*

Carmen suddenly had an idea. She knew exactly what to do to put an end to the discussion. She took out a pen and scribbled some figures on a piece of paper then slid it across the desk to the boy. She sent the pen sliding toward him too. "Can you tell me the answer to this?" She had written: "⅓ *is to 3 as 3 is to* ___."

Jessie glanced down at the paper, his face registering a look of disgust. He slid the page back to Carmen, never touching the pen.

"Well then," Carmen said smugly, "Why don't we continue with the *Math Discovery* class until the end of the year?" She didn't really intend to humiliate the boy; she was just trying to make her point. He needed to prove he deserved a seat in an algebra class before he got one. He obviously wasn't ready. Carmen smiled stiffly at Jessie. "If your grade improves in Math Discovery, well, I'll see what I can do about getting you into algebra in the tenth grade. Okay?"

"Twenty-seven." Jessie growled the answer at her. "Is that the hardest one you got, lady?"

Carmen turned to the boy's mother. "I'm sorry, Mrs. Diaz. It's already midyear. Jessie will be too far behind."

Jessie grunted into the tabletop. "X times one third equals nine, so x is twenty-seven."

Well, I'll be damned was what Carmen was suddenly thinking. But she wasn't referring to the words Jessie had just spoken, or to the scene inside her office. Her attention had switched to a movement behind Mrs. Diaz and her son. A movement she noticed outside her window—out in the parking lot. A caramel-skinned muscleman had just stepped out of Carmen's Lexus. He was at least six-three, broad-shouldered, and smooth-shaven except for a neat mustache and goatee that framed full lips. The owner of *At Your Service* was less than twenty feet from Carmen's window, standing near her car, casually scanning the row of buildings for a clue to which direction he should head in. The brother was wearing an expensive white velour jogging suit, which made him look like something from a Rodeo Drive display window. This fine specimen was gorgeous. *Figures,* Carmen thought instantly. The shady way she had been treated by this so-called proud black businessman should have clued her in that he was crooked, crazy, or cute. This one was obviously all three. Carmen felt the heat of the coming confrontation warm her face. *Oh yes,* she thought, *one more beautiful egomaniac to knock down a few pegs.* This was going to be fun.

She stood abruptly, gathered the pile of folders on her desk into a stack, and plopped them all into her already overflowing in-basket. She had suddenly decided what to do about Jessie.

"Come in first thing in the morning, Jessie. We'll get you into an algebra class. We'll rework your entire schedule, okay?" She reached her hand out toward him, but he didn't reach to shake it, which prompted his mother to smack him again in the back of his head. He stood up, and without looking at Carmen, shook her hand limply.

"Thank you for meeting with us," Mrs. Diaz said, the tone of victory in her voice turned up just enough for Carmen to catch it. She shook Carmen's hand one quick time and corralled her son toward the door ahead of Carmen, who was now obviously rushing them out of the room.

Jessie stopped abruptly in the entrance to the outer hall.

"I'm not the only one who shouldn't be in that math," he said, challenging Carmen matter-of-factly. He looked boldly into her face and waited for her to respond.

Carmen didn't even acknowledge that she'd heard the boy's comment. She was finished with Jessie and his mother, and was more than anxious to get to the confrontation waiting for her in the parking lot. She followed the two into the main hallway and dismissed them both by muttering, "See you first thing in the morning, young man," then she filled the long corridor with the sound of her Kate Spade pumps clicking their way toward her prey.

⇒ 3 ⇐

A Perfect Stranger

The moment Carmen pushed open the heavy door leading outside, the man's eyes found her, and he headed in her direction with what looked like a *Can you help me?* expression on his face. He'd had the good sense to park in the employee lot and had managed to find a spot sixty or so feet from the entrance to the administration building, but he was carefully navigating his way through the maze of tightly packed-in cars, and was taking those slow, cool steps beautiful men tend to take. It was making the wait impossible for Carmen.

She stood in the open doorway and glared at him coolly, letting the door close behind her. When he smiled broadly at her and shouted, "*Excuse me,*" she did not smile back. Instead she started in his direction, covering the forty or fifty feet left between them with bold, angry steps that made her hips sway back and forth like a Vegas showgirl making a stage left exit.

She did not break her stare, and only broke her determined stride when she was about two feet in front of him. She stopped abruptly then, glaring coldly into his startled face. Without saying a word she flipped her wrist out in front of her with a snap, holding her hand out expectantly.

The man looked rather amused, but he didn't say a word to Carmen. Instead he waited patiently for her to let him know what she was expecting him to put in her outstretched hand. As if he didn't know what she wanted. It was only obvious that she was asking for—no, *demanding*—the return of her car keys, but he just stood there with his hands in the pockets of his jogging pants, looking at her with a cocked eyebrow and a jovial smile on his gorgeous face.

"Well?" Carmen scowled. She was not about to smile at the man. She was trying to let him know she was not a woman to be trifled with.

He stared at Carmen's outstretched hand, his eyebrow still raised curiously at it. Then he removed his right hand from his pocket, placed it gingerly on top of Carmen's upturned palm, and grasping it firmly, he turned her little attempt at boldness into a friendly handshake.

"Well, I am very glad to meet you too, Ms. DuPrè." He pumped the handshake dramatically, and two deep dimples suddenly appeared at the corners of his smile.

"Very funny," Carmen grunted. She dove right in then. She didn't ask him for his name or bother with nice-to-meet-you pleasantries. "Look Mr. . . . Mr. At Your Service. I don't know who the hell you think you are, but I've been trying to reach you for three days now, and all I could get was the damn runaround. I left several messages with your employees, and was assured by them that I would hear from you, but do you have the courtesy to at least pick up the phone? Of course not."

Carmen barely took a breath before she started in again. "And another thing. Who gave you permission to replace my distributor hat without my consent? I didn't ask for any damn distributor hat to be replaced, and if you thought it needed to be replaced, then you should have called me and *asked* me if I wanted my distributor hat replaced."

The smile on the man's face widened suddenly, showing those damn dimples again, which only served to piss Carmen off more. She raised her voice to a near shout. "And while I'm at it . . ." She kept her eyes fixed squarely on his, while pointing a rigid index finger in the direction of her car. "I had that car diagnosed by a reputable Lexus mechanic, and he told me all it needed was a new alternator. Now, the only reason I even brought my car to your little shop was because an acquaintance of mine assured me you were honest, and you *supposedly* do excellent work, and I was trying to give a black man's little community-based shop some support. I will certainly never make *that* mistake again."

Carmen stuck her hand out again; this time she thrust it rigidly into the space just under his nose and left it there expectantly. "Now. Can I have the key to my automobile . . . puh-*leez*?"

"Of course you may." He was totally unruffled by Carmen's dramatic display. He had returned his hands to his pockets, but he didn't bring out any keys. Carmen stared into his face, still waiting expectantly for him to do what she'd asked. She raised her eyebrows as if to say, *Well?* and smirked angrily. But still no keys. It was then that something happened that wiped the smirk completely off Carmen's face.

She watched the man's smile fade, then seriously, almost sadly, he spoke words she should have known were coming—words for which she usually had one of many snappy comebacks—but when the words came out of his mouth, something in the tone of his voice when he said them kept her quiet.

"You are a *beautiful* woman."

Carmen didn't say thank you. She didn't respond in any noticeable way. Instead she stood there, waiting for the pickup line that was sure to follow. He would ask her if she was married, or if she was dating anyone. He would ask her if she'd like to have coffee with him sometime, or maybe take in a movie. She would turn him down curtly, and he would act as if he might actually take no for an answer. But as gorgeous as he was, the challenge of being turned down by a beauty like Carmen would be too much, and he would surely try a different approach. Offer to take her to dinner or a concert—something with a greater monetary value than just coffee. Carmen was sure it was coming, so she shifted her weight to one hip and waited for it.

He shook his head slowly and gazed seriously into her eyes. *"Tan hermosa y tan infeliz."*

Ugghh. Carmen curled her lip in disgust. She hated when people who could speak English perfectly well spoke Spanish to her. It just irked her. She could barely tolerate it when a parent or student who wasn't able to speak English did it; as if, because her name was "Caaa-r-rmen," she was supposed to be able to just *ah-blah ess-pan-yol* right back at 'em. But at least those who weren't able to speak English had a legitimate excuse. When someone who was obviously fluent did it, it just plain pissed her off.

"English, please." She didn't smile.

The man looked into her eyes and translated solemnly, "You are too beautiful to be so unhappy."

His obvious sincerity made Carmen's throat tighten, and she swallowed uncomfortably. When she cut through the thick silence with a sharp "I am perfectly happy, actually," the lie hung in the air between them like a puff of stale cigarette smoke. She pretended to brush something from the shoulder of her blouse. She cleared her throat, glanced over at her Lexus, down at her Kate Spades, and back into the man's face. "Why wouldn't I be?"

She felt his eyes moving slowly over her then. Not like every other man whose stares melted the fibers of her clothing like acid. This man was studying her, reading her like she was some work of classic literature—like he might uncover clues to some barely decipherable mystery buried beneath the prose.

"The worms are going to get that, you know." His voice was soft and sad, and though Carmen didn't have a clue why the man was talking about worms, she softened her tone too.

"Excuse me?"

"Sorry. Something my son said to me." His eyes glistened.

"My little boy was in the hospital all last week—which is why I wasn't able to get back to you." He pulled his right hand out of his pocket, Carmen's keys dangling at his side. "I'm sorry I didn't ask your permission first, but I left a message for the mechanic to go ahead and fix your car when he couldn't get ahold of you on Saturday. I didn't think you should be charged two hundred and eighty dollars for a perfectly functioning alternator, when all you needed was a thirty-two-dollar distributor cap."

Carmen felt an icy current of shame rush down her spine. She wished she could just suck all the words she'd spit out in the past five minutes right back into her mouth and swallow them whole. All that fussing she did about her distributor hat or cap or whatever it was called and she was dead wrong about the man's intentions. He had actually tried to save her money, and in the midst of it all, his son had been sick. She should have just waited to find out why he hadn't returned any of her calls before jumping all over him like that. Carmen mumbled a pitiful "Oh. I—I'm sorry your son was sick."

He nodded acceptance of her apology.

"I hope he's feeling better." It was a weak attempt at making up for her attitude.

"He passed away Thursday."

Carmen didn't utter a sound. She wanted to crawl underneath her car and wait there until he disappeared. He smiled compassionately at her. "You had no way of knowing that."

"I really am sorry," she blurted anxiously. *Oh God, get me out of this conversation,* she thought. Carmen didn't do death. It was out of her league. In the three years since her father had died, she still hadn't allowed herself to really feel the impact of it. She knew the man standing in front of her had to be in some incredible pain, and she didn't want to be reminded of what it felt like. She hoped to God he would quickly change the subject and just let her go ahead and pay for the car repairs and get on with her day.

"My son had a brain tumor." He offered her the information as though she had asked for it.

"I—I . . ." She couldn't say another "I'm sorry," so she decided to be quiet.

"I miss him." He uttered the words with the matter-of-factness of a parent whose child was away at summer camp, but his eyes told Carmen he was suffering terribly.

"Nothing could ever prepare you for losing your only child, you know?"

Carmen nodded knowingly at the man, but inside she was thinking, *No, I don't know, and I really don't want to know.* She scanned the parking lot nervously, then the rows of windows on the buildings lining the edge of the lot, hoping a fight would suddenly break out or a fire alarm would be pulled. The campus was unusually quiet, so she allowed her eyes to settle back down on the man's face.

He seemed totally oblivious to her discomfort. "A few months ago, before the doctors finally admitted there was nothing more they could do, my boy said to me, '*Don't be sad for me, Poppi.*' He said he was giving his body back to Mother Earth to use. That's when he told me, '*The worms are going to get it, Dad.*' "

Carmen was horrified. She could not believe the man was

sharing such an awful story with her. She didn't want to think about hospitals or chemo or . . . worms. God. What a grotesque thing to tell a perfect stranger. How could she politely say something to let him know she was sorry for his loss, then get her keys from him, and get back into the building?

He smiled genuinely and stared deep into Carmen's eyes. She was sure then that he was crazy. The man was standing there confirming Carmen's belief that the gorgeous ones usually were anyway. Crazy. Certifiable.

"My son told me, 'Poppi, if this body was that important, God wouldn't let the worms get it.' He held Carmen's eyes with an intense gaze. "A nine-year-old said that to his dad. Can you believe that?"

Suddenly, quite unexpectedly, something in the way his dark eyes were piercing hers sent a wave of calm through Carmen's body. She felt her nervousness evaporating in the warmth of his gaze, and in that instant she forgot about the bell the classes and the students. Inexplicably her anxiety vanished, and in the small space between her and the stranger a universe of calm had been created. She liked the feeling it gave her. Peace. Like there was nothing in the world more important in that moment than being where she stood.

His voice softened, barely above a whisper. "I know you think I am crazy. You're thinking, Who would share something so personal in the middle of a parking lot?"

Carmen nodded.

"There are some experiences in life that are meant to be shared. Loss is so personal, but in the pain there is healing. Bad things sometimes happen to good people, but that's not always a bad thing. I choose to tell people about my son's battle, because for me it has changed everything."

He had her. He had somehow banished all of Carmen's discomfort and had reeled her completely in. "Changed everything?" she questioned.

"You have to ask yourself what this life is really for, you know?"

Carmen stared curiously at him.

He reached for her hand. Holding it in his, he gazed solemnly into her eyes. "When I get up in the morning, I sit on the edge of my bed and ask myself, 'Pedro Camacho, what is the most important thing for you to accomplish today? I used to answer that question from some ridiculously long list of things I needed to do. But now . . . I have only one answer."

He turned Carmen's hand over and placed her car keys in it, then glanced over his shoulder at a tow truck parked nearby. "That's my mechanic over there. He's waiting to take me back to the shop." He let go of Carmen's hand abruptly and began walking away, calling to her over his shoulder, "It was a pleasure to meet you Miss DuPrè, and don't worry about payment—it's on me." He took a few hurried steps, then stopped to pat the top of her Lexus. "Your car is in excellent shape, I don't think we'll be seeing each other anytime soon." With that he turned his back on her and headed for the truck.

Carmen was stunned by his leaving. As she watched him walk away, the feeling of calmness he'd given her seemed to drain with each of the long strides he took. Something about his departure hurt, as if he had invited her in, then shut the door in her face. She wanted him to stay. She wanted him to turn around and come back—and the fact that she wanted that annoyed her. She watched as he hopped in the truck, and it rolled toward the street.

Suddenly the truck lurched to a stop. Pedro Camacho stuck his head out of the window and shouted, "Hey."

Carmen waited for it. She just knew he would ask her if he could call her sometime. She held her breath hopefully.

But the only words he had for her were ones that seemed to ring even louder than the passing bell that sounded just before he had spoken them. They were words that would echo in Carmen's head for many months to come.

"Be happy."

As the truck pulled out of the lot, Carmen ignored the rush of students pouring out of the buildings around her. Watching the taillights of the disappearing truck, she tried to shake off the uneasy feeling that settled on her heart. *What important thing?* She wanted to know. She really did. She regretted letting the man get away without telling her the answer to his daily question. Carmen knew she would be haunted by it the whole day, like a song lyric you try to remember, but just can't seem to get off the tip of your tongue. *What?* Carmen wondered in exasperation. *What is the most important thing you do each day?*

⋛ 4 ⋚

What's Wrong with This Picture?

If she thought there was the slightest chance of getting away with it, the moment the final bell sounded Carmen would have rushed to her car and raced out of the parking lot. She knew there was no way Schuyler would tolerate her missing one more so-called emergency meeting, and, since she would need a favorable reference from the man when she went after that Talented and Gifted counseling position, she decided to just buckle down and suffer through the torture of another mandatory staff discussion.

When she arrived in the crowded cafeteria, most of the tables were already packed with dozens of worn-out and impatient-looking teachers. The entire social studies and science departments, as usual, were camped out in the back rows, most of their noses stuck between the pages of newspapers. The English teachers took up the entire two rows up front, and the math department huddled together at two long tables pushed end-to-end smack dab in the middle of the room. Eugene was huddled right along with his colleagues, seemingly engrossed in the announcements the principal had begun making from the front of the room. Carmen held a hand over her nose to block out the lingering odor of the green chile enchiritos that had been served for lunch, as she sauntered over to her usual perch in the wide-ledged windowsill near the back door.

Schuyler was standing at a microphone at the front of the room, his fat belly protruding so far over his belt, he was forced to stand nearly a foot from the mic. His eyes followed Carmen to her perch and rested for a brief moment on her before he went back to his address.

"As you all know," the stern-faced Schuyler bellowed loudly into the unnecessary microphone, "there was a near-fatal stabbing under the D building stairwell last week, and the victim is refusing to name his attacker."

Grumbles of recognition rippled throughout the room at the mention of the already well-known incident. The words "near-fatal" and "stabbing" seemed to barely register with the group.

"We have a violent perpetrator in our midst," Schuyler proclaimed gravely, "and since the hoodlums are probably both gang members, it's not likely the victim will name him." More grumbles of recognition reverberated through the room, though the reactions lacked any real sense of alarm.

"Yesterday evening the snack stand was vandalized *again*," Schuyler continued in a matter-of-fact tone, "and two of the vending machines outside the library were broken into. So I have no choice but to call for a moratorium on all after-school activities."

Carmen fought the urge to roll her eyes. She hated it when Schuyler used big, unnecessary words. *Moratorium. Half the teachers in this room probably have no idea what the hell you're talking about,* she thought smugly. She searched the room, as if looking for evidence to support her theory, when her eyes rested on Francine Dominguez, a first-time U.S. history teacher with some kind of art degree—ballet or drama or something along those lines. To Carmen, Francine was nowhere near qualified, and given the fact that the woman was at Overland with an emergency teaching credential, Carmen could not understand how Francine was always the first one to speak up during staff discussions. As Carmen expected, Francine was already on her feet. Apparently she had some clue what "moratorium" meant.

"Excuse me Señor Schuyler, but that doesn't seem fair to the rest of the students." Her petite frame didn't fit the loud, feisty insistence of her voice.

"Yes, well, thank you for your input Miss Dominguez, but as we all know, these are desperate times, therefore we have no choice but to institute the most desperate of measures. As of today, all after-school activities are immediately canceled until further notice."

"But the Academic Decathlon is less than a month away," Francine complained loudly. "Our team meets every day after school and we'll need—"

The cafeteria erupted with laughter, drowning out the rest

of her comment. A voice from the back of the room shouted, "Come on, Overland's AcDec team places last every year." Another voice grumbled, "The team's a joke."

Francine shot a disapproving glance in the direction of the insults. "Just because Overland's never actually *won* the decathlon doesn't mean we shouldn't enter the competition. It's a good experience for the kids."

Carmen couldn't resist jumping on the comment. She *had* to throw her two cents into any argument that involved Overland students making fools of themselves. "Since when is it a good experience to be a *loser*?" Carmen's tone said she was clearly agitated.

Francine turned abruptly to face Carmen. "Overland's team competes with schools from Beverly Hills, Palos Verdes, and Malibu. Schools that actually have textbooks and lab equipment. Our kids know they're going into that competition on an uneven playing field, but it doesn't stop them from trying."

Carmen didn't care for the smugness in Francine's voice. She couldn't tell if the woman actually cared what happened to the kids, or if she just had something to prove to her own undereducated self. "So"—Carmen put a hand to her hip and frowned sarcastically at Francine—"basically you're saying it's all right to put an underprepared, ill-equipped person in a position where they can't win, just for the *experience* of it?" There was no mistaking the reference Carmen was making to Francine's emergency credential status—the entire room caught it and fell immediately silent.

Francine glared at Carmen. "Our kids work very hard to

prepare for that competition. Just because they've had a life-time of substandard education and *very little guidance,* that doesn't make them losers." Before Carmen could launch a nasty comeback at Francine, Schuyler jumped into their disagreement.

"Ladies, we can put an end to this discussion right now. The bottom line is, the AcDec team will have to meet elsewhere. I just cannot afford to hire any more security guards. We've already spent all of this year's choir and debate traveling funds on the guards we have. Not to mention money we are supposed to be using for building improvements."

Francine wasn't about to take no for an answer. Her voice rose in persistence. "Perhaps we could solicit volunteers from the community—parents and grandparents to be on campus after school so that—"

"*Perhaps* I haven't made myself clear, Miss Dominguez. There really is no debating this. To avoid further violence and vandalism, this campus will be *off limits* to students after school. Any student who is found on campus without very good cause will be immediately suspended." Schuyler peered sternly over his black-framed glasses, daring anyone to interject. "Now, for the next agenda item. Timms, I believe you requested fifteen minutes to present your department report."

Eugene wasted no time getting to the front of the room and to the point. The first words out of his mouth were in praise of Francine's crusade for the decathlon team. He glanced nervously at Carmen as if asking forgiveness for what he was about to say, then set his eyes warmly on Francine. "I'm up here to talk about math, but I just want to say thank you to

Miss Dominguez for believing our students can benefit from the preparation they receive when they compete in the Academic Decathlon." He smiled at Francine with sincere admiration, which Carmen found quite upsetting.

How dare he take her side were the words that came to Carmen's mind just as Eugene turned to face her with a beaming smile.

"I also want to acknowledge the concern Miss DuPrè has for the impact such a significant competition can have on our students if we send them in there unprepared." Carmen raised an eyebrow at Eugene, and offered him a sarcastic little smile—a smile that said he'd barely saved himself on that one.

When Eugene returned his attention to the audience, Carmen watched as he addressed the mostly attentive teaching staff. She couldn't understand why they all seemed to have so much respect and admiration for the man. He was a nerd and a math geek, and probably the most old-fashioned human being Carmen had ever met. He arranged their dates at least three days in advance, wouldn't let Carmen step foot out of the car until he opened her door, and would never hear of Carmen paying for anything when she was in his company. Actually, that was the part about him she liked most—the old-fashionedness. In some ways he reminded her of her father; and, something about her time spent with Eugene always left her feeling well protected and taken care of. Unfortunately, his nerdiness got on her last nerve.

The strange thing was, Eugene didn't seem to be so nerdy in situations such as this one—among his colleagues. Sounding more like a civil rights attorney than a math geek, Eugene was up at the front of the room going on and on about the importance of a rigorous math curriculum for all kids, especially for kids who plan to go on to college. Carmen marveled at the fact that no one made snide remarks when Eugene mentioned the possibility of Overland students getting into college. And he even managed to get a few laughs with a couple of well-placed jokes about the condition of Overland's textbooks. He had the entire room spellbound, and Carmen took note of how self-assured he looked in front of all of them. Nothing like the stumbling, stuttering man he became when they were alone together. *If he acted more like this on our dates,* Carmen found herself thinking, *I might actually be able to develop some kind of attraction for the man.*

"The truth is," Eugene's voice rose excitedly as he picked up a file folder and pulled a transparency from it, "our kids deserve better than we are giving them, and that's why I requested this opportunity to talk to you all today." He placed the transparency on the overhead projector and pointed at a row of brightly colored bars on the chart looming on the screen above.

"These bars represent the mathematics test scores of our incoming ninth graders. Look at what we have here." Eugene pointed an index finger at one of the bars. "As you all might expect, we do have a large number of students who appear to be lacking in basic skills, *but* we also have two hundred ninth graders who have already scored above the fiftieth percentile on this test." A murmur of disbelief erupted from the back rows, which Eugene quickly addressed with a loud "That's right. I said *two hundred* scored above the fiftieth." The murmuring instantly stopped. "That means they outscored half of the students in the country. Now . . ." He reached into the file folder for another transparency and placed it on the projector. "This is our master schedule." He let the room study the image on the screen before bringing his point home in a very loud voice. "As you can see from our master schedule, we only have *three* freshman algebra classes. That means even if we pack them in, there are only one hundred and twenty available seats." He looked out over the unmoving faces of his colleagues. They didn't seem to be getting his point. "I ask you," he continued, "how can we put these two hundred *undeniably capable* ninth graders into one hundred and twenty algebra seats?" Eugene removed his glasses and stared dramatically at the crowd. "Does anyone see what's wrong with this picture?"

Carmen saw it immediately, but only because Jessie and Mrs. Diaz had made it so painfully clear to her just a few hours earlier. The picture Eugene was painting with his little slide show was quite upsetting to Carmen. She was the one who had to face the wrath of parents when there weren't enough seats in advanced math classes. She stood up and raised her hand. "I see the problem," she said, loud enough for Eugene to hear.

He was obviously surprised to see Carmen responding to his presentation. She was usually quiet during staff meetings.

"Miss DuPrè?"

"You have six, eight, ten . . ." Carmen was counting the spaces on the schedule that represented the class offerings called Math Discovery. "Eighteen. There are eighteen offerings of Math Discovery, but only six algebra classes, and half of those are already filled with upperclassmen." Carmen's mouth twisted into a frown. It dawned on her suddenly exactly what that meant. "That means an awful lot of freshmen who could handle algebra won't be able to take it because there aren't enough seats for them." Carmen was surprised at the intensity in her own voice. Eugene's point was a damn good one. No wonder she couldn't do her job in this godawful place. There were a lot of kids—just like Jessie—who could and should be in an algebra class. Kids who might be on their way to higher, college-preparatory math, but there wasn't any place to put them. Carmen scolded the room with her tone. "How can we expect these kids to be ready for college, if we can't even offer them algebra?"

Eugene raised both of his palms heavenward and beamed at Carmen as if she had descended into the meeting on angel's wings. "Thank you, Miss DuPrè," he gushed. "You have hit the nail right on the head." He turned his attention back to his audience, his voice pleading. "We have got to get rid of some of these Discovery classes and somehow manage to triple our algebra offerings if we hope to—"

Schuyler interrupted loudly from his seat. "Harrumph. Well. Now, now, let's not get ahead of ourselves, Timms." He rose to his feet and headed for the mike. "You have no idea what you're suggesting."

Eugene did not make room for the principal at the microphone. He stood his ground and spoke into the mike himself. "I think every single one of our freshmen should get algebra, regardless of what these tests say, but that's another conversation. What I'm suggesting today is that there are at *least* two hundred students whose test scores say they should be in college-prep math, but they aren't—and no one can say it is because they're not capable."

Schuyler did not look happy. He glared sternly at Eugene and commanded in an angry tone, "Timms, have your Discovery teachers stand." He placed his fists on his rotund hips.

"Excuse me?" Eugene responded.

"Stand up." Schuyler bellowed at the teachers in the middle rows. "If you teach Math Discovery, I want you to stand up."

Six teachers rose hesitantly from their seats.

"Raise your hand if you have a teaching credential." Schuyler was trying to make a point, but nobody in the room seemed to know where he was going. Three of the six teachers raised a hand. The other three glanced at one another sheepishly.

"Now, raise your hand if you are prepared to teach algebra. If you were a mathematics major, or if you are confident that you are expert enough to teach at that level."

Two of the teachers, one an older Latino woman, the other a young black man, slowly lowered their hands and sat down. Two of the three uncredentialed teachers sat down too. A young Latino man and a gray-haired white woman were the only ones left standing. They and Eugene were the only teachers on campus qualified to teach higher math. Schuyler's point was made.

"We simply don't have the personnel to teach twelve algebra classes." Schuyler glared at Eugene in irritation.

Eugene spoke enthusiastically into the mike. "We are already working on that problem in our department. Every single one of the Discovery teachers you asked to stand up has volunteered to attend professional development sessions to get them up to speed. We can have them ready to teach algebra by September. If we do this right, we can be ready for the incoming freshmen this fall."

"And who's going to pay for that, Timms?" Who is going to pay for subs while these teachers attend these development sessions, and who's going to pay the developers? We just don't have it."

"We were thinking we could get some of the money from Title I funds and some from—"

Schuyler's face became a swollen tomato, his voice exploding angrily from his throat. "Title I? Absolutely not! Those funds are already allocated." He motioned Eugene away from the microphone and waddled up to it himself. "I'm the first one to admit there are a lot of changes we need to make around here, but believe me, if it were that easy, I'd be the first one to make 'em."

Grumbles of protest erupted from the back rows, but Schuyler pretended not to notice. When he realized that most of the room was still studying Eugene's chart, Schuyler quickly switched off the overhead projector.

"I appreciate your concern, Mr. Timms," Schuyler offered with a hint of embarrassment in his voice. He shrugged his shoulder apologetically and added, "I assure you I will consider your ideas during our budget planning session this summer."

Carmen felt her face heating up. *I assure you I will consider your ideas?* Schuyler knew good and damn well it would be too late by then. Too late to have the math teachers ready to teach algebra by September. Too late for one more class of freshmen who would end up getting enough basic math to earn a diploma—but far from enough to prepare them for college.

Carmen glared at Schuyler from her roost in the back windowsill. She wondered how many lives would be impacted by the principal's little shoulder shrug. She wondered how many times she'd shrugged her own shoulders because some kid's life was going to be screwed up, and there was nothing she could do about it. The thought crowded her head and made her temples pulse painfully. Why hadn't she thought of it that way before? Eugene's charts and diagrams made her see all too clearly that every student who didn't get a chance at the hard classes couldn't hope to go to college. The idea of how much the adults in the room impacted the lives of students suddenly seemed too much to be responsible for. She stared out the window and let her mind drift to thoughts of meeting the superintendent and convincing him to give her that TAG position. Talk about a dream job. Gifted student after gifted student academically prepared and hungry to get into college. No weight on her back about who does or doesn't deserve to be in an algebra class, and no attempted murders under the stairwells. She glanced at her watch, anxious for the staff meeting to end. If she was going to be ready for her date with Eugene—her chance to meet the superintendent—she needed to get out into the traffic within the next fifteen minutes.

Schuyler wasn't talking anymore, so Carmen took that to

mean the meeting was over. She rose from her perch in the windowsill and picked up her purse, preparing to head for the door, but no one else stood up. It was then that she realized Schuyler was staring straight at her like a dazed deer caught in her headlights. Finally he wiped his brow with the back of his shirtsleeve and cleared his throat with a loud *harrumph*. "If there are no further announcements," Schuyler seemed to be shouting directly at Carmen, "this meeting is adjourned."

⋚ 5 ⋛

Some Kind of Trouble

"*He put his* tongue where?"

Carmen held the phone a foot away from her ear and winced. Her younger sister, Lindsey, had the loudest mouth in the entire DuPrè family, and she was using it on Carmen now—full force.

"You heard me girl," Carmen said calmly into the receiver. "That creep put his tongue in my ear."

"And what did you do?"

"Nothing." Carmen was ready for it this time. She held the phone at arms length, anticipating the high-pitched squeal Lindsey was sure to use on her.

"Nothing!?" Lindsey was livid. "That old geezer put his tongue in your ear, and you didn't slap his old creepy face?"

"No I didn't," Carmen responded matter-of-factly. She

should have known Lindsey wouldn't understand. Lindsey was barely twenty-five, she had a job doing something she loved, and she'd had some amazingly lucky breaks in her career as a software designer—breaks she didn't have to kiss up to some dirty old geezer to get. Carmen didn't bother trying to explain how different it was working for the school district.

"Carmen, please tell me you at least told him he was a disgusting creep."

"No, of course I didn't. I asked him out to lunch."

She held the phone away again, anticipating an angry onslaught, but she heard only silence on the other end. Apparently Lindsey didn't have a snappy comeback this time, which could only mean she was really upset. What was the big deal anyway? So what if Carmen was going to have lunch with the man? It wasn't like he could attack her across a restaurant table. She was smart enough to know how the hiring game had to be played. She just wanted to stack the deck a little in her own favor; what harm could there be in that? Lindsey was being naïve. Sometimes a woman's just gotta do what she's gotta do.

Lindsey still hadn't spoken.

Carmen stayed quiet too, cursing herself for telling her sister in the first place. She knew better. She had managed to hold it in all night—but she couldn't keep it to herself forever. She had to tell somebody. In the past she would have called Yvette, but since *the incident,* that bitch was now her *ex*-best friend, so that was no longer an option. Who else was she going to tell but Lindsey? She'd almost told Eugene, but then thought better of it. It would serve her much better if no one inside the district knew that Dr. G. Harold Browning, the superintendent of schools, had tongued her in her ear—while Eugene Timms stood right beside her, never suspecting a thing.

The moment Carmen had been introduced to Dr. Browning she began trying to maneuver her way into a private conversation with the man—hoping to get a chance to tell him how very interested she was in the Talented and Gifted counseling position. But wasn't she more than surprised when he slithered up next to her and let her know *he* was interested in *her* for the position? Browning whispered in her ear that he had been informed that she was an excellent counselor. Of course Carmen was ecstatic. The words the man whispered were music to her ears. She just pretended not to notice the tongue. It might even have been unintentional. He had had a few drinks, and it was entirely possible that he didn't actually mean to lick her inner ear. *Yuk.* The thought of it made her cringe. She had to admit it was pretty disgusting, but she could definitely overlook it if it meant she'd finally be moving up and out of Overland High. How could she expect anyone to understand how important this was to her?

Lindsey was still silent on the other end of the phone. She wasn't taking the ear-licking news too well.

"I'm *not* letting this opportunity pass me by, Linn," Carmen insisted. "You don't know what it's like."

Lindsey still hadn't said anything, so Carmen took a deep breath and tried harder to sound convincing. "I hate my job. I'll do anything to get out of Overland."

Still no sound from Lindsey.

"Linn?"

"I'm still here," the younger DuPrè muttered quietly. "I told you, you should just quit that damn job."

"And do what, Lindsey?" Carmen responded sarcastically. "Move back in with Mother and let her tuck me into my frilly pink canopy bed every night?"

"You know you're welcome to stay here with me. I've got an extra bedroom."

"No, thank you, Linn." Carmen couldn't tell her why. She would never in a million years consent to living with any of them. Never. She'd live in a homeless shelter first. On top of everything else Mavis could find to criticize her about, the last thing she wanted to do was hand her more ammunition. Living with her baby sister would only make her a bigger laughingstock than she already was.

"You're still a young woman, Carmen. You could go back to school. You can stay here with me until you find something you love."

"No, thank you, Linn." Carmen repeated her words with a tone that let her sister know she was finished with the conversation.

Neither of them spoke for a few painful seconds. Lindsey finally broke the silence. "So what did you want, anyway?" she muttered dryly. "I'm sure you didn't call me at six in the morning to tell me you're planning to sleep your way to the top of the counseling hierarchy."

"I *said* I'm having lunch with him. I have absolutely *no* intention of sleeping with that creepy little man." Her voice softened suddenly. "I can't believe you would think that."

"Well you can believe he has *every* intention of sleeping with you," Lindsey said quietly. Her tone softened too when she added, "Be careful, Carmen, okay?"

Carmen brushed off her sister's warning by quickly changing the subject. "Anyway. You're right. I didn't call for that. I called because I need you to do me a favor."

Lindsey waited in silence.

"I have a doctor's appointment Thursday at two-thirty. If you're not too busy, I"—she cleared her throat nervously—"I was wondering if you wouldn't mind going with me."

"Aww, Car, I told you I'm going to Atlanta on Wednesday. I won't be back until next week. We're running a multimedia demonstration at the NetTech conference and I'm the lead technician on the team." Lindsey listened for her sister's response, but Carmen was quiet. "Maybe Della can go with you, or if you can postpone it . . ."

"I do *not* want Della to go," Carmen interrupted crisply. "and I'd appreciate it if you didn't mention this to her, Linn." Della was their older sister and Carmen's archrival. The two couldn't be in a room together for more than five minutes without all hell breaking loose. Carmen didn't trust Della as far as she could throw her, and with Della's two-hundred-and-fifty pound ass, that wasn't too far at all. All Carmen needed was to have Della calling all the DuPrè family members to voice her "concern" over Carmen's medical appointment. By the time Della was finished with the newscast, she'd have the whole family believing Carmen had contracted the damned AIDS virus.

"Are you and your friend Yvette still—"

Carmen didn't let Lindsey finish. "You know better than to mention her name to me, Linn."

"I understand you're still angry, Car, but—"

"Lindsey. *Don't*, okay?" Carmen would just have to change the subject. She wasn't ready to talk about what kind of so-called friend Yvette had turned out to be. *Two-faced traitor.* The truth was, there was nobody Carmen could ask to go to the doctor with her but Lindsey. Not Della. Not their brother, Maxwell, and definitely not their mother. If Lindsey couldn't accompany Carmen, she'd rather just go alone.

"I will let you know how my doctor's appointment went when you get back," Carmen muttered.

"I'm sorry, sis. I can tell you're worried about it."

Carmen *was* worried about it. She wished like hell she could postpone the appointment again, but her doctor would never go for that. Carmen had already postponed three times, which is what prompted all those "urgent" messages she kept getting at work. Finally Dr. Lee's receptionist lucked out and called while Carmen was sitting at her desk—she said the doctor had already put Carmen down for Thursday.

"Carmen, are you okay? Is something wrong with you? I mean something serious?" The slight tremble in Lindsey's voice said it had finally occurred to her that there might be something seriously wrong with her sister.

"No. No. I—I just . . . You know how I am, Linn. I'm just a big baby when it comes to going to the doctor. It's just a routine physical. I—I'd just rather have you come with me if you could, but you can't, so don't even sweat it, sweetie. Really, Linn. I'm fine."

Carmen was lying through her pearly white teeth. She'd already had the *routine* part of the physical. This appointment was a follow-up. All Dr. Lee's receptionist would tell her was that one of the many tests she'd taken looked "irregular," and Dr. Lee wanted her to come in to discuss it. Carmen tried to get the receptionist to tell her on the phone what the problem was, but the woman wouldn't give up any information.

"I'm absolutely sure there's nothing wrong with me, Linn. Call me when you get back to town and I'll whine all about it to you then, okay?"

"I'm sorry, Car—"

"I said it's no biggie, Linn. *Really*. Listen, I gotta go. I'm going to be late to work if I don't get on out in that traffic. Don't worry, sweetie, I'm fine, okay?"

"Okay, Carmen." Lindsey hesitated, then said quietly, "Carmen?"

"Yeah?"

"How many times have I asked you not to call me sweetie?"

Carmen laughed softly into the phone. "Kill 'em in Hotlanta, Linn."

"Thanks, Car. I'll call you when I get back."

"Bye, sweetie," Carmen whispered before she lowered the receiver softly to the cradle.

⋛ 6 ⋚

A Date with Miss D

"Who let you in here?"

Carmen walked briskly across the counseling center to her partitioned cubicle. She quickly checked her desktop to make sure no items were missing, then angrily opened and closed both of her file drawers. Everything seemed to be in its place.

"You said—" Jessie Diaz began, but Carmen cut him off hastily.

"I *said* meet me here first thing in the morning. But I expected you to wait in the outer office like every other student knows to do. And I did not expect you to bring company." Carmen turned to look at the gruff-looking Chicano boy seated at the table next to Jessie.

"This is Angel." Jessie nodded toward the boy, "He's one of 'em I was talking about."

"One of *what*?" Carmen asked impatiently.

"He don't belong in there either. Like me."

Jessie's slightly overweight friend stood immediately and offered his hand to Carmen. Before shaking it, she looked the boy over. He seemed older than his age—too old to be a freshman. He could easily pass for eighteen or nineteen, and he looked even more like a hoodlum than Jessie did. He wore a black hooded sweatshirt unzipped over a plain white T-shirt, and the crotch of his gray Dickies sagged nearly to his knees. The peach fuzz on the boy's caramel-colored face was the only hint that he might actually be fourteen. Carmen finally took hold of the boy's outstretched hand and shook it, noticing the same homemade tattoo Jessie had—"malo" written in blue ink across the knuckles.

She raised an eyebrow. "Angel, huh?" He certainly did not fit his name.

"Angel Huerta. I'm in the same math with Jessie. Mr. Hoyle. Second period."

The sound of the first bell, signaling to students that morning classes were about to commence, filled the counseling room. Carmen took the opportunity to excuse Jessie's visitor. "It was a pleasure to meet you, Angel," she said curtly. "You'd better hurry on to class."

Angel frowned at Jessie. "Man, I thought you said—"

"Come on, miss," Jessie interrupted. His voice lost its nonchalance. "I'm telling you. That's baby work we do in there. *Please*?"

Carmen sighed in exasperation, but she wasn't as irritated as she pretended to be. She was actually a bit impressed. Jessie was trying to go to bat for his friend, and it touched Carmen somewhere. For all of the young man's exterior hardness, he had an obvious soft spot for his buddy.

Angel began testifying on his own behalf. "Count to a hundred by twos. Tell how many fourths in a half a pie." At the end of each sentence, the young man's voice rose as if his statements were really questions. He twisted his barely mustached upper lip into a snarl. "We watch a lot of movies 'cuz the subs don't know we don't have no textbooks, and nobody tells 'em to bring their own worksheets with 'em to our class. When we *do* work in that class—that's the kind of stuff they give us. Count to a hundred by twos."

"Well, I'm sure that is just for review," Carmen offered weakly. "In the beginning of the year the Discovery teachers have to determine how far behind the students might—"

Jessie cut her off. "That pie question was on the final last Friday, miss. We been doing that easy stuff all semester."

Carmen glanced back and forth between the two young men. Eugene had just made it clear at the last staff meeting that there were no more seats available in any of the algebra classes. How was she going to explain stuffing two more students into an already overflowing class that was heading into the second half of the year?

I'll just tell him I was doing my job. She motioned Angel back into his chair. "Have a seat, Mr. Huerta." She pulled a stack of transfer forms from the tray on her desk and opened her file drawer to find a pen. It was then that she noticed a little blue box tucked in between a carton of staples and a spare roll of Scotch tape.

It wasn't just any blue box. Right away Carmen recognized the gold embossed crown—the Royalson Jeweler's insignia. Royalson was top-of-the-line and exclusive. They had only three distributors in the entire country, and one of them was just off Rodeo Drive in Beverly Hills.

Carmen picked up a pen and closed the drawer quickly. She sat still for a moment, trying to decide whether to excuse herself and take the little box somewhere private—or just go ahead and peek inside it right there in front of the two boys. She looked at the boys blankly while she mulled the idea over in her head. Her behavior must have seemed odd to them, because they were both staring curiously into her face. Carmen made her decision quickly. As much as she was dying to know what kind of jewelry was waiting for her in that box, and who had given it to her, her curiosity would have to go on hold until she could get the boys out of her office.

She started on Jessie's schedule changes first. The transfer form consisted of two mandatory components—one giving a written justification for the transfer and the other requiring an official recommendation from Carmen to move the student to the preferred class.

By the time Carmen had gone over each of the forms for both boys, the entire period had passed, and in the time she'd spent with them it had become clear to her that the two boys were very bright. Despite her initial concern about their being too far behind, she thought they might actually be able to adjust to the midyear shift to algebra. But, just in case, she pulled a flyer from a folder in her drawer and handed one to each boy. "These are places in your community where free tutor-ing is available—if you find yourself falling behind."

The boys did the exact same thing at the exact same time. Each promptly put the flyer Carmen had handed him down on the table and, placing a hand on top of it, slid the page back in Carmen's direction. "We won't need it," they said simultaneously.

Carmen raised an eyebrow and slid the flyers back to them. "No need to be embarrassed about possibly needing help, you two. Just fold it up in a little square and hide it somewhere—just in case.

The boys looked at each other and grinned knowingly. Jessie was the first to explain.

"We already got a math tutor. The best. That's how come we already know algebra." He slid his flyer toward Carmen again. "This dude from the barrio named Paid. He works with some of us at night and sometimes on Saturdays."

"Paid?" Carmen's imagination conjured up the gangbanger drug dealer whose moniker could be something as ridiculous as "Paid." She didn't try to hide the look of suspicious sar-casm on her face.

"Paid is the man. He's the carnal, for real," Angel offered enthusiastically.

"Car-*nal*?" Carmen repeated the word slowly. It sounded like something sinister to her.

"Carnal. You know. The . . . uh . . ." Jessie looked to Angel for help.

"The homie." Angel said matter-of-factly.

Carmen nodded knowingly. "And just what is it about this

Paid character that makes him the homie?" The conversation was making her feel old.

"Let's see . . ." Jessie began. "He got mucho dinero. He got a ba-a-ad Benz. And he got every fine lady in the neighborhood wanting him to be their papi chulo."

Laughing out loud, Jessie and Angel slapped each other sideways "five" and each landed a playful punch against the other's shoulder. "He's the man," they said in unison.

Carmen wanted to ask what their friend did for all that "dinero." She thought to remind them that those things they mentioned weren't what makes a man a man, but she kept quiet. If they hadn't learned it by now, who was she to try to school them about such things? What could she expect from boys like them anyway? No fathers at home. Tattooed knuckles and gang attire. Of course they would be taken in by the "Paids" of the world. Carmen herself had had a few run-ins with those "high-roller" types since her breakup with Randall. She'd had offers of expensive gifts and trips to the Caribbean from men with brand-new Benzes and no business cards. "Illegits" was what she called them. Imagine trying to bring one of them to a family reunion. Hah. She would never allow herself to stoop that low—no matter how much money was involved. She hoped the boys would realize what she already knew—the only reason a character like that would be interested in offering them so-called math lessons was so they would owe him a debt that could be collected at a later date.

"You two must remember that you never get something for nothing in this life." Carmen heard herself sounding maternal. She liked the way it made her feel.

"You saying we owe *you* something, Miss D?" Jessie misunderstood her point. She decided to capitalize on his confusion. She hadn't felt like a real counselor in a long time. Maybe these boys didn't have much of a chance at getting into college, but just getting into an algebra class was a major accomplishment. It made her feel good to help. Carmen let a smile spread across her face.

"Yes. Both of you owe me at least a B in algebra."

Jessie elbowed Angel in his ribs. "You got that B, homes?"

"I got that *A,* man. You just better try to keep up."

They were competing for Carmen's approval, and she liked it. "I tell you what." She looked back and forth at the two eager young faces. "If either of you gets an A, I'll take him to lunch. My treat."

What on earth was she saying? She didn't spend her hard-earned money on students. That was her golden rule, and she never broke it. She'd just gotten caught up in the moment. *Well, it's just this once.* It wasn't like it was going to break her bank account.

Both of the young men sat up straighter in their chairs. "I got a date with Miss D," Angel whispered, smiling shyly.

Jessie shoved his friend playfully. "*I* got a date with Miss D, foolio."

"Can I get a date with Miss D too?" a deep voice growled from across the room. Gordon Iverson had stepped unnoticed into the counseling center, and they all watched him as he made his way over to Carmen's cubicle with a basketball tucked under his arm.

"You two in trouble again?" Gordon teased. He palmed the

ball in midair, then held it out to Jessie, snatching it back abruptly when the boy reached for it.

Before either of the boys could answer Gordon's question, the room was filled with the loud ringing of the bell signaling the start of second period. Carmen handed each boy a carbon copy of his reworked class schedule. "If you hurry you can make it to your new algebra class on time."

They gathered their backpacks and notebooks from the table and thanked Carmen again on their way toward the door. "Thanks for helping us out. We won't let you down Miss D," Jessie announced sincerely as they disappeared into the hall.

"Well, can I?" Gordon sat on the edge of the table nearest Carmen's desk and set the basketball down beside him.

"Can you what, Gordon?" Gordon was a tall, slender black man with an athlete's broad chest and muscular legs. He wore a closely trimmed beard on his plain, maple syrup–colored face, and his thick, curly eyelashes saved him from being less-than-interesting to look at. He was no prize, but with his athletic physique he probably got his share of attention at the local gym. At the moment he looked as if he'd just come off the basketball court. Carmen could see the wet perspiration stains in the underarms of his Lakers T-shirt.

"Can I get a date with Miss D too?" He put his hand over his heart and smiled slyly at her. "I promise I'll be good." They both knew what he was trying to imply.

Carmen ignored the innuendo. Any other time she would have reprimanded Gordon's attempt at a dirty joke, but she had something else on her mind at the moment. She'd gotten so caught up in helping Jessie and Angel, she'd almost forgotten about the jewelry box hidden in her file cabinet. Now that she'd remembered it, she was hoping Gordon would either confess to having left it or just get on out of there so she could open the box and put an end to her burning curiosity.

"I don't know, Gordon, I'm really busy this week." Carmen was thinking about the lunch date she'd arranged with the superintendent at noon on Thursday. After that she had to go see what Dr. Lee was all worked up about. Depending on how that turned out, she might not feel like being bothered with Gordon on Friday night.

"Lakers game is Friday. I need you in that seat next to me, lady."

"I don't know, Gordon . . ."

"Clippers," he reminded her. Gordon picked up his basketball and cradled it in his lap. "Grudge match."

Carmen couldn't say no to a Lakers-Clippers game. She was a Los Angeles Lakers fan through and through, and it always irked her that the Clippers had the audacity to lay claim to the L.A. name. She could use an evening of watching the Clippers get massacred. She smiled at Gordon in defeat. "What time do you want to pick me up?"

"I'll be there at six sharp." Gordon got up from his perch. "And Carmen, would you mind doing me one little favor?"

She raised a suspicious eyebrow. "What kind of favor, Gordon?"

"Would you wear that?" Gordon gestured toward Carmen's lap. She had on a knee-length gray wool skirt and black tights. Certainly not something Gordon might think sexy enough to wear on a date. She looked at him incredulously. "You want me to wear this?"

He leaned his long self over her desk and motioned for her to lean in. He surprised her with a bold kiss on the lips then pulled open her file drawer. "No, baby. That." He was pointing at the Royalson's box.

"You put that—"

Iverson put his index finger to her lips. "I'm taking the team to that invitational in San Diego, but I'll be back in town Friday morning. I'll be at your place at six." He placed another kiss on Carmen's lips and hurried out of the room.

≡ 7 ≡

All That Warm Flesh

Dr. G. Harold Browning was balding on top, but had the idea that if he swept the longer side hairs over the bald spot, somehow the world would overlook the freckled yellow skin showing itself mercilessly through the graying strands. Blatant denial. It was obviously a theme the man lived by—a theme that would repeat itself throughout the hour and a half Carmen spent with him.

She had used a sick day to make sure her lunch date with Dr. Browning went off without a hitch. She'd spent the morning getting a manicure and pedicure, and since her doctor's appointment wasn't until two-thirty, she figured she'd be able to get her message across to the superintendent and still have plenty of time to make it to Dr. Lee's office in Westchester. She had arranged to meet Browning at the McCormick and

Schmicks on Rodeo Drive, and when he arrived at the restaurant, she was already seated and waiting for him.

"I understand you attended Spelman," he said after they had each ordered lunch. Carmen ordered the glazed pecan salad and salmon cakes just as Browning had, but instead of the Chablis he ordered for himself, she'd requested an iced tea.

"Spelman? Oh yes," Carmen spouted. "Attending Spelman or Morehouse is an undying tradition in our family." Carmen emphasized "our family" in a way that would express to Browning that despite her mediocre position in a cubicle in the counseling center at Overland High, she was anything but run-of-the-mill or ordinary. She took a prim little sip of her iced tea before continuing.

"Every DuPrè woman since God knows when has graduated from Spelman. Pledged AKA. You know." With the "you know," Carmen smiled and waved a limp-wristed hand at him, then picked up and unfolded the maroon swan, which was her napkin, and laid it gingerly across her lap.

"Yes, yes," Browning muttered. "I am a Morehouse man myself. I was quite the lady killer in those days. Yes, sir."

Carmen winked at him and flashed her dimpled smile. "Oh. I'm sure you were, Dr. Browning." She wasn't really so sure, but she thought it was possible. If the man didn't have a gut hanging six inches over his belt, a set of false teeth that clicked when he talked, and that half-hidden dome-of-shame up there on his head, he *might* have been a lady killer back in the day.

"Oh yes indeed," he continued. "Quite the lady killer, I must say." He stuck his chest out importantly. "I was the captain of the football team my junior and senior years, you know." Before he thought it through, he blurted out, "Matter of fact, I knew your father, Wilfred, quite well. He was a very good athlete. Broke the hundred-meter record, if my memory serves me correctly."

The mention of her father made Carmen choke on her tea, and she began coughing uncontrollably. She brought her napkin up to her mouth and made an attempt to quiet the loud hacking that was drawing attention to their table. Browning rose immediately from his seat and was instantly at Carmen's side with his hand against her back. The way he was patting and rubbing his hand back and forth between her bra straps made her sit up arrow-straight.

"I—" Carmen coughed and patted her chest gingerly. "I'm fi—" Another cough, and several more pats. She reached for the iced tea glass and took a tiny sip as she waved him back to his seat. "I—I didn't know you knew my father," she was finally able to say. Dr. Browning was a lifelong New Yorker who had moved to California to fill the district's superintendent position some months after her father died. Carmen had no idea the two men had met.

"Wilfred DuPrè?" Browning reached out a plump hand and put it on top of Carmen's. "Knew him well. Your mother too." He picked up his glass of Chablis and tipped it toward Carmen. "Class act, your mother. She must be very proud of you."

Snake. Carmen knew exactly what the man was doing. The mention of her father was an obvious faux pas—it would only remind them both that the old geezer had no business trying to hit on Carmen. But mentioning her mother? That was strategic. If he knew Mavis DuPrè, he knew she was anything but proud that one of her daughters had turned out to be a guidance counselor at one of the poorest and worst performing schools in the district. Browning was surely luring Carmen in for the kill. She decided to take the bait.

"Yes. Of course Mother is proud of *all* her children," Carmen crooned sweetly. "And the fact that I've chosen to make a career out of helping young people find their way to college makes her especially proud of me. But you must know she'd be just a bit prouder if I were to be promoted to that TAG Academy position." Carmen smiled broadly at Browning and placed her left hand gently on top of the hand he had already used to clasp her right one. With all that warm flesh stacked up together, she knew he got the point she was making.

"Well, now." He squeezed her fingers gently. "In that case, I believe we can help each other."

Carmen removed her left hand from atop his and placed it lightly against her ample bosom, leaving the other hand still held firmly in his grasp. "Well, yes. I mean, I can see how very helpful you can be to me, Dr. Browning. But . . . what exactly is it that I can do for you?"

For a split second Carmen thought she saw a look of shame cross the superintendent's wide yellow face. A barely perceptible tinge of embarrassment—that at his age, not only was he a hound dog, he was chasing the tail of a college buddy's offspring.

"I—um." His turn to cough. He stared at Carmen for a

long moment before he spit out what he was trying to say. "You know, Miss DuPrè, you really are very beautiful."

Carmen smiled. "Why, thank you. I'm very flattered that you think so."

"I really . . ." There was that embarrassed look again. Only this time it lingered and made his face turn pink. "I'm so very glad you asked me here today. I—I want to apologize for what happened the other evening."

Carmen looked at Browning with an expression that said, *I have no idea what you're talking about.*

"I had a few too many glasses of wine, and—"

"Dr. Browning—"

"Please," he interrupted. "Call me George."

George? Carmen swallowed hard and smiled demurely. "Okay . . . George." Carmen was waiting for him to get to his point, but she continued pretending, acting as if she hadn't noticed that he'd jammed his tongue into her ear at that dinner party. "I'm sure I don't know what you're talking about," she said with simulated sincerity.

"Well, that is very gracious of you, Miss DuPrè. And it shows how much of a lady you obviously are. But we both know I was way out of line. I'd really like a chance to"—he squeezed her hand gently—"to spend some time with you. I hope you will please accept my apology and allow me to begin again. This time as the gentleman that I am."

Carmen could hardly believe her ears. The man was actually trying to *date* her. Did he think there was a chance that she might consider some kind of *relationship* with him? She needed to take another sip of tea and figure this one out—quick.

"Dr. Browning . . ." Carmen pulled her hand away from him and used it to take a drink from her glass.

"George," he reminded her.

"George. I never thought you were anything less than a gentleman. If I did, I wouldn't be sitting here with you, would I?" She shook her head no in answer to her own question. "I think we . . . I mean honestly, George . . . You know how very interested I am in working with the students at the Gifted Academy, and I think . . ." She put her hand back on top of his. "You are absolutely right. We *should* spend some time to-gether. What better way is there for you to get a clear idea of the skills I can bring to the position."

Browning blushed a deep crimson. This was a blush Carmen had no desire to see. One she'd recognize in her sleep, she'd seen it so damn many times in her life. G. Harold Browning was smitten with her. Wide-eyed and attentive—just like Gordon and Eugene. *Be careful what you ask for, Carmen,* she thought. Then she thought about her tiny cubicle back at Overland and thought again. *Sometimes a woman's gotta do what she's gotta do.* She smiled warmly at Dr. Browning and picked up her fork. Stabbing it into her lettuce greens she spouted coyly, "So is it true, *George,* that the position at the academy might be available as early as May?"

⇒ 8 ⇐

Firm and Round and Perfect

After the hour and a half—which seemed to stretch into forever—of smiling sweetly and answering G. Harold Browning's hundred and one personal questions, the last thing in the world Carmen wanted to do was take her clothes off and sit around half naked, but that was exactly what she was being asked to do.

She stared at the cloth gown her gynecologist was holding out to her and just folded her arms stiffly across her chest, refusing to reach for it. Carmen had no intention of giving Dr. Lee the impression that she might actually agree to her ridiculous suggestion. She was insisting Carmen undergo some kind of urgently needed test—a test with the word "needle" in the title. Carmen damn sure wasn't interested in any more tests. She had tried to listen to what the doctor said to her about the mammogram results that had come back irregular, but she still wasn't really getting the point.

"What do you mean by 'irregular,' anyway, Dr. Lee?" Carmen grumbled impatiently.

The slightly exasperated look on the doctor's face said she did not want to have to repeat herself a third time, but she inhaled a deep breath and did just that.

"Carmen, as I explained to you before, it is absolutely essential that we perform an aspiration biopsy of that small mass in your left breast. There's a shadow on your mammogram that is significantly larger than it was on the film in May. With a woman your age, it is rare that I schedule a second mammogram, but I had to make sure that shadow was nothing to worry about. As it turns out, it has increased significantly."

Carmen stared blankly at her. She was waiting for the woman to get to the point.

"It still may be nothing to worry about, but it is too important to risk doing nothing. Which is why we really need this test."

"What will the test tell you that you don't already know?" The question was a waste of breath. It did not matter to Carmen what the answer was; she had no intention of having the procedure done. She was more than willing to take the risk of doing nothing and hope for the "probably nothing to worry about."

"What we do know, Carmen, is that you've had substantial tissue growth. We want to make sure it's just fibrous and not malignant. African-American women have an increased incidence of fibrous masses, so that in itself is not anything for you to be alarmed at. Nearly eight out of the ten masses we biopsy are completely benign. However, breast cancer *is* diagnosed in two hundred thousand women each year, and African Americans are more than two times likely to die from breast cancer than white women."

Carmen's pulse began to race. *Do I really need to hear all this?*

"And when it is detected early, it is nearly one hundred percent curable. The needle biopsy is a necessary precaution. Really. I wouldn't suggest if it I thought otherwise. We really need to be certain."

Carmen stood up abruptly, gathering her jacket and her purse and clutching them to her chest. "You assured me when we did the mammogram that it was an optional test at my age. I am not even thirty years old, Doctor. *Really,* it isn't likely that it's anything serious, right?" Carmen didn't wait for an answer to the question. She headed for the door, trying her best to sound firm when she spoke again. "I will come back in a few months. How's that? If you still think you need to do your—" Carmen frowned. "What was it?"

"Needle biopsy," the doctor offered. "But, Carmen, we really cannot risk any more time getting by us. We have to have the test right away or—"

"We?" Carmen interrupted. She stuck her hand up in front of the woman's face, signaling that she did not want to hear anything else. "*We* is not who you mean, Dr. Lee. The only *we* about to get stuck with a needle is *me.* And *I* don't want the damn test. You said yourself that a woman my age has a low risk of breast cancer. You told me that when I consented to the damn mammogram in the first place. Now you're telling me you want to poke a needle in my breast? In *my* breast, Dr. Lee—not *our* breast."

The doctor's expression turned gravely serious, and she scolded Carmen firmly. "It's true that it is less common to find cancer in a woman your age, Carmen, but it does happen." She softened her tone when she added, "And really, if there is a problem, I mean, if there is a malignancy, we want to catch it early—believe me. Breast cancer is a swift and vicious killer. I have seen it too many times."

Swift and vicious? Carmen got a mental image of a million cancerous Pacmen munching away at her breast.

"At this point the mass is simply suspicious, but if it is cancerous, Carmen, knowing that now might mean the difference between losing a small amount of breast tissue and losing your life."

Carmen didn't want to lose anything. She wanted her breasts to stay firm and round and perfect. She didn't want to be hearing any of this. Why had she consented to that damn mammogram in the first place?

"When?" Carmen whispered painfully. "When do you have to do this test?"

"Today." The doctor held the gown out to Carmen again.

Carmen looked blankly into her face. "I can't today. I have to work tomorrow. And I'm going to the Lakers game. I—" She realized how ridiculous she sounded and stopped talking.

"You will be able to do all those things, don't worry." The doctor smiled warmly. "A needle biopsy isn't an invasive operation. It's done with a very fine needle, is nearly painless, and leaves no scar. And you will be able to go back to work to-morrow *and* catch the Lakers game. I promise you."

Carmen exhaled a loud breath of defeat and sat back down. Finally she reached for the gown Dr. Lee was once again holding out to her and as she grasped it, she gave the doctor the most pitiful, pain-filled, *Why are you making me do this?* expression she could manage.

"I promise to make this as quick and painless as possible, Carmen. Why don't we just put the gown on and get started, okay?"

"Yeah, sure." Carmen muttered sarcastically. "Why don't *we?*"

⇥ 9 ⇤

Sharpened and Ready to Slice

Mavis DuPrè's home was decorated mostly in ivory and gold, with a few gaudy walnut and mahogany pieces thrown in for not-so-good measure. After Lindsey graduated from high school and moved on to Spelman, Mavis had plush off-white carpet installed in the living room and bought herself a brand-new drawing room set—an obnoxious ensemble of pale birch end tables gilded around the edges, two stiff ivory and gold brocade upholstered armchairs, and a matching settee. With the exception of a silk shingle lamp she found in New Orleans a few years back and an antique curio shelf Della had given her last Mother's Day, Mavis hadn't added or changed a thing since.

Carmen always found it difficult to sit in her mother's living room, and, as if Mother DuPrè knew it caused Carmen distress, she made sure to begin Carmen's visits home with a sit-down-and-have-a-cup-of-tea discussion there. Carmen would be forced to endure an hour or so of who in the family had accomplished what, who was on the verge of bringing shame to the DuPrè family name, and who had managed to behave like a total fool.

Normally the very last place on earth Carmen wanted to be on a Friday afternoon was her mother's living room, but after having spent the previous day suffering first through lunch with Dr. Browning and then that awful needle test with Dr. Lee, there Carmen was, perched at the edge of her mother's brocade settee, sipping chamomile from a china teacup, and silently asking herself why she had even bothered to come.

Mavis was seated in an armchair across the room, concealing her ever-growing plumpness under a roomy red satin jogging suit and sporting a pair of fuzzy black slippers. Her fingernails were perfectly polished in candy apple red, with her lips painted to match. Carmen took note of the thick, two-shades-too-light layer of beige foundation Mavis had too generously applied on her perpetually scowling face. *She's getting old*, Carmen thought. Mavis was sixty-three years old, but she looked closer to eighty.

"So, what brings you out to visit your mother on a school day, Carmen?" Mavis sipped from her teacup tentatively, carefully studying her daughter over the edge of her glasses.

"I took the day off today. I just thought I'd drop by."

Mavis raised a suspicious eyebrow. "Didn't you take the day off yesterday?"

"Yes, I did. I had an important lunch—"

"Yes, I know." Mavis interjected. "I know all about your luncheon with Dr. Browning."

Carmen just stared at her mother in awe. How in the hell did this woman do it? She always managed to get her nose in the middle of Carmen's business. And it wasn't good enough to just *be* in her business—no, Mavis DuPrè had to sniff and sniff until every last trace of possible impropriety was discovered.

"Rowena Matthews's niece's husband's sister LaDonna saw you two at McCormick's." Mavis narrowed her eyes at Carmen. "You getting fired or something?

"No, Mother."

"Well, it certainly can't be a demotion. You work in just about the worst hellhole in the district now. What are they going to do, send you to the *projects*?"

Carmen ached to roll her eyes and send a twisted frown in her mother's direction, but she stifled the urge and smiled stiffly at Mavis instead. "I'm getting a promotion, Mother."

"A promotion, huh? So are they finally taking you out of that big uni-office you've got and giving you one with a door?"

Carmen sighed heavily and put her teacup down on a coaster on the table in front of her. "I'm being promoted to the college counseling position at the Talented and Gifted Academy." It wasn't all the way true yet, but Carmen tossed the bone to Mavis anyway. "I'm very excited about it, Mother."

Mavis looked at Carmen as if it pained her to feel even the slightest tinge of pride about something she had accom-

plished. She didn't comment at all on her daughter's announcement, and instead Mavis's tight little smile widened
suddenly, and she scooted herself to the end of her chair.

"Did you hear Della's news?"

Carmen shook her head. "What news?"

"She sold that estate out past Malibu. She'll be getting a
quarter-of-a-million-dollar commission check. Can you imagine earning all that money on one sale?"

Carmen felt her stomach tightening into a hard ball. Soon her
abdomen would begin cramping—and then there'd be those
sharp shooting pains in her chest. And if she didn't get out of
there quick, she'd have a migraine headache to go with that.

"Um. That's very nice." Carmen managed to push the
words out without too much sarcasm. "I'm sure Daniel must
be very proud of her."

"Well, of course he is. She manages to take such good care
of him and the twins, and she still finds time in her day to sell
multi-million-dollar real estate *and* visit her mother regularly."

Carmen stood up abruptly. She picked up her purse and
halfheartedly flashed Mavis the least phony smile she had.
She walked over and planted a stiff-lipped peck on her
mother's wrinkled beige cheek. "I've got to be going now,
Mother."

"Hmph. You haven't been here half an hour, Carmen. It's
the middle of January and I haven't seen you once since
Christmas. Your sister Della manages to come by a couple of
times a week. But you—it's a good thing I don't hold my
breath in between visits; I'd have turned every shade of blue
and dropped dead by now."

Carmen hated herself for coming. There was just no good excuse for wasting a day off being persecuted by Mavis; but she needed to talk to someone. She had awakened with such a strong feeling of dread that morning. Fear really. Though she was trying desperately to believe Dr. Lee's assurances that the chance of a malignancy in a woman her age was unlikely, Carmen lay in the bed half the morning enveloped in a cloud of doom. She was more than a little worried about the results of that damn test, and though things with Mavis never ended up any different than they had today, she thought maybe, just maybe she should at least try to go home.

"I'm sorry I haven't been by more. I've been very busy lately with the semester change and all." Carmen wanted to just blurt it out. Put it right out on that ugly little coffee table. *Mother, they're afraid I might have cancer.* I'm *afraid I might have cancer. I'm afraid I'm going to die alone, Mother—never having a husband or children or any of the things you are so proud of Della for having.*

Carmen felt a burning pressure building behind her eyes. She fought the urge to cry and smiled stiffly at her mother instead. She tried to picture herself getting what she really wanted from Mavis. She tried to picture Mavis leaping to her feet to gather her daughter in a comforting embrace—tried to imagine how her mother's voice might sound telling her some soothing words about having faith—about family being there for you. She tried to picture her mother simply telling her not to worry, that everything would be okay. *Never in a million years.* Carmen knew better. *Knowing Mavis, she'd ask me what stupid thing I'd done that could cause me to get cancer. She'd go on some long tirade about how bad my diet is and then she'd tell me all about some special she saw on shark cartilage on channel forty-eight.*

Carmen cleared her throat tersely, blinked back the tears behind her eyes, and dismissed her fantasy of receiving any kind of maternal comforting. She quickly made her way to the front door instead. "I really do have to go, Mother. I'm going to the Lakers game in a couple of hours, and I don't want to be late."

"Lakers game? Why don't you call Maxwell and see if he wants to go? That poor baby works so hard, you know." Mavis hoisted herself from her chair and followed Carmen to the entryway. "Ever since they made him a partner at the law firm, he just seems so tired all the time. Carmen, you do your brother a favor and take him with you."

"I'm going on a *date,* Mother." Carmen pulled the door open and stood in the threshold. Just a few more seconds of torture, then she could make her escape.

"A date? A date with whom?" Mavis asked the question like there was absolutely no chance it was none of her business.

Carmen let out an exasperated breath. "He's not a doctor or a lawyer, if that's what you want to know."

"Don't you get testy with me, Miss Carmen Marie." Mavis put a hand to one hip and shook an index finger at her daughter. "I have every right to ask my own child who she *is* spending her time with—since she isn't spending much of it with *me*." Mavis had that *Look at what you've done—you've got me on the edge of tears* thing in her voice. "Since your father passed, I don't have anything on this earth to live for except my children and my grandchildren. And you think it doesn't interest me to know who you're going out with? You think I don't care that it looks like you're going to end up an old, barren maid?"

The words "*old*" and "*barren*" were knives Mavis kept sharpened and ready to slice Carmen with when she meant to cut her extra deep, but Carmen pretended not to feel the pain they inflicted. She just held her breath and stepped out onto the porch, taking hold of the doorknob and glaring indignantly at Mavis. "I'm dating a basketball coach, Mother, not a racehorse. I'm not getting impregnated by the man; I'm just going to the Lakers game."

Mavis's face suddenly shone with pleasure, as if she had just sunk her teeth into a Dove bar at the end of a chocolate fast. "You're going out with the coach of the Lakers? Oh my goodness, Carmen—Rowena will be green."

"Goodbye, Mother," Carmen muttered sadly as she pulled the door closed behind her.

10

Seven or Eight Carats

Carmen had never been as glad to see Gordon as she was when he arrived at her door, and she let him know it by giving him an especially passionate kiss. She hadn't spoken to him since he'd left for the basketball tournament in San Diego, and this was the first chance she'd gotten to talk to him about the little blue box he'd left in her desk drawer. And now that she was with him face-to-face, she could feel her heart swell a little in her chest at how highly he must think of her to buy her such an exquisite gift.

"What did I do to deserve that?" he asked, half joking. He knew Carmen put more of herself into that kiss than any she had given him before.

She stayed put in Gordon's arms for a couple of minutes and basked in the feel of his hands sliding gently up and down her back. She didn't tell him she was happy not to have to be alone after the day she'd had, and she didn't tell him how worried she was about the biopsy Dr. Lee had performed the day before. Even if she tried, there was no way she could put into words how absolutely terrified she was that sometime after Monday, when the doctor gave her the verdict about her breast, she might not be able to find a man willing to take her to lunch—let alone one who might be willing to consider walking her down the aisle. "Barren and alone" was how Mavis had so aptly put it.

With all the thoughts and fears crowding Carmen's head, all she really wanted to do was just lay her head on Gordon's chest, feel his arms around her, and cry like a little girl. She ached to tell him all about the effect a few minutes with Mavis had had on her. She wished she could tell him how much she yearned for her father—how she wished he were alive to provide the kind of comfort Mavis never would. She wished she could let Gordon know how good it felt to have his arms around her. Instead she just got into his car, focused her attention on the bracelet on her wrist, and didn't talk about much else the entire ride to the Staples Center.

"Oh, Gordon, look how the light makes a million tiny sparks jump off the diamonds." It wasn't like Carmen to gush like a schoolgirl, but that was exactly what she was doing. And she'd been doing it from the moment Gordon opened her car door and helped her settle down into the passenger side of his '94 Buick LeSabre. Carmen's voluptuous curves were wrapped in a pair of skin-tight jeans and a snug-fitting pink cashmere sweater, and she had her nails and toes French-tipped, as if she needed to do one more thing to prevent poor Gordon from being able to concentrate on the road.

When they'd arrived at the arena and made their way to Gordon's courtside seats, Carmen turned to him and tried once again to let him know how grateful she was for the gift he'd given her. She stretched her left hand out in front of her dramatically—turning her wrist this way and that—oohing and aahing at the sheer beauty of the bracelet. It was the first time she'd actually worn it, though she'd almost put it on for her lunch date with Browning, but then thought better of it. She was glad now that she'd decided to wear it for the first time on her date with Gordon.

By the end of the first quarter Carmen must have thanked him at least five times. Grinning from ear to ear, every few minutes she spouted some giddy remark like "Oh, I can't believe how beee-utiful this is" or "You must have spent a small fortune on this, Gordon." But each time she showered him with thank-yous, he just grinned at her and repeated that he was so very glad she liked the gift.

Liked it? She had no idea diamonds could have such an effect on her. From the moment she opened the little box, lifted the diamond-studded bracelet from it, and watched it sparkle before her eyes, Carmen knew she was in love—with the bracelet, that is. And Gordon? She had to admit that his generosity had made him much more attractive, and interesting, and amusing, and—well—*generous*. One thing was for sure; he was beginning to edge out Eugene in the competition for her attention.

As she sat next to Gordon, waiting for the Lakers to run

out the final two minutes left in the half, Carmen turned the bracelet over and over in her lap, watching the arena lighting shatter into a thousand little sunbeams. The thoughtfulness of Gordon's gift had her overflowing with an emotion she didn't quite recognize, and she was trying desperately to think of a way to give him an idea of just how grateful his gesture was making her feel.

Carmen rested her hand lightly on top of Gordon's muscular thigh, watching the bracelet send little shards of light onto his black nylon sweatpants. She gave his thigh a gentle squeeze, which was enough to get Gordon to momentarily take his eyes off Shaquille O'Neal. He glanced down briefly at the hand Carmen had placed on his leg, then, with raised eyebrows and an astonished look on his face, he looked deeply into her eyes. She stared back into his eyes suggestively and fluttered her eyelashes ever-so-softly, smiling at the man like she was a teenager with a crush.

Gordon's Adam's apple made a slow up-and-down motion that Carmen interpreted as a nervous gulp, then he took Carmen's hand in his and lifted it from his leg just long enough to plant a kiss against it. He returned her hand to his thigh and his attention back to Shaq.

It was the first time Carmen had seen Gordon at a loss for words—with no snappy sexual innuendo to fire at her. He bounced his knee slightly up and down a few times, nervously directing his attention back and forth from Shaq to Kobe Bryant—who were passing the basketball to each other in an attempt to run the clock down. Without looking away from the court, Gordon whispered to Carmen, "If I could afford to, I'd put one on the other wrist and both ankles too—especially if it made you smile at me like that more often."

Carmen felt her smile widen uncontrollably. She knew she should settle down and just act like her old nonchalant self, but it was impossible for her to keep still. She had been trying to concentrate on the game since the starting tip-off, but she just wasn't able to give her beloved Lakers her full attention. Not tonight. There had to be at least seven or eight carats wrapped around her wrist, and with every movement of her hand, the bauble flashed and sparkled at her, reminding her that Gordon Iverson was turning out to be more of a man than she had initially given him credit for.

"Gordon?"

Gordon patted Carmen's hand absently. His eyes were now fixed on Kobe, who was standing at the free-throw line with just six seconds remaining in the half.

"Gordon?"

This time he squeezed Carmen's hand to let her know he'd heard her, but his attention was steadfastly fixed on the leather sphere in Bryant's hands.

Kobe bounced the ball two quick times and aimed for the basket.

"Take me home please, Gordon." She squeezed his thigh with a gentle massaging motion.

Gordon didn't see Bryant's shot bounce disappointingly against the glass and back down onto the court. His eyes were fixed unblinkingly on Carmen's.

"Home? But we just got here." He searched her face for

some sign that she was upset or bothered by something he'd said or done, but she was smiling provocatively at him.

Carmen let her fingers slide back and forth suggestively along Gordon's inner thigh. "Let's go, Gordon. We can go to my apartment . . . if you want."

The roar of the crowd was the only signal either of them had that Bryant had had better luck with the second free throw. The entire crowd rose to its collective feet just as the buzzer sounded to signal the end of the half. Carmen and Gordon seemed to be the only ones still sitting down.

Carmen waited in silence for Gordon's response. She was more than a little surprised that he didn't make a dirty remark—something about how he might finally get a glimpse of her breasts, or something equally crass. But Gordon's Adam's apple just did that slow gulp thing again, and, uncharacteristic of him, he remained speechless. Finally he rose slowly to his feet, and holding a hand out to Carmen, he helped her stand too. Without a word, he guided her through the crowd toward the arena exits.

Carmen followed behind as Gordon pulled her through the mass of people. It seemed every one of the thirty thousand spectators had decided to take advantage of the halftime intermission, and it was all Carmen could do to keep a tight grip on Gordon's hand.

When they'd finally made it out into the main foyer, she gave his hand a tug—a signal that she needed to stop at the entrance to the women's restroom.

A line of women stretched twenty or so feet along the wall and wrapped down a stairwell, where the line disappeared into the bathroom. The wait would be at least fifteen minutes, so Gordon offered to go get the car and come for Carmen through the valet parking lane. She returned the quick peck he placed on her lips and agreed to meet him out front, then took a place at the end of the line and watched as Gordon walked away from her. She was relieved to watch him go. Carmen didn't really even need to use the bathroom. She just wanted a chance to get away from Gordon for a few minutes so she could give some thought to what she was getting herself into.

She leaned her shoulder against the wall and watched as passing men took double and triple takes while their women looked Carmen up and down with salty stares. One man made the woman he was with go stand in the concession line for him—so he could stand nearer to Carmen and try to pass his business card to her without getting caught.

Carmen was used to that kind of ridiculous behavior from men. If she were really on the hunt for a long-term relationship, she believed she could snag just about any man she wanted. But she wasn't near ready. Her plan was to wait until she was standing firmly on her own two feet, making good money and having no need to depend on a man for anything. No man would ever put her out as if she were an unwanted alley cat—as Randall had so cruelly done. Never again. Carmen intended to own her own home, upgrade her automobile and her wardrobe. Then she'd be ready to go after some big game. Maybe an NBA player or a high-powered attorney. Certainly not someone as crude and low-class as Gordon. A high school basketball coach with a dirty mouth? Definitely not husband material, but with his newfound generosity and his puppy dog admiration of her? He might just be the temporary company she needed right now.

Carmen closed her eyes and imagined what it might be like to let Gordon get what he'd been after all these months. She imagined herself resting against his muscular chest, feeling his arms enfold her. She wanted to be close to him, to let him absorb some of the fear and loneliness she was trying so hard to deal with on her own. She wanted to take him back to her apartment, but she wasn't quite sure if she was ready for what that really meant. One thing she did know for sure—if she let him make love to her, there would be no going back to the way things were before. He would begin to see her as his "territory." He would try to put her on a string, and then little by little he would reel her in until every last bit of her freedom was gone.

When Carmen's section of the line finally made it inside the bathroom door, she bypassed the stalls and stepped behind a woman washing her hands in one of a long row of occupied sinks. Carmen was not at all ashamed to stare at herself in the mirror in the crowded restroom. She gazed at her own reflection as if it were a piece of fine art—studying the way her emerald eyes sparkled back at her from a face the Creator had blessed with flawless skin and fashion-model cheekbones.

Finally the woman in front of her stepped away, leaving Carmen with a full view of the way her pink cashmere sweater hugged the round perfection of her breasts. She thought of Dr. Lee's words "swift and vicious" and tried to picture one of her breasts missing. *What's left when a woman's breast is cut off?* she thought. *A hideous mangled scar. A woman who would always be less than a woman.* If that happened to her, what man would want her? How could she face the rest of her life knowing she'd end up just as Mavis had said, "barren and alone"? The mere thought of it made her eyes water.

A loud "ahem" erupted behind Carmen, so she quickly leaned over the sink to turn on the faucet, acting as if she'd come in to wash her hands. She just let the water run into the sink, checking her face, making sure her makeup was all right. She wasn't in need of a lipstick touch-up, and her hair fell perfectly around her face in a cascade of shiny auburn curls. Carmen looked fabulous, but she stood in front of the mirror primping anyway. Stalling.

A tall redhead in a gold and rhinestone-studded denim suit let her know with an irritated smirk that she was waiting to use the sink Carmen was blocking, so naturally Carmen took her sweet time.

Carmen slowly brushed the palms of her hands down the front of her sweater and took a long look in the mirror. *Lose a breast?* God would not do that to her. He created a work of art when He created Carmen; He wouldn't let anything so drastic happen to a sculpture like this. Carmen cocked an eyebrow at herself and turned to smile slyly at the irritated woman behind her, then she used the hand with the bracelet on it to smooth some of her curls behind one ear—making sure the impatient woman caught an eyeful of the prize on her wrist.

"It's all yours now," she said to the woman with a sugary smile. Carmen didn't need any more time at the mirror anyway. She didn't need any more time to think about what she was going to do with Gordon either. She'd made her decision—Gordon was finally going to get what he had waited all these months for. Carmen was going to let Gordon Iverson make love to her tonight.

⋛ 11 ⋚

Get Some of This

Carmen showed Gordon the way to her bedroom and left him sitting stiffly on the edge of her queen-sized bed. She retreated in haste to the bathroom to find the nerve she seemed to have misplaced somewhere on the ride from the sports arena to her apartment—nerve she desperately needed now. It wasn't that she was trying to back out of what she'd started. She actually wanted to be in Gordon's arms. It was just that it all seemed so . . . planned.

She turned on the faucet full blast so Gordon couldn't hear her brushing her teeth, gargling with Listermint, and performing the various other hygienic activities she felt the need to undertake before getting naked with a man. After ten or fifteen minutes she emerged from the bathroom smelling like Givenchy body lotion and wearing her silk bathrobe—tied tightly at her waist—with nothing on underneath but the diamond bracelet.

Gordon was exactly where Carmen had left him—perched stiffly at the end of her bed. But there was one startling difference—the man had removed every stitch of his clothing. When he leaned his totally naked self back on straightened arms and smiled suggestively at Carmen, she spotted a condom package, already conveniently ripped open, on the bedside table.

Gordon gave her a cocky grin, patted the bed's lavender satin comforter, and rubbed his hand in slow circles on the spot next to him where he wanted her to sit.

"Are you gonna come over here and get some of this"—Gordon raised a sly eyebrow, then looked down at the huge erection that had propped itself up awkwardly against his muscular thigh—"or are you going to make me chase you down and give it to you?"

Carmen swallowed hard and smiled apprehensively. Gordon's shy nervousness had sure disappeared in a hurry. Chase her down? Give it to her? Since when was making love supposed to be like that? Wasn't it supposed to start out slow and work its way *gradually* toward big, bold, frontal nudity?

She stared down at Gordon's erection with wide eyes. Though Randall had been her first, and she didn't have much to compare him to, she had always considered him well-endowed. But compared to Gordon . . . *Ouch.* She took a deep, resolute breath and inched toward him. Swallowing hard, and trying not to look nervous, she slowly fumbled with the belt on her robe.

"That's it, baby." Gordon was still leaning back on his straightened arms, feasting on her scantily clad body with his eyes. He sat up straight and motioned for Carmen to come to him. She wordlessly obeyed, still fumbling with her belt and trying unsuccessfully to calm her nervousness. She attempted to smile confidently at him, but all she could do was hope she didn't look as scared as she felt.

"Ohhh. I've waited a long time for you to share these with me." Gordon didn't bother trying to help her undo the knotted belt. Instead he peeled her robe back around the outer edges of her breasts and buried his face between them like they were oxygen and he needed them to breathe.

"Damn, baby. Damn." Gordon's mouth was all over the place—sucking and licking all over Carmen's breasts like he was a starving puppy. Carmen wasn't enjoying it nearly as much as he seemed to be. Maybe she could enjoy it more if he would slow down a little, and if he wasn't pressing her damn breasts together like he was trying to make them into one big melon instead of two.

"Gordon." She stared down at him in irritation.

Gordon stopped the tongue bath abruptly and opened his eyes. "Yeah, baby? Oh yeah. Here, let me get that." He'd assumed she wanted him to untie the knot in her belt, which he immediately began fumbling with. At least that kept his hands busy, but he went right back to licking and kissing all over her cleavage.

Carmen was trying desperately to relax and catch up with Gordon—to follow him to the place of wild abandon he was obviously on his way to. So when he finally loosened the knot on her belt and reached into her robe to fill his huge hands with the firm, warm flesh of her behind, she welcomed the hot glow that crept between her thighs. Placing her hands on either side of Gordon's head, Carmen pulled his face gently into her cleavage, then guided his lips slowly up the slope of one of her breasts. Out of the corner of her eye, she caught sight of the intoxicating glint of the diamonds on her wrist, and a shiver of pleasure instantly snaked its way up her spine. Just at that moment, Gordon took one of her nipples gently into his mouth, and Carmen closed her eyes and let out the tiniest of moans. The sound of it seemed to drive Gordon wild. He pulled Carmen to him, pressing his hardness against her thighs. His lips traveled from her waist to her thighs, then back up to her breasts and down again.

Carmen's inhibitions melted away and she let the heat of Gordon's passion thaw what Randall had left in deep freeze. When Gordon stuck his tongue in her navel and traced a soft, slow line around it, her breaths came in quick little gusts, and her legs began to weaken beneath her. A wave of fire was sizzling now beneath Carmen's flesh, and when the desire to feel Gordon inside her welled between her thighs, she felt a strong urge to push Gordon down onto his back and climb on top of him and—

"*Owww!*" Carmen screamed it—loud. Gordon had licked his way back up to her left breast and had bitten her nipple. Hard.

She backed away from him angrily. "Ouch." She stared down at him like he'd lost his goddamn mind, rubbing the injured breast with the palm of her hand, and waiting for him to respond with something besides the silly grin he had plastered across his face. "That hurt, Gordon."

"Aww, come here, girl," he growled. "Let me kiss it and make it better." He reached for Carmen, but she backed farther away and glared at him. She frowned and reprimanded him firmly, "If you want to do this with me, Gordon, we're going to have to lay down a few ground rules."

"Oooh. I like a woman to take charge in the bedroom." He grunted excitedly, reaching for her again. This time he caught the front of her robe and pulled her to him, making her tumble down awkwardly on top of him as he lay back on the bed.

"Gordon, I'm serious." Carmen struggled to free herself from his grasp. She managed to raise up on one elbow—to stare Gordon down with a *Don't mess with me* expression on her face. She wanted him to know she meant it. It had been too long. She had waited too long to finally choose a man to go to bed with for Gordon to treat her like she was some common street whore.

"We're supposed to be making love, Gordon . . ."

"I know, baby. I know." He lifted his head from the bed to press his lips to her mouth, but she turned her head, avoiding his eager lips.

"Look, Gordon, I already have reservations about this." She exhaled a loud, frustrated breath. You don't need to make it any more diffi—"

The wounded look that took over Gordon's face made Carmen stop midsentence. From the look he was giving her, you would have thought she had accused him of rape. He stared at her sullenly. "What did you say?" There was the tiniest hint of anger in his voice.

"You heard what I said, Gordon."

"You have reservations about this?" He searched Carmen's face for a long moment. Suddenly, softly, he closed his eyes and let his head fall back against the bed.

"What I meant was I've waited a long time to do this, Gordon, and—"

"You have reservations about this?" he repeated, his eyes still tightly closed. When she didn't answer, he rolled Carmen off him and lay motionless on his back.

Carmen suddenly felt uncomfortably aware of her nakedness and struggled to pull her bathrobe around her exposed body. "It's—it's not easy for a woman to just put her guard down and let—" She didn't bother to finish. She knew Gordon understood exactly what she was trying to say. She really wasn't ready for what they were doing.

Gordon sat up abruptly and stared at her, a look of sadness reflected in his eyes. Finally he reached a hand out to slowly finger one of her silken ringlets. "You have no idea what this means to me, do you?" His voice quivered with an emotional quality Carmen didn't think Gordon was capable of. He sounded almost . . . *vulnerable.*

Gordon let the lock of Carmen's hair fall from his fingertips as he whispered, "*You* invited *me* here, Carmen. If you have reservations about having sex with me, why are you doing it?"

His words seemed to slide their way right down Carmen's arm to the bracelet. She quickly hid the glint of the diamonds inside her bathrobe, but that just made her look guilty. Gordon raised his eyes to Carmen's. He glared sullenly at her, behaving as if it had not occurred to him before that moment that the piece of jewelry on her wrist was the real reason he had finally been invited into her bedroom.

Letting himself fall back down against the bed dejectedly, Gordon stared at the ceiling in silence. Finally he muttered quietly, "I didn't buy the damn bracelet, Carmen. Timms did."

Carmen knew she didn't hear Gordon say he didn't buy the bracelet. She just knew there was not a butt-ass-naked lying motherfucker on her bed telling her she had almost—

She jumped up from the bed frantically, tying her bathrobe closed and screaming like a madwoman. "*Get out!*" She grabbed Gordon's clothes, which he'd left in a sloppy pile on the chair near her bedroom door. "Get *out* of my house, goddammit."

"Now, Carmen . . ."

"*No!*" She headed for the living room with Gordon's clothes in her arms, still screaming at the top of her lungs. "*No! Hell No!* You lying son of a *bitch!*"

Gordon leaped from the bed and followed behind her into the living room, trying desperately to make his case. "Hey. Come on, Carmen. I didn't want it to matter, baby. I just wanted you to want me for me. That's all. I—"

Carmen stood at the front door and yanked it open. She heaved Gordon's clothes out into the darkness of her private porch and turned on him, her eyes seething with hatred. Her words came out in a snarled whisper. "You get the hell out of my house."

Gordon hop-stepped his nude self out onto the porch, desperately trying to gather up his clothes before a nosy neighbor called the apartment security patrol—or the police. He grabbed his boxers from the potted palm and his sweats from the flower box, then tried to make it back to Carmen's door in time to get back in. She quickly slammed it in his face and bolted it.

Still holding on to the deadbolt with one hand, she leaned her forehead to the door, barely whispering the words she had screamed at Gordon a few seconds before—"Lying son of a bitch." She closed her eyes and listened as Gordon, struggling to get into his clothes, muttered apologies to her from the other side of the door.

"Let me make it up to you," he begged. "Try to understand how I feel about you, Carmen. Please. I didn't actually lie to you. I—I never actually said I bought it. I just didn't tell the truth when I should have." Gordon knocked softly. "Let me in, Carmen. I really am sorry." Finally she heard him open and close the latch on the gate, open and close his car door, and drive away.

Carmen stood with her forehead pressed against the door, her anger turning suddenly into overwhelming terror. She tried desperately to avoid the thoughts materializing behind her eyes. The thought of Dr. Lee's test—of probably losing her breast. She thought of Randall. Of how lucky he was to have dumped her when he did. She wondered if she would ever again have a man make love to her the way Randall had. And then it struck her suddenly, painfully, that this date with Gordon, as humiliating as it turned out to be, was quite possibly her last date—ever.

An agony Carmen recognized began welling up deep inside her—an agony she wasn't equipped to face again. She raised her hands high above her head and pressed both palms to the door, her cheek pressed against the wood as if she were being held at gunpoint by an invisible assailant. She stood in that position of surrender for a long, excruciating moment, feeling herself sinking into a terrifying place she distinctly recalled. A place you fall into when everything you were sure you knew about your life and your future was suddenly and brutally snatched away, and you could hardly wake to face day after miserable day. She'd barely survived it—the loss of Randall. And now all Carmen could feel in the tight space behind her breasts was that same terror. The terror of once again losing everything that made her anything. The awful dread that when it was all said and done, there would be nothing left of her that would be worth anything to anyone. In the end she would die just as Mavis predicted—*barren and alone.*

Alone. The word swam around in Carmen's head in a harsh whisper, joined by other, more terrifying words that Carmen could not keep out. *Swift and vicious. Cancer. You have cancer.* She was sure of it. Carmen imagined the tiny Pacmen Dr. Lee had called to mind, chomping away at her breast—chomping away at her life. *Cancer.* She saw a clear picture of Pedro Camacho waving to her from his truck—the man whose son had died of it. She heard his words ringing ominously in her ears. Words he had tossed so carelessly at her—words that were impossible for Carmen to believe she would ever see materialize in what might be left of her life. *Be happy.* He'd said it like it was really the simplest thing to achieve.

The sound of her own raspy breathing loosened the tenuous grip Carmen had on her emotions, and the urge to sob surged behind her rib cage. *I will not cry.* She tried to battle it, to stand firm against the wall of tears building up behind her eyes. *I will not cry.* As her chest heaved with heavy, painful breaths, Carmen turned slowly, leaning back despondently against the door and gazing around at the emptiness of her apartment.

Letting her eyes roam the ivory tones of her sparsely furnished home, she was struck suddenly by how pale everything in her life was. Her carpet, ivory. Her corduroy sofa group, off-white. Her vertical blinds, beige. Her coffee and end tables, clear glass. Then Carmen's eyes settled on the only thing in the entire room that held the slightest hint of warmth or color. She gazed up at the one treasure she had managed to salvage from the years she wasted with Randall. She gratefully shifted her focus away from her pain and studied the four, limited-edition, hand-tinted J. L. Wright photographic prints hanging side-by-side on the far wall. A collection entitled *Sisters of Eve.* A soulful compilation of beautiful but lonesome-looking black women draped in colored linen—sisters tinted in shades of gold, teal, lavender, and sienna who stared solemnly at Carmen from frames of platinum and glass. Carmen had managed to sneak them all out of Randall's apartment the day he put her out, and she had always been somehow comforted by the private joke she shared with the kidnapped Eve and her sisters. But not even they could soothe Carmen's torment tonight. Instead they seemed to taunt her with their sorrowful stares. *Be happy.* She shut her eyes tightly and pressed herself back against the door, still fighting to hold in her tears. What could possibly make her happy? A man? A bracelet?

Who gives a damn about a bracelet? She looked at the diamonds on her wrist, her heart swelling with a blazing fire of hatred. She hated the damn bracelet. Hated Eugene for buying it. Hated Gordon for using it to get into her bedroom. The thought of how close she'd come to giving Gordon her body sent a wave of rage through Carmen, and she slammed her fist against the door, doubling over in immediate agony. Grabbing the injured hand and holding it tightly to her chest, Carmen fought the hot tears gathering in her eyes. *Why me? Why is this happening to me?*

In one slow, sullen move, Carmen unhooked the clasp on the diamond bracelet and watched as the bauble slid, as if in slow motion, off her wrist and onto the floor, making the tiniest *clink* that seemed to echo loudly in the lonely apartment. For a moment Carmen just stared down at it. Stared at its stones. At the way the tiny lights danced in patterns on the tile floor.

When Carmen's anguish exploded suddenly from her chest in painful, breathless sobs, her body shook with spasms that sent her sliding down inch by inch against the smoothness of the enamel door. And when she felt the icy hardness of the tile against her skin, she curled into a despondent ball and cried until she couldn't cry any more.

≋ 12 ≋

Just This Side of Strange

Carmen slammed the Royalson's box down on Eugene's desk as if it were the winning bone in a South Central domino tournament. She stood facing him with one hand planted firmly against her hip and a sour expression planted just as firmly across her face. Glaring at the man with venom even she didn't know she had, she growled, "Who in the *hell* do you think you are, Eugene?"

His mouth hung open slightly. A look of bewilderment camped out on his face and refused to budge. The rest of him didn't budge either. He sat stiffly at the paper-strewn desk in his deserted classroom just staring at Carmen—waiting for her to finish her angry onslaught. She glared at him icily, daring him to say something she didn't want to hear.

Carmen knew Eugene hadn't a clue that she had almost

given her body to a man she didn't love for a bracelet Eugene had bought. She also knew he had no idea that the person Carmen was most angry at was herself.

Eugene opened his mouth slightly, as if he was about to speak, but no words came out.

Carmen filled the silence herself. "What is it, Eugene?!" You don't have enough finesse to *talk* your way into my god-damn panties? Huh? You think you can *buy* me with some . . . some . . ." Her eyes searched the room as if the word she was looking for might be written somewhere on the walls. When she didn't find it, she swiped at the little blue box with every ounce of her anger, smacking it so hard it flew across the room, bounced off a wastebasket, and skidded to a stop underneath a bookshelf near the far windows. Carmen's eyes shot bullets of rage into Eugene's startled face. "I am *not* anybody's whore, Eugene Timms, and you . . ." She pointed a stiff index finger in his face. "You will never get in my panties. *Never.* No matter how much money you waste on crap like that. Do you understand me?"

The expression of bewilderment on Eugene's face finally broke, and the one that replaced it was not one Carmen was expecting. Eugene was suddenly smiling at her. Seated at his desk with his white dress shirt buttoned up to his neck, looking every bit the nerdy math professor, he sat up straighter in his chair. He smiled softly at Carmen. "Your panties?"

"How much did it run you, Timms, huh?" Carmen leaned on straight arms against the edge of Eugene's desk, leaning into him until her face was a few inches from his. The peacock blue V-neck sweater dress she wore strained with the weight of her breasts, creating a cave of cleavage for Eugene to explore. But he didn't so much as glance away from her eyes. Carmen looked down into her dress herself, looked at her round, golden breasts straining against her white lace bra, then looked back up into his eyes. "How much, Eugene? Hmh?" she cooed sarcastically. "How much is it worth to you to get next to these?"

Eugene didn't flinch. He held Carmen's stare for a few quiet seconds, then, as if he hadn't heard a word of Carmen's angry tirade, he raised himself from his chair and walked slowly, silently toward the back of the classroom.

Carmen watched in silence as Eugene made his way leisurely through the rows of empty student desks, stopped at the bookshelf near the windows, and turned to look directly into Carmen's angry face. He slowly unbuttoned first his left, then his right cuff, and pushed his sleeves up onto the muscles of his forearms. Without taking his eyes off hers, he grasped the bookshelf and slid it away from the wall. When he had retrieved the box from behind the shelf, he calmly returned to where Carmen stood, and, looking her boldly in the eye, he placed the box down gingerly in front of her on the desk.

Eugene seemed to have found some secret strength to challenge her wrath, and Carmen wondered where it was coming from. His voice had a tinge of indignation in it when he spoke. "Be assured that I am not trying to"—his smile had faded and was replaced by a slight blush of something that looked like embarrassment—"to get into your"—he obviously didn't want to say the word again, but he muttered it again—"your *panties.*"

Carmen rolled her eyes at him immediately, then looked at the box, twisting her upper lip into a sarcastic snarl. "Hmph. Then what is *that* for?"

"It's for you, swe—" Eugene corrected himself. "It's for you, Carmen."

"For what, Eugene?"

"For *you*."

"For me, for *what*, Eugene?"

"It's not *for* anything, Carmen. It's a gift. It's a gift I can afford to give to a beautiful woman whom I would like to have it."

Carmen eyed Eugene suspiciously. "And just what do you think you're supposed to get in return?"

Eugene shook his head wearily. "Carmen, let me set your mind at ease, okay? There is . . . there's something you should know about me. I mean . . . I'm not . . ."

He searched her eyes with a burning intensity. She had no idea what he was searching for, but she thought it might help if she softened the scowl on her face slightly. She let some of the angry tension in her face ease, but crossed her arms defensively across her chest. "You're not *what*, Eugene?"

"What I'm trying to say is, if you knew me a little better you would know that that little gift . . ."

Carmen's eyebrows arched involuntarily at his choice of words. The *little gift* he was referring to had to have cost him at least five or six thousand dollars. She picked up the box and held it out on her flat palm. "Little gift? You call this a little gift, Eugene?"

"What I mean is, what difference does it make how much

money I spent on it, Carmen?" His voice rose slightly, along with his exasperation. "Look, I enjoy giving, and I especially like when the gifts I give are appreciated." Eugene cleared his throat and lowered his voice to a calmer tone. "I'm quite interested in you, but I'm not . . ." Carmen waited anxiously for him to finish the sentence.

He walked slowly around the desk and reseated himself in his chair. Focusing his eyes on the windows along the back wall, he placed both elbows on the desk in front of him and clasped his hands together. He looked as if he wanted to pray—or as if he was weighing whether to share with Carmen some unspeakable secret. Carmen wished he would just spit it out.

Eugene stared down at his clenched hands when he spoke to her.

"What I'm trying to tell you, Carmen, is that . . . there is something you should know about me . . ."

Carmen braced herself. *Know about you? Know what?* Something about Eugene *had* always struck her as odd. Just this side of strange, actually. She thought of the countless times Eugene had left her at her doorstep with a tender peck on her lips and no pressure to take things any further. Now here he was telling her there was some monumental secret he'd been keeping from her? She shifted uncomfortably and cleared her throat with a scratchy little "*harrumph*" that was meant to get Eugene to look at her, but he kept his eyes on his clasped hands. Carmen's mind was racing through all the possibilities. *What has he been hiding? Is the man impotent? Gay? Oh God, he has AIDS.* She couldn't take the suspense any longer. "What, Eugene? What in the hell are you talking about?"

Before Eugene could answer, the door to his classroom burst open, and a noisy group of students barged through it. He rose immediately while Carmen stood her ground and eyed the group angrily. School was out for the day, and they had no business in the building. The new policy said students were not supposed to be anywhere on campus after school, but there had to have been two dozen or more of them, all boys, pouring into Timms's classroom, each and every one of them totally clueless to the idea that they might have interrupted an important conversation.

"Excuse you," Carmen barked at the oblivious mob, though they hardly took notice. They were noisily plopping their graffiti-covered bookbags onto desktops and seats all over the room. Some of them were milling around by the windows, pointing outside and loudly exclaiming things in Spanish Carmen didn't even try to decipher.

One of the students had stepped up to Eugene's desk, and without seeming to notice her, he rested his butt down on it as if it were a bench in the gymnasium instead of the math department chairperson's personal workspace. But Eugene didn't seem at all bothered by the boy's actions. He greeted the student with an enthusiastic handshake, while a few more boys burst through the door and migrated to individual desks, nudging, joking, and insulting one another along the way.

Carmen had suddenly become invisible, and Eugene did not so much as glance her way. He seemed totally engrossed in the conversation he was having with the student who had seated himself atop his desk, and it wasn't until Carmen paid closer attention to the two that she realized they were speaking Spanish to each other. At least the student was. Eugene's responses made him sound like a tourist in a Tijuana souvenir shop.

"Cuan-toes ess-too-dee-antays po-dees-tay in-cone-trar?" Eugene looked proud of himself.

"Your Spanish is getting good, Teach." The student stuck a fist out, prompting Eugene to pound it awkwardly with his own clenched fist. "I brought all the guys I could find on the quad. Jessie's bringing one more."

"Bway-no, bway-no," Eugene said with a nod of his head. He finally looked over at Carmen, catching the look of irritation on her face. "I'm sorry Miss DuPrè, but I'm going to have to finish our talk at another time."

"Excuse me?" Carmen's face said she was not about to be evicted from her conversation by a roomful of hooligans.

"I have promised these young men my undivided attention." Eugene smiled apologetically at Carmen, then glanced out across the sea of faces that had all seemed to turn in unison to listen to the exchange taking place between the two adults.

Carmen sneered. "You do know that our new security plan does not allow students to be in the building past the three forty-five bell?"

"These young men are under my direct supervision, and I accept all responsibility for them." His eyes said, *Please don't mention this to anyone.*

Carmen made sure the look on her face didn't give him any

121

idea whether she would or wouldn't give away his little impropriety. "Whatever you say, Eugene," she muttered sarcastically. She started for the door, aware of the many pairs of eyes following her every move. When she reached the door, it opened before she could grab the knob. Jessie Diaz and Angel Huerta were standing in front of her, both of them smiling broadly at her as if they'd just arrived at her front door for a first date.

Carmen stepped aside to let them pass, still in a huff from having been asked to leave. She didn't smile at them, but they didn't seem to notice her sour mood.

"Hey, Miss D." Angel was the first to speak. His oversized jacket made him look fifty pounds heavier than the two hundred he was. "Me and Jessie was just looking for you."

Jessie and I were looking . . . Carmen thought but didn't say. It would've been a waste of breath, she knew. The grammar these students used in their daily lives was atrocious, and Carmen had given up on correcting it.

"Yeah, we went by your office." Jessie rummaged around in his backpack. He pulled out a sheet of paper and held it out to Carmen. Angel had produced one as well. She looked down at the pages in each boy's hand. Math quizzes. The heading across the top of the pages read: "Algebra 1B—Quiz #2." In the upper right-hand corner of each page was a capital letter A written in red ink.

Carmen forced a fake smile. "That's very impressive," she muttered dryly.

Angel and Jessie looked hurt. They simultaneously stuffed the pages back into their packs, staring at each other blankly.

She felt the disappointment radiating from the two previously eager faces, so she mustered a more genuine smile and quickly added, "You two must be working very hard."

That was all it took to put the grins back on their faces.

"Cheesecake Factory." Jessie winked playfully at Carmen as he stepped past her to find a seat in Eugene's classroom.

"Yeah. Cheescake Factory would be the bomb, Miss D." Angel stepped past Carmen too.

"Miss DuPrè . . ."

Carmen turned to find Eugene walking toward her. He grabbed her wrist gently, placed the Royalson's box in her hand, and without smiling he whispered in her ear, "I'd like to call you tonight if I could, to finish our conversation. Would that be okay with you?"

She looked down at the box, now dented at one corner, and didn't answer Eugene's question with so much as a grunt. Instead she shoved the box into the pocket of her coat, walked out the door, and left Eugene to figure out the answer for himself.

⋛ **13** ⋚

Hanging Up

The moment Carmen heard Dr. Lee's voice, she cursed herself silently for picking up the telephone. She had been screening her calls for days—erasing a couple of Eugene's attempts at "checking on her" and missing three or four of Dr. Lee's urgent "Please call me, Carmen" conversations. She had forbidden Gordon to ever call her again, and she'd left a message in Eugene's box that said she "needed space." Carmen wouldn't have picked up the ringing phone at all, but Superintendent Browning had left a message saying he'd call her at home around six P.M., and his was a call she didn't intend to miss.

"Hello, Dr. Lee," Carmen muttered unenthusiastically. She wasn't ready to deal with those damn test results Dr. Lee was surely calling to share, results Carmen had spent the last few days talking herself into believing that she really didn't care to know. Good or bad, positive or negative, she'd just as soon not have them floating around in her already stress-filled head.

"Oh Carmen. I am so glad I caught you at home."

Carmen recognized the genuine caring in Dr. Lee's voice, but she didn't respond in kind. Instead she fought the urge to "accidentally" hang up the phone and offered a terse "What is it, Dr. Lee?"

"Is it possible for you to come and see me tomorrow?"

"I'll be at work tomorrow."

"I will be in my office until late in the evening."

"I don't know if—"

Dr. Lee cut her off abruptly. "Carmen. I cannot adequately discuss your biopsy results with you over the phone, or I most certainly would. I don't want to alarm you, but I want you to understand that we are dealing with your health, and that is a very precious thing."

Carmen didn't speak.

"Please tell me you will stop in to see me tomorrow."

Carmen rolled her eyes to the ceiling and cursed herself again for picking up the phone. She frowned at Eve and her sisters in their frames on the wall then sent them an irritated smirk, as if they somehow might be in on Dr. Lee's conspiracy to destroy Carmen's life.

"Carmen?" Dr. Lee's voice was sharp and insistent. "Carmen, please say you'll be here tomorrow evening. Is five o'clock good for you?"

Carmen took in a deep breath and exhaled loudly. "Fine. *Fine*, Dr. Lee. I will stop by around five." With that she quickly returned the receiver to the phone's cradle and stared at it, fighting to drive out the thoughts crowding her mind. Of course it had to be bad news. She'd expected it from the moment Dr. Lee suggested the mammogram. She thought about calling the doctor back right away. Just call back and postpone. *I can tell her I'll come in first thing next week.* She tried to think up a reason why tomorrow wouldn't do. *I'll just reschedule.* Then she would get caller ID. With that and the call screening she could avoid the doctor's little announcement until she was ready to hear it.

Before Carmen could sink any deeper into her avoidance scheme, the phone rang again. She stared down at it—uncertain whether to risk another unwanted call—then lifted the receiver, hoping it would be George Browning.

"Hello?"

"Yes. I'd like to speak with Miss DuPrè, please." Carmen recognized the voice. It was the superintendent.

She gave Eve and her sisters a look of triumph. She smiled at them slyly and winked, as if to say, *This is it, girlfriends. This is what we've been waiting for.* "Oh, Dr. Browning," she cooed into the phone. "What a pleasant surprise."

"Carmen. Haven't I made it clear to you, my dear? Please call me George."

"Of course, George. Please forgive me. I have been looking forward to your call."

"Yes, well, I've been quite busy with these union contract negotiations. But I certainly haven't forgotten about you. I have been pulling a few strings here and there since we last spoke, and . . ."

Carmen held her breath. This was where he would tell

127

her the position was officially hers. "And . . . ?" Carmen could feel her skin tingle with anticipation. *Goodbye, Overland hellhole.*

"I'd like us to meet once again. Could you have dinner with me tomorrow evening? Say around eight o'clock?

Carmen didn't miss a beat. She gushed, "Of course, George. Just tell me when and where you'd like to meet."

He didn't answer right away, and Carmen waited impatiently in the uncomfortable space left by his silence. What was he doing anyway? Why couldn't he just give her the damn job? Why did he have to drag this thing out?

Browning finally breathed his answer in a husky voice, "You don't have to worry about where to meet me. As I told you before, I'm a gentleman." He sounded as if he was out of breath, as if he'd just worked out. "I will come for you, of course."

Come for me? Carmen was hoping to make this more like a meeting than a date, but Browning apparently had other intentions. "Ummm," Carmen hedged. "You really don't have to do that, George."

"Yes, Carmen. I really *do* have to do that. I'll be there to pick you up promptly at eight." When the phone clicked and Carmen heard the dial tone in her ear, she didn't know what to be more startled by, the authoritative voice Dr. Browning had used on her or the fact that he hung up without saying goodbye. She hung up too, staring at the phone for a moment in disbelief. Not a second lapsed before it began ringing again. *Browning.* Calling to apologize for his abruptness, no doubt.

"Hello," Carmen said with a hint of attitude.

"Hey, Car." It was Lindsey.

"Hey."

"I just got in. I'm calling to check up on you."

"Back from A-T-L huh?

"Never mind Atlanta. Tell me about your doctor's appointment. And don't leave anything out."

"Well, let's see. I was diagnosed with cancer, started chemotherapy, and had my colon removed while you were gone," Carmen blurted matter-of-factly.

Lindsey didn't speak.

"Linn?" Carmen was instantly sorry.

"Don't do that to me, Carmen." Lindsey's voice was tinged with anguish—it turned quickly to anger. "That's not funny."

"I was just teasing you, sweetie. I'm sorry. My doctor visit went just fine. I'm just fine."

Lindsey's silence said she was beyond disturbed.

"I'm really sorry, sweetie. I will never play like that again. I really am fine. Really." Carmen quickly changed the subject. "So . . . Atlanta was. . . ?"

"Atlanta was cool," Lindsey said softly.

"That's it? You spent a week in the land of gorgeous, successful black men, and all you can say is, 'Atlanta was cool'?"

"No, actually, Carmen, Atlanta was amazing. Really amazing." The warmth had returned to Lindsey's voice, and Carmen could hear a nervous excitement oozing all over her sister's words.

"You better tell me everything. I can hear it in your voice. What happened? Did you get another promotion already?"

"Carmen . . ."

"What girl? Spit it out."

"I met someone."

"You *what?*" Carmen could not believe her ears. Not Lindsey. Not the never-had-a-serious-relationship-never-getting-married-never-having-kids-never-gonna-be-tied-down-to-no-man Lindsey DuPrè.

"Can you believe it, Car? I mean, I know how these conference things go. I know we just met, and I'm not trying to rush into anything, but—"

"Rush into . . ." Carmen cleared her throat dramatically. "What the hell are you talking about Lindsey? Rush into *what?*"

"Carmen . . ." Lindsey hesitated. "Do you . . ." She seemed to be choosing her words carefully. "Do you believe there is such a thing as a soul mate?"

"Lindsey, *what happened* in Atlanta?" Carmen was playing the big sister role now. She was past being happy for Lindsey. Now she was concerned.

"Nothing happened. I mean. Nothing happened *like that.* It's just . . . It's just that Kenny and I have so much in common. We can talk about anything. Or we can just be in each other's presence and not talk at all. We stayed up into the late hours every night doing nothing but enjoying each other's company. We love the same things. And, Car, Kenny is the CEO of a web-based design and marketing company. Vizinet. I'm sure you've heard of them. They're huge. They're on NASDAQ."

Carmen feigned enthusiasm. "NASDAQ? Wow." Lindsey was suddenly reminding Carmen of herself. Her old self. The self that had fallen so hard for Randall. She had to at least try to warn her baby sis. "Sweetie . . ."

Lindsey didn't let her finish. "Please don't 'sweetie' me, Carmen. And don't start with that tone of voice. I shared this with you because you're my sister and I know you want me to be happy. I'm asking you not to criticize this, because I am ecstatic about it. I mean—I don't even know what this is yet, but I'm asking you to support me, Car, and if you can't, please just leave it alone."

Carmen fought to keep silent. She held back a rush of words the big sister in her was dying to let out.

"This is not what you think, Carmen. I'm not being foolish or reckless. I *know* how badly you want to lecture me right now, but I'm asking you not to."

Carmen didn't know what to say to that. Lindsey was right on the money. Carmen *was* getting ready to lecture her. She was about to launch into that lecture called "better be having safe sex 'cause men can be dogs and make sure you don't give up too much too soon and how do you know he isn't married and . . ." The list was endless. Carmen bit her tongue. Finally she whispered, "Can I just ask you one tiny little question?"

Lindsey let out a slow, irritated breath.

"Please tell me you had safe sex," Carmen whispered. Lindsey's silence sent a wave of terror through Carmen. *Oh God,* she thought, but kept it to herself. She managed to sound very calm when she added, "Lindsey, please tell me you did not have sex without protection."

"Carmen. I said we just met. We didn't have sex at all. I haven't even kissed Kenny yet. Dag, you are such a big sister.

I am not as naïve as you think I am. Just because I've never had a serious relationship doesn't mean I'm going to be a mindless airhead the first time I find something that looks like it could be real. This . . . Carmen, this really is different."

"Different, huh?"

"Yeah."

"Good. Then I won't have to tell you to slow down. And I won't waste my breath telling you to be careful," Carmen said softly.

"Good," Lindsey tossed back at her with playful defiance. "Then I won't have to tell you to butt out and mind your own damn business."

"Good," Carmen quipped back. "'Cause then *I* won't have to tell *you* that my baby sister's business is my business."

"Good," Lindsey returned. " 'Cause then I won't have to tell my *much older* sister that if she had a *life* and some business of her *own,* she wouldn't have to get all up in mine."

Carmen didn't have a comeback for Lindsey's last jab. She felt the full weight of her sister's use of the word "older," and the reference about her not having a life sounded a little too close to what might literally be true. Carmen felt a sudden stinging in her eyes.

Lindsey sensed her sister's unease immediately. "Actually, Carmen . . ." All the playfulness had left Lindsey's voice. "What I really want to say is, I know how much my older and *wiser* sister has been through in the love department, and I appreciate her concern. And I know she only lectures me because she loves me and is just trying to be there for me."

Carmen didn't dare speak. She couldn't let Lindsey hear

the fear swelling in her heart—fear that was sure to come bursting out in tears if she tried to talk. She desperately wanted to tell Lindsey about her biopsy. About Dr. Lee insisting on seeing her to discuss what was sure to be terrible news. She wished she could let Lindsey help her carry the weight of her fears.

"Carmen, you still there?"

Carmen considered it. She turned the idea of it over and over in her head—how she might actually let Lindsey in on her secret. She weighed it in her mind and tried to believe Lindsey might be able to keep something so critical to herself. *No way. Lindsey would mean well. She would intend to not tell anyone else in the family, but she wouldn't be able to carry the weight of it. Della would get it out of her. Then Mavis would find out. Once Mavis knew, the entire DuPrè clan would be chattering about poor little Carmen and how her life never seemed to go right.*

Carmen faked a couple of throaty coughs and whispered loudly into the phone. "I love you too, sis. I gotta go now, sweetie. I'll call you tomorrow, 'kay?

"Carmen, wait. . . ."

Carmen pressed her fingertip firmly against the "end call" button and held it there, choking back her tears. Before she could return the handset to the cradle, the phone rang loudly, startling her fingertip from the button—an action she immediately regretted. She didn't want to talk to Linn. She didn't want to talk to anyone.

"Carmen. Carmen is that you?"

It wasn't Lindsey's voice at all. It was a deep, husky voice

Carmen knew well. A voice she'd be happy to never hear again as long as she lived.

"What do *you* want? Carmen welcomed the opportunity to trade the anguish in her heart for the anger that quickly flooded in.

"I know you told me to stay away from you at work. And I have, Carmen. I've done that." It was Gordon. The day after the bracelet incident, he'd called begging to see her, so Carmen threatened him with a sexual harassment lawsuit if he came to her home, stepped foot in her office, or came anywhere near her while they were on campus. So far he'd abided by her demand. He'd even skipped the last Overland staff meeting. This was the first time she'd heard his voice in nearly a week.

"Like I said, what do you want?"

"I need to see you, Carmen."

"Yeah. And I need a chateau in the South of France. So what?"

"Carmen, how many ways can I say I'm sorry?"

She glanced toward the kitchen, glaring at the three mangled boxes of long-stemmed roses she'd stacked on top of one another near the trash. "How many ways can I say leave me the hell alone?"

"It was wrong. It was stupid and it was wrong, Carmen." Gordon's voice dripped with begging. "I was jealous. I hated that he could afford something like that, and I was jealous of it. And then when I came to pick you up and you kissed me the way you did . . ." She heard him draw in a deep breath. "Still. There's no excuse for me letting you believe I bought it. It was stupid and wrong, Carmen, and I really am sorry.

"Stupid and wrong?" Carmen uttered dryly. "No, Gordon. *It* wasn't stupid and wrong."

She heard him exhale with relief. She heard in the breath he let out that he actually thought he could be forgiven. Before he could lead himself too far down that path, Carmen repeated her words, letting each syllable roll slowly off her tongue with a tone of utter disgust. "*It* wasn't stupid and wrong, Gordon. *You* are stupid and wrong. What you *did* was evil and unforgivable."

"Carm . . ."

"I'm going to say this one more time, Gordon Iverson, and you are going to hear it. Don't speak to me at work. Don't call my home. Don't send me flowers. Don't utter my name. Don't remember I'm alive. Got it?"

"All but that last one," he said sadly.

"Goodbye, Gordon."

"I didn't wash my clothes," he suddenly blurted.

What the hell? She considered hanging up in his face, but the tone in his voice bothered her. What could she say in response to Gordon's strange announcement about his laundry?

"Your scent is all over that sweat suit I wore to the Lakers game, and I haven't washed it yet. I— I'm not ready to lose those memories I have of our last night together. I'm so sorry, baby. I wish I would have told you the truth about the bracelet the day I saw Timms put it in your desk. I just . . . I really am sorry."

Carmen was speechless.

"I wish I could live that night all over again, and wake up next to you, baby. I miss you. Carmen, I—I love you."

Carmen let the sound of the handset sliding onto its cradle be her response to that.

≋ **14** ≋

A Grave Mistake

Carmen stared blankly into the steaming liquid, absently stirring her tea bag into a tiny whirlpool. She watched the water darken gradually, not seeming to notice that tears had begun sliding down her cheeks and into the swirling current.

"Carmen, is there someone I can call? Someone who will be there for you through this?"

She didn't look at Dr. Lee, but held the teaspoon limply, slowly circling the interior of the ceramic mug with it, mixing her tears into the brown liquid. She didn't respond to the doctor's question—couldn't respond.

Dr. Lee gently wrestled the teacup from Carmen, setting it on the nearby counter. She took Carmen's hand in hers and held it firmly. "I know this is not the news you were hoping to hear. But I must tell you that you are very fortunate to have caught this so early."

Carmen finally looked up at Dr. Lee. She hated the woman for having suggested the damn mammogram in the first place. Hated her for having performed the biopsy. Hated her for finding cancer. Hated her more for daring to use the word "fortunate." Carmen snatched her hand from the doctor's grasp.

Dr. Lee took a Kleenex from the box on her lap and held it out, but Carmen didn't take it. Instead she wiped her tears with the back of her hand and swiveled her chair away to face the opposite wall. A large poster of an attractive, bare-breasted older woman loomed above her. The woman had one hand raised high above her head, the other pressed flat against one of her full breasts. The poster's caption read, "Breast self-examination can save your life!" Carmen stared at the words blankly, then covered her eyes with both hands and tried un-successfully to stop the flow of tears. "How dare you call me fortunate," Carmen grumbled.

Dr. Lee didn't let Carmen's anger unsettle her in the least. Instead she moved swiftly, squatting in front of Carmen, handing her another tissue. "Please look at me, Carmen."

Carmen glared directly into Dr. Lee's eyes.

" 'Fortunate' is a very appropriate word to use in your case. What we found is a stage one, node-negative cancer that could easily have spread if left unchecked. Breast cancers in very young women typically spread much more quickly, but yours is localized at this point. It is not too late for a simple lumpectomy."

At the word "lumpectomy," Carmen's eyes widened.

"I'm confident that with the lumpectomy and aggressive radiation therapy your cancer is completely curable."

Carmen wrapped her arms tightly around herself and held on. "Lumpectomy? Radiation? I already told you," Carmen fumed, "that's out of the question."

"A lumpectomy is necessary to remove the mass. We must schedule the surgery right away."

"I won't let you do it." Carmen tightened the grip she had on herself and glared menacingly at the doctor. "I won't let you cut off my breast. I'd rather be dead." She said the word "dead" with a startling conviction.

"You do not mean that, Carmen."

"Look at me." Carmen let her arms fall limply to her sides, exposing the fullness of her bosom. "Do you think I want to lose a breast? Do you think I want to live without one of these? You might as well be threatening to cut off my hair or my—my head, for God's sake."

The doctor stood up, her cheeks red with frustration. "As I explained to you before, a lumpectomy is just a removal of the offending tissue. It is not a removal of the entire breast. You will have some minor scarring, perhaps a slight indentation, but you will not lose your breast."

"What about the radiation? What is that going to do to me?"

"It's going to save your *life*, Carmen. That's what it's going to do."

Carmen scowled. "You *know* what I mean. What kind of damage will it do to me? What kind of side effects? Is all my hair going to fall out?"

"No, there's no hair loss with radiation. The treatments last no more than twenty or twenty-five minutes. You will need to have them daily for about five weeks. It might be a little uncomfortable. Some women complain of a slight burning sensation, but it is not painful. Some patients experience darkening of the skin, scarring, and some soreness in the area of —"

"No."

Dr. Lee locked eyes with Carmen and frowned at her impatiently.

Carmen repeated herself firmly. *"No."*

"No? What do you mean, *'no'*?"

Carmen stood up abruptly. "I don't want to hear anything more. I do not want to hear anything more about any of this. I will find someone willing to treat this without all the slicing and burning you seem so gung ho to do."

"Carmen . . ."

"No." Carmen grabbed her purse from the counter and headed for the door.

"Carmen, please. You're making a grave mistake. As your doctor I must insist—"

"You are no longer my doctor." Carmen swung the door open angrily. As she stomped hurriedly off down the corridor, she could hear Dr. Lee calling after her.

When she reached her car, Carmen groped the interior of her Vuitton purse, realizing there were no keys inside. It was more than she could take. She fought the overwhelming urge to have a nervous breakdown right there in broad daylight. She leaned heavily against the car as she allowed the reality of what was happening to her sink in. *I have cancer.* This wasn't something she could manipulate her way out of. There was no one to smile coyly at—no talking her way out of it. *I don't have to do this.* What if she just didn't accept it? How valuable was one stupid doctor's opinion anyway? *I do not have to do this. Not now.* She'd have to face it eventually, but for now . . . She took in a deep breath, stood up straight, and looking at her reflection in the tinted windows of her Lexus, she ran her hands through her hair. She had more important things to concentrate on in her life now. Like getting out of her miserable job. Like proving Mavis's predictions wrong. Perhaps it was time to start thinking about finding a man to settle down with. A man who could deal with whatever her future might bring. She'd get a new job, a new man, and a new attitude. Spending day after miserable day in Never-Never Land certainly wasn't going to help her feel any healthier. *I will get that promotion.* It was time to get moving on her goals, and this cancer business would just have to leave her be for now.

Carmen caught the reflection of Dr. Lee approaching from beind her, and she turned around abruptly to face the woman. The doctor held Carmen's keys in her hand. "Carmen," she pleaded. "Let's talk about this, okay?"

Carmen took the keys from Dr. Lee and jammed them into the door lock. "Goodbye," she muttered gruffly, not looking into the doctor's eyes.

Dr. Lee took a small step backward. "Goodbye Carmen. I hope to see you again very soon."

The last thing Carmen saw as she pulled out of the driveway of the medical complex was Dr. Lee's head shaking sadly from side to side as Carmen's Lexus disappeared down the street.

≋ **15** ≋

Something Hot and Wet

"*That color is* absolutely *divine* on you."

Carmen turned slowly in front of the three-way mirror, admiring the calf-length chiffon dress. She let her eyes travel along every one of her curves, taking delight in the way the dress clung to the small of her back, the front of her toned thighs, her plump breasts, her round behind. "Yes, this red is fabulous, isn't it?" She smiled broadly at the beautiful self she saw smiling back at her in the mirror.

"Versace is calling it 'garnet' this season. But a rose by any other name is still a rose, now isn't it? Whatever the color, madam, it is marvelous on you. And your figure is just— well—it is *perfection*. You really are blessed with the perfect body, now aren't you?"

Carmen winced, her smile fading into a tight, straight line.

The word "perfect" was a sharp little dart that pricked her happy mood. The shopping high she had worked so hard to attain began to deflate immediately. No, her body wasn't *perfect,* and she didn't care to be reminded of that just now, thank you very much.

Carmen's excursion to Saks Fifth Avenue was intended to have a healing effect on her spirits; it was something she could always count on shopping to do for her. Though she really should have been on the 405 driving home to prepare for her meeting with George Browning, she decided to give the Valley-bound traffic a chance to disperse by wasting a little time pampering herself at the shops along Rodeo Drive. Never mind Dr. Lee. Carmen definitely had it in her to do nothing—to put that ridiculous lumpectomy business in the back of her mind until she was good and ready to deal with it, which she certainly wasn't. And until now, until this very moment, she had been doing a damn good job of forgetting all about the "C" word. She didn't appreciate this pushy little saleswoman raining all over her shopping parade.

Without another word to the woman, Carmen disappeared into the dressing room and came out with the Versace she couldn't afford draped over her arm and a scowl draped over her face. "I'll take this dress and those silver and red Gucci sandals right there." Carmen pointed to a disheveled pile of open shoeboxes—a dozen pairs of shoes she had just spent the last thirty minutes trying on. She didn't attempt to hide the irritation in her voice. "And while you're at it, I'll take that silver shoulder wrap as well."

"Can I interest you in some jewelry to go with—"

"No, you cannot. I am late for an appointment. Please just wrap my things now."

The saleswoman silently prepared Carmen's packages and completed the sales transaction, the whole time staring attentively at her. She didn't seem to be able to take her eyes off Carmen, and every time Carmen looked at the woman, she quickly looked away. But within seconds her eyes would dart right back to Carmen's face.

"What?" Carmen finally said tersely.

"Excuse me?"

"What are you staring at?"

"I—I didn't mean to be rude. It's just—it's just that—I don't believe I've ever seen anyone so beautiful." The woman's porcelain skin suddenly flushed pink. She pushed a lock of blond curls behind one ear and fluttered her blue-gray eyes nervously. "I mean—I mean that in the most sincere way. Really. You really are stunning."

Carmen didn't respond.

"Please don't be offended, miss. I—"

"Are you gay?" Carmen put one hand on her hip and raised an eyebrow at the woman. "Because if you are, you can forget it, sister. I'm not like that."

The woman's face flushed a deeper shade of pink, and a shadow of irritation coated her voice when she spoke. "I have been happily married for fifteen years. I just thought I'd pay you a compliment, that's all." The customer service smile and voice had disappeared.

"Oh well, thank you," Carmen offered halfheartedly.

"Would you like to have someone carry this out?" the

woman asked blandly, holding up the plastic-enclosed dress on a hanger in one hand, a shopping bag in the other.

"Yes, I would. I'll be in the gold Lexus." Without another word, Carmen turned on her heel and headed for the valet.

At seven forty-five, when George called from his car phone to inform Carmen that he was en route to her home, she had barely managed to navigate through the Valley-bound traffic, make it home, shower, and apply some styling mousse to her hair. She didn't want Browning to have any reason to come inside her apartment, so she dressed hurriedly, touched up her red toenail polish, applied the finishing touches to her makeup, and was just putting the new Gucci sandals on her feet when her doorbell rang.

Carmen quickly grabbed her new wrap and her purse and headed for the door. When she opened it, George Browning was standing on her front porch with a huge bouquet of yellow long-stemmed roses and an expression of lustful appreciation on his jowled face.

"Well, hello, George." She took in the sight before her. George's baldness was covered with what had to be a very costly hairpiece—she wouldn't have had the slighted clue it was fake if she hadn't already seen his freckled bald head with her own eyes. She instantly recognized the three-button Ermenegildo Zegna sport coat Browning was wearing—the one she thought she remembered Samuel L. Jackson wearing on the cover of *GQ* a few months previous. George had even replaced his thick tortoiseshell glasses with a pair of sporty wire-rimmed specs. *This old geezer is trying to make an impres-*

sion, she thought, taking a little step back. "*My,* don't you look handsome," she offered in a sugar-coated tone.

Browning stepped toward Carmen, thrusting the roses at her and backing her up into the apartment. "I thought these were fabulous when I bought them, but in your presence they're mere weeds." His eyes feasted on her red-sheathed body. "You, my dear, look absolutely edible."

Carmen accepted the roses and motioned Browning toward an armchair near the door. "Let me put these in water, George. I'll just be a minute." She retreated to the kitchen, and as she pretended to be searching for a vase for the flowers, she called to him over her shoulder, "So is it a surprise, or are you going to tell me what restaurant we'll be dining at this evening?" She got no response to her question. Carmen chalked it up to the old guy being hard of hearing. She turned the faucet on and off quickly, plopped the roses into the sink, and hurried back to the living room so she could rush the man out of her home.

She found Browning admiring Eve and her sisters.

"I know this artist." Browning was bent over, peering over the edge of his glasses at the artist's signature. He straightened, puffing his chest out and raising a self-important eyebrow at Carmen. "I can arrange for you to get an original of his work, if you'd like."

"A Wright original?" Carmen gasped. "Oh. I could never afford something like that on my salary." She welcomed the opportunity to mention her inadequate income level. She hoped he'd take the bait and tell her she'd been promoted and her income would soon be rising. He didn't bite.

"Well, of course I wouldn't expect you to pay for it." He reached out and gave Carmen's bare upper arm a gentle squeeze. "A few years back . . . '93, I believe it was, I helped that young man put together a ten-campus art show through a friend at the University of California. I believe Mr. Wright would be happy to donate a piece to your collection if I asked."

Carmen took a nervous step backward. "You really are too generous, George." She didn't let her face reflect her repulsion at Browning's touch. She smiled coyly, her eyes wide. "He is my favorite artist. This collection of prints is one of my most prized possessions. I would be forever grateful to you for adding an original of his to my wall."

"Consider it done." Browning stepped forward, closing the space between them Carmen had created. He pressed a hand to each of her bare shoulders and slid his palms gently down her arms. She stiffened at his touch, again backing away from him with a nervous little step that left her with her back against the wall. Having no more room for retreat, she tried a different tactic.

"Well, we had better get going. Where did you say you made reservations for dinner?" She hoped Browning would hear the insistence in her voice and start moving toward the door. He moved toward her instead.

"It's getting a little late for that, don't you think? Why don't we order in tonight instead?" He placed his right hand against the wall just above Carmen's shoulder and leaned in close enough to give her a whiff of the alcohol on his breath. "I know a great little Thai restaurant nearby that will deliver anything on the menu." His eyes traveled down the entire length of Carmen's Versace, then back up to rest in her cleavage. His next words came out in a throaty whisper. "Or we could just eat something else."

Carmen was calmly weighing her options. She had no intention of letting this thing get out of hand. She knew quite well how to get a man to eat out of the palm of her hand, any man. And though she could see he'd had a little too much to drink, George would do exactly what Carmen intended for him to do—promise her that counseling position without so much as a kiss on the lips from her in return. She'd just have to play along with him until he told her what she wanted to hear.

Browning mistook Carmen's silence for submission, and it emboldened him. He placed his left hand against the wall and looked her directly in the eye. Now she was getting the full effect of the liquor on Browning's breath. She held hers.

"If you'd prefer, little lady, you can just let me order from your menu instead. How about it, Carmen? You can count on me to deliver, but can I count on you to give me what I want?"

This was where she'd make it clear to him that he was about to upset her. She'd already figured the whole thing out in her head. Of course he was going to push to see how far he could get with her, but once he realized she wasn't some kind of cheap pushover, he'd apologize for his behavior and would finish the evening like a gentleman. "If I didn't know you better, George, I'd swear you were trying to—"

Browning pressed his wet lips onto Carmen's, prying his tongue into her mouth like a crowbar.

She uttered a loud "mnnnh" that was meant to be "no," twisting her head to the side to escape Browning's slobbering kiss.

"George!" She put both hands on Browning's chest and pushed him as hard as she could. The ex-college fullback must have still had some athlete in him—he didn't budge. Carmen wasn't frightened. She knew she could handle this old geezer with a couple of harsh words. "What do you think you're doing, Dr. Browning?" She stared threateningly into his eyes, raising one of her eyebrows defiantly. "Are you sexually harassing a district employee?"

He laughed. "Not yet, young lady. But I fully intend to." He pressed the full weight of himself against her, pinning Carmen to the wall and rubbing his ample pelvis desperately against hers. She felt his erection through the layers of his sport coat and trousers, but it still didn't occur to her that she was in any real danger. Browning had a career to consider. A reputation to protect. He certainly wasn't going to try to force himself on her. The alcohol might make him believe he could get away with grinding up against her, but he certainly wouldn't be stupid enough to try to rape her.

"George Browning. Stop this right now." Carmen's tone was calm but firm. She was not going to escalate things any more than need be. She was determined to end this little encounter on a positive note. Just as with the tongue-in-the-ear thing. She'd been able to salvage that situation to her benefit. She would somehow manage to salvage this too.

"I've gone to a lot of trouble for you," he breathed angrily. "You're not acting very appreciative, young lady."

Carmen's face suddenly registered a look of complete disgust. George had managed to unbutton his jacket, and his hand was emerging from his open trousers, jerking busily back and forth along his aroused penis.

"George!"

Carmen was finally scared. Terrified. She took in a breath to begin her scream, but George anticipated that and caught her with her mouth open—locking his mouth on hers, his tongue sliding against hers like a thick, wet slug. She struggled with every ounce of her might to get away from him, but he was too strong for her. As she wrenched to one side to free herself from his grasp, the heel on her Gucci sandal caught in the carpet and stuck. Carmen lost her balance, twisted her ankle painfully, and fell to the floor in a heap at George's feet.

In a split second he was on top of her. "I knew you wanted it. I knew you wanted to give it to me." He held a sweaty hand firmly to Carmen's mouth and began rubbing his body rhythmically against hers. With his free hand he grabbed a fistful of her dress and jerked it up, but the weight of both of them on the delicate fabric was too much. Carmen heard the Versace rip, the sound of it giving her an extra boost of anger and energy. She writhed and struggled beneath Browning, but it only seemed to excite him more, his pelvic movements becoming even more intense. Carmen attempted a scream, but all she heard was her own muffled yelp trapped pitifully in the back of her throat.

Tears of frustration and terror dripped from the corners of Carmen's eyes as she felt herself conceding defeat. She let her body go limp under Browning's weight, unsure of what was going to happen to her next. It was then that Browning's body began jerking uncontrollably against Carmen, and in a second he was completely still, his weight suffocating her, his breaths hot and wet against her ear. She felt something hot and wet against her thigh too.

He lay still on top of her for what felt like an eternity, giving Carmen time to wonder fearfully what could possibly be coming next. Did he expect to just get up and walk away from this? Did he think she wouldn't report him? She took in a swift, sudden breath as a terrifying thought invaded her mind. *He plans to kill me.* Her chest began to heave with short, impossible breaths.

Browning finally raised himself up on one elbow until he was looking directly into Carmen's tear-streaked face, his hand still pressed firmly against her mouth. The few seconds of silence between them seemed like hours to Carmen.

"Congratulations . . . Miss . . . DuPrè," Browning finally whispered into her face. "You are now *officially* the college counselor at the Talented and Gifted Academy."

⇒ 16 ⇐

On the Outside Looking In

Carmen crouched in the shadows near the entrance to the aging brick building wearing only her torn Versace and an old pair of house slippers. Shivering with the panic Browning's attack had drenched her in, she emerged slowly from the shadows, glanced furtively around the deserted parking lot, then limped pitifully toward the double-doored entry to the building. When she reached the locked glass doors, she peered into the darkened foyer of the law offices of Preston, Carr, Bombeck, and Winston.

Seeing no signs of life in the outer office, she pressed her cheek to the cool glass, craning her neck at just the right angle to get a view of the far end of the interior corridor. At the end of that corridor was his office—at least that's where it was the last time she'd been there. And just as she had hoped, there was that familiar line of soft yellow light glowing from beneath the last door on the left.

She pressed the buzzer softly, staring expectantly at the faint glow of light, praying for it to widen into the brighter glow of an opened door. It didn't. She pressed the buzzer again. *Maybe he isn't here,* she thought. *Maybe he doesn't work late anymore. Maybe he'd rather be at home with his wife.* When she pressed the buzzer a third time, she left her finger against it for a few hopeless seconds.

A sudden crackle of static from the intercom jerked Carmen's finger from the button just as Randall's voice, hushed but warm, floated from the speaker. "Baby, you're early. I'm just about finished. Come on in. Use your key, okay? The sweetness in his voice when he said "baby" seared Carmen's heart and brought hot tears to her eyes. She knew that tone. Remembered when its warmth was intended only for her. *He calls someone else baby now.* She fought the emotions welling up in her chest. Fought the urge to turn and run as fast as she could.

"Chelle? Did you hear me?"

"Randall . . ." Carmen attempted to announce herself, but she couldn't get past his name. "R-Randall . . ." she tried again, but this time his name erupted from her throat along with the tiniest of suppressed sobs, and before she knew it, with breaths that wheezed softly in and out across her vocal cords she was crying his name in whispered moans. "Randall . . . Randall . . ." It was all she could manage.

It only took seconds for him to emerge from his office. He raced down the corridor, and when he arrived in the foyer and

154

stopped in front of the glass doors, he looked solemnly into Carmen's face and froze. He stepped back from the door a few feet and just stared at her. Her face was obviously not the one he'd expected to see on the other side of the glass.

Carmen recognized the tiniest glimmer of something that looked like caring in Randall's dark eyes, but it was instantly replaced by a veil of nervous apprehension. He was afraid of her. She could see it plainly. He was afraid she might be at it again. "Stalking" was what he had called it back then. It was what he told the judge who issued the restraining order against her. It had been over a year since Carmen had gone crazy on him, but it was the last memory Randall had of her.

"What are you doing here?" She couldn't hear his words through the closed doors, but she read the message clearly on his lips.

Carmen pressed a palm to the glass and spoke in a shaky voice. "I—I need your help. I need your help, Randall. Please. I'm not here to bother you. I-I need to talk. *Please.*" She couldn't tell if he heard a word she'd said, but something in her facial expression must have made him let his guard down a little. He approached the doors hesitantly, finally taking in the sight of her. Her dress, stained and torn, hung sloppy and crooked on her frame. Circles of black mascara framed puffy eyes. Her hair was pulled back into a messy ponytail, and on her feet were a pair of fuzzy pink slippers.

Carmen stared hopefully into his eyes, letting him see the tears welling up in hers.

He took a step toward her, glancing down at the keys in his hand, then at the door lock. When he looked in Carmen's face apologetically, his eyes told her he cared. She could see it clearly. He wanted to let her in. He just needed to know he wouldn't regret it.

Carmen spoke into the crack between the double glass doors, her tone pleading. "I'm really sorry for everything. Please. I won't give you any trouble. I just need someone to talk to. Please?"

He took a few small, cautious steps forward, the whole time studying her face. He stared into her eyes, searching for signs of instability. When the frozen lines of intensity that had etched themselves across his brow began melting, and the hint of a gentle smile appeared on his lips, Carmen knew he'd made up his mind.

Randall pulled the door open, still wary of her. She limped awkwardly past him into the darkness of the foyer, favoring her twisted ankle dramatically as she moved. Turning to face him, she let her eyes travel from his beautiful ebony face down his sweat suit–clad body to his well-worn Adidas. Even in a pair of old sweats and a baseball cap the man was as gorgeous as ever. Carmen withstood an excruciating moment of nervous tension before Randall finally reached both arms around her and hugged her cautiously.

"It's good to see you, Carmen." he said quietly, sincerely. He led her past a black lacquer reception desk to a stylishly decorated waiting area and motioned for her to have a seat. As she lowered herself delicately onto the black calfskin sofa, Randall remained standing, waiting silently for her to tell him why she had come.

She made a weak attempt at straightening her dress, then

ran a nervous hand over her hair. "I—I didn't know where to go—what to do. I—I was nearly raped by—" She stopped and took in a labored breath, letting it out slowly as she tried to find the words to tell Randall what Browning had done to her.

"This evening I had a dinner meeting with the superintendent—"

He cut her off. "George Browning did this to you?"

She nodded. Tears welled behind her eyes. "He told me he wanted to meet with me regarding a promotion."

Randall's eyes fixed on Carmen's exposed left thigh—exposed where her dress had been ripped halfway up the side.

"I tried to insist on meeting him at the restaurant, but he wouldn't hear of it."

Randall listened intently to Carmen's story, shaking his head in disgust when she described how Browning jammed his tongue in her mouth as she fought him off. When she got to the part in her story where she'd fallen to the floor and Browning climbed on top of her, then ejaculated on her leg, Randall knelt down on one knee in front of Carmen and held her hand tightly.

"That sick bastard."

The outrage on his beautiful, chiseled face made her feel protected. Made her feel like there was somebody in the world who would fight for her. She ached to throw her arms around his neck and feel his arms around her. Instead she frowned softly at him and murmured, "I'm just lucky he didn't—"

He didn't let her finish. "Have you been to the police?"

The police station was the last place Carmen wanted to go. She didn't want a cop; she wanted a lawyer. A lawyer with no hidden ties to Browning and no favors owed to him or his political cronies. She wanted a lawyer who could sue the daylights out of George Browning and win. She wanted Randall.

"I want to take that son of a bitch to court. I want him to pay for what he did to me. And I want you to help me."

Randall was quiet. He rose from his kneeling position and stood looking down at Carmen. She wondered if he was feeling the same electricity she was. She wished Randall would pull her into his arms and tell her how stupid he had been to let her go. But he just stood there looking at her with a sad expression on his face. Finally he asked softly, "Is there anyone who knew about this meeting you had with Browning?"

Carmen shook her head.

"When he attacked you, did you scream or make any sounds that might have been heard by a neighbor?"

Another negative head shake from Carmen. "He held his hand over my mouth." A look of angry exasperation painted itself across her face. "Is this where you tell me it's my word against his?"

"I'm afraid it is." His eyes traveled again from her face down to her torn dress. "You certainly look as though you've been through hell. But your attorney will have to prove the man assaulted you. That's difficult to do without witnesses or evidence."

Carmen felt her face warming up, and when she spoke, her words were hot and angry. "Are you telling me that bastard nearly raped me, and he's going to get away with it?"

"I'm telling you it will be difficult to prove. Difficult, but not impossible." Randall's look of absolute sympathy softened

Carmen instantly, making her want to crawl into his arms and feel the warmth of his chest against her face. Her bottom lip puckered into a pout. "You could make him pay for this, couldn't you, Randall?" she purred.

He turned away from her abruptly and walked over to the reception desk. He quickly opened and closed a drawer and returned holding a business card. "I can't represent you, Carmen." The tone in his voice said having him as her lawyer was not going to happen, and the certainty of it sliced Carmen's heart. She wanted him to fight for her. She wanted him to want to.

"Here is the name and number of one of my colleagues. Cynthia Bombeck is an excellent lawyer. You should call her first thing in the morning."

Carmen swallowed Randall's dismissal, choking silently on his rejection. When she reached for the card, she looked longingly into his eyes, praying he might change his mind, but he didn't return the gaze. He looked toward the door instead. "You'll have to report this right away. There's a police station two blocks from here. You have to tell them what happened. It will be your word against his, but that doesn't mean you don't have a case."

At the mention of the police, Carmen wrapped her arms tightly around herself and rocked slowly back and forth at the sofa's edge. She closed her eyes for a long, dramatic moment. When she opened them again, Randall was staring intently at her face. "I know what you think," she whispered sullenly. "You think I asked for it. You think I did something to deser—"

He interrupted her. "I think . . ." He smiled softly at her. "I think you are a beautiful woman." His eyes roamed her face—as if she were a neighborhood he'd moved away from, but yearned to drive through for old time's sake. "Sometimes beauty can lead a man to do stupid things, Carmen." His lips formed a soft smile, but his eyes said he had something to hide.

Carmen didn't smile back. She sensed his words had nothing to do with George Browning. She didn't know what he was getting at, and she wanted him to do more than hint. "What's that supposed to mean?"

He didn't answer. He turned his back to Carmen and stared blankly toward the door. He seemed to be looking for something outside, something in the darkness on the other side of the glass. He took a few slow steps away from her. "I want to apologize for something I did to you, Carmen," he blurted nervously, turning to face her. "I've been carrying this around for a long time, and I think you deserve to know the truth. I did something terrible to you that you never suspected—"

She cut him off in a dry, matter-of-fact tone. "I already know, Randall." She rolled her eyes dramatically. "You were cheating on me. You broke up with me to be with her." The cocky tilt in her left eyebrow meant she was dead sure of the conclusion she'd jumped to. "Please. I figured that out a long time ago. Why do you think I went so crazy?"

Randall perched himself on the edge of the desk and folded his arms stiffly across his chest. "I did not cheat on you, Carmen." He frowned in exasperation. "I tried to tell you that then, but you wouldn't listen. I did not leave you for another woman. I didn't even *talk* to women for three months after you moved out." He looked offended. "Our breakup devastated me."

"Mmph. Well that's pretty unlikely since you were married within six months of breaking up with me."

"I married Michelle because . . ." Whatever he was about to admit to, he thought better of it. "Carmen, that has nothing to do with what I'm trying to apologize for. I'm trying to tell you how much I regret not being honest about why I stayed with you all those years."

Why you stayed? Carmen had no clue where he was going with that. She already knew why he stayed. He stayed because she'd worked so hard to be everything a man could possibly wish for in a woman. He stayed because she'd supported everything he dreamed of and strived for. And, of course, he stayed because he loved her with all his heart. *Why you stayed?* She suddenly did not want to hear whatever was coming. She didn't want to hear another word of this so-called apology.

"An apology really isn't necessary, Randall. Really." She shook her head no, for added emphasis. She did not want to hear anything that would change her crystal-clear vision of the perfect love they once shared.

"Carmen, do you remember that argument we had—the last big one?"

What is this man talking about? she thought. They never argued. Never. "We never argued, Randall. I'm sure I have no idea what you're talking about."

"Proposition 187. You said you agreed with it, remember?

Carmen stared blankly at him.

"It was a ballot measure to keep the children of illegal immigrants out of public schools."

Carmen's face registered a look of absolute cluelessness. "I really don't remember any argument about that, Randall."

"It was the same day I asked you to move out. We argued about 187 that morning. I can't believe you don't remember it. You suggested all Latino students should have to carry a special pass—that they should have to prove they were Americans to be allowed in the school building. I, uh, I said some pretty mean things to you."

An uncomfortable little half smile appeared suddenly on Carmen's face. "Oh," she said in a voice of sudden recognition. "When I said all those illegal kids were sucking money out of the school system that could be used to give teachers better pay? Yes, I do recall that conversation. You called me a shallow, selfish bitch." She scowled at him for a moment, then instantly replaced the scowl with a tolerant smile. "I forgive you, Randall. There's no need to apologize for that now."

Randall's chin dropped to his chest in exasperation; when he lifted it to look seriously into Carmen's eyes, she lost herself in his gaze.

"Umm, no, Carmen. That's not what I'm apologizing for either. Please. I need you to hear this. I've been carrying this around with me for too long, and I've always hoped for a chance to make this right." He faced her resolutely, then walked slowly over to where Carmen sat. He held his hand out to her and waited expectantly for her to grasp it. She eyed his outstretched hand with uncertainty. She wanted to reach for it. Ached to hold on to it for the rest of her life. But she couldn't move. Right in front of her face, right there under her nose was Randall's golden wedding band, and the sight of it on his finger turned Carmen to stone.

He knelt down on one knee at Carmen's feet, taking her hand into his. "As strange as it may sound to you now, Carmen, it was that argu— that *conversation* we had that made me see the truth about myself. I was pretending. The last few months of our relationship I spent pretending we had the same values, pretending I would one day be your husband . . ." He shook his head slowly and gazed deep into her eyes.

Carmen's heart beat wildly and her entire body glowed with the warmth of being so close to him again. He looked so perfect. So irresistible. Randall Winston was down on one knee at her feet—the position she had waited all those years before to see him in, and now here he was, already married to another woman, and begging for her to forgive him—*for what? For not marrying me?* Had Randall had some kind of change of heart? Was his marriage less than he expected—not everything he could have had with Carmen, and now he wanted to take the chance to get her back? Carmen held her breath.

"I don't know how to say this to you, Carmen."

Her voice came out soft and hopeful. "Just say it, Randall." She smiled. "I want to hear whatever it is you want me to know."

"Breaking up with you was one of the most difficult things I've ever done, but . . ."

"But what, Randall?"

"If I hadn't found the courage to do that, I would never have found my soul mate, and . . ."

Soul mate? Carmen's heart leaped into her throat, closing off any possibility that she might have a response to Randall's cruel announcement.

"I'm not saying this to try to hurt you any more than I already have; please know that."

Carmen gulped and blinked a few quick times, but she didn't try to speak.

"When I met Michelle, I knew." Randall's face seemed to radiate light. A light that was blinding Carmen—making her eyes water. "From the very first conversation I ever had with her, I knew she was the one. I don't know how to explain it to you, Carmen, I just knew."

Carmen could feel an attitude coming on. What the hell was this man doing down on one knee in front of her confessing to some kind of mystical love for somebody other than her? Like she came all the way over here in a ripped-up dress after nearly being raped to hear this shit?

"What I'm trying to say is . . ." He squeezed her hand gently. "I would never have met the love of my life if I had stayed in that relationship with you, and the worst fear I have is that . . ." Randall's face reflected some kind of deep sadness Carmen couldn't quite identify. Shame? Was that what was hidden behind his eyes? What had he done to her that he would be so ashamed of?

She raised an angry eyebrow and waited.

". . . in my selfishness I may have deprived you of finding yours."

Finding mine? Carmen wasn't getting whatever he was supposed to be apologizing for. Didn't he know he was her true love? Didn't he know *she* was supposed to have been his soul mate?

"It's not that I didn't love you, Carmen, because I did—very much."

"But . . . ?" she heard herself say in an irritated voice.

"I'm afraid that I spent too much time pretending. That I didn't break up with you when I should have. I'm afraid that you might have missed out on the kind of true love you deserve . . . because . . . because of the years you spent with me."

Carmen glared hard into Randall's face, but he wouldn't look at her. She cleared her throat tersely, fighting with every ounce of her self-respect not to spew curses in Randall's pretty face—curse him for ruining her life—for destroying the chance at happiness she had wanted so desperately with him. She was feeling those crazy feelings again. She wanted to throw herself at him and dig her nails into his beautiful face—to give him a tiny taste of the pain he'd inflicted on her. Instead she stewed in her angry silence, waiting for whatever could possibly be coming next.

"I was mesmerized by you from the beginning, you know. I loved the way it made me feel just to be in your presence. The way people looked at us when we were together." He finally looked directly in her eyes. "I loved what it did to me somewhere in here"—he placed a hand over his heart—"what it did to me just to look at you from across the room." He looked away suddenly. "But I always knew there was something missing. Even with all the love I had for you, I knew I couldn't ask you to marry me, because I knew the glue holding us together was superficial and—"

"Superficial?" Carmen interrupted him with furious disbelief in her voice. "*Superficial?*" she repeated angrily. "You were in love with me, Randall Winston. Don't you try to deny that now."

Randall's eyes settled softly on hers. "I did love you, Carmen. I'm not denying that. I still do. But I never believed we were meant for each other. Never. I never had the kind of faith that's required to turn a relationship into forever. Into marriage."

Carmen eyes squinted into two angry slits, and she leaned toward him menacingly. "You *never* said anything like that to me in all those years, Randall. You said you needed time. You always said we were headed toward marriage. You had me believing one day I was going to be your wife, and the whole time you were waiting to get the courage to *dump me?*"

He nodded a silent, guilty *yes* to her question before he muttered quietly, "I'm ashamed to hear myself say this, Carmen, but I . . . I couldn't convince myself to leave something . . . someone as beautiful as you."

Carmen glared coldly at him. "That's bullshit."

"It's the truth. It's the truth, Carmen, and I'm asking you . . . I'm hoping that you can forgive me."

She scooted to the very edge of the sofa and stared angrily into his face. "You're sitting there trying to tell me you stayed with me seven years because I *look good?*" Suddenly she was on her feet. A wince took over her face as she put too much weight on her injured leg, but the pain in her voice had nothing to do with her ankle. She stood over Randall, her eyes glazed over with hurt and anger. "I dedicated my life to you. I betrayed my own family to move in with you, and you have the nerve to sit there and tell me you never *loved* me?"

"You deserve to be loved for who you are inside, Carmen. I'm sorry that I didn't give you that. I hope there is a man in your life now or in the future who will."

Randall stood up to face Carmen. He stood close to her with his hands at his sides and his face wide open to her rage, as if he were anticipating a well-deserved slap, but Carmen had suddenly become a statue. Her face had lost every trace of anger. She seemed to actually be contemplating what Randall had finally admitted to her, and a peaceful smile broke suddenly across her face. Randall stood motionless before her with a look that begged her forgiveness.

She took a slow step toward him, reaching her arms up around his neck. "I forgive you, Randall," she finally crooned at him.

He wrapped his arms around her, holding her in a long embrace. "I will always care deeply about you. Please know that," he whispered into her ear. She knew he meant it. She also knew he had no idea that they were no longer alone.

Carmen smiled provocatively at the woman peering in at them from the other side of the glass. All the fantasizing she had done over the last year had finally come to fruition, and though the sweet reunion scene wasn't quite the way she had envisioned it in her dreams, Randall was in her arms again, and the woman who had stolen his heart was getting a taste of what it felt like to be on the outside looking in.

≋ **17** ≋

Maybe God Is Trying to Tell You Something

Carmen sat in stunned silence in the passenger seat of Mrs. Michelle Winston's Toyota Land Cruiser, staring into the dark blur of scenery along the shoulder of Interstate 405. She counted the cars they passed that were moseying toward the Valley in the slow lane, counted the office buildings along the highway—even counted the number of still-glowing office windows. Anything to give her mind something besides the current circumstances to concentrate on.

When the brightly lit, jewellike structure that was the Getty Museum shone up ahead in its setting of hilltop timber, Carmen fixed her eyes on its radiance, distracting herself from the thick, uncomfortable silence surrounding her and her ex-boyfriend's wife.

"It's beautiful, isn't it?" Michelle said in a quiet voice.

Carmen stole a glance at her—took note of what looked like thirty extra pounds packed onto a plump, nothing special figure. Michelle's square, makeupless brown face held large, deep-set eyes, a wider-than-cute nose, barely noticeable cheekbones, and full lips. And her hair. How she managed to get all those unruly little twists tied down under that bandana was beyond Carmen. The woman wasn't exactly unattractive, but she wasn't anything to write home about either. Carmen had no choice but to wonder, *How on earth did this woman do it?* How had she managed to accomplish in three months, or to hear Randall tell it, in three minutes, what Carmen hadn't been able to coax him into in seven years? She ached to ask the woman—tried to hear herself saying it out loud. *So how exactly did you trick Randall into marrying you?* Instead she muttered, "Mm hmm, the Getty is beautiful,"

"Randall has a photo in one of his albums of the two of you there together." She turned to look at Carmen. "I thought the *photograph* of you was gorgeous"—she smiled, a barely perceptible but obviously sincere gesture, then turned her attention back to the highway—"but you really are much more stunning in person."

Carmen forced a barely audible "Thanks," but all she could think was *Why is Randall showing pictures of me to his wife?* From the looks of the woman, she had an awful lot to be insecure about, especially compared to Carmen's assets. It was just plain mean of Randall to flaunt Carmen's beauty in his wife's face like that.

"I'm surprised . . ." Carmen let a sarcastic little puff of air escape her lips. "I'm surprised he kept any pictures of me. I was pretty sure he hated me after . . . after everything we went through."

"I'm sure you know Randall could never hate anyone. Least of all you." Michelle's eyes fixed momentarily on her rearview mirror, on Carmen's eyes, then back to the road ahead. "Randall started that war with you, Carmen." She sent Carmen a no-nonsense look. "I love what you did with the garage door. And I told him so."

Carmen heard no trace of sarcasm in Michelle's tone, and all she saw on her face was a calm expression of straightforwardness. Why wasn't the woman teasing her? Why wasn't she flaunting her man in the face of the more beautiful but jilted ex? Carmen would have. If the tables were turned, she would have surely rubbed chubby little Michelle's face all up in her defeat. Would have made her understand exactly what she lost—and that it had been found—and promptly married. But Michelle didn't seem to want to do that at all, and Carmen wasn't sure how to handle it. The woman's generosity unsettled her, and her kindness was rather irritating, actually. There was something about her, some kind of an air that was bothering Carmen to no end. The moment Randall had turned the key and let his wife into the foyer of his office building Carmen noticed it. It was beyond strange that Michelle had no trace of jealousy on her face—not even for a split second—despite the fact that she had walked in on her husband wrapped tightly in the arms of his ex—a drop-dead gorgeous woman he had spent nearly seven years loving. But no, she just walked right through the door, gave Randall a little peck on his face, then turned to Carmen and extended a hand in greeting.

"Hi, I'm Michelle." No dirty look. No evil eye for Randall.

Carmen was left with no choice but to shake the woman's hand. She didn't introduce herself in return, but just stood there, dumbstruck. Didn't Michelle catch the grin Carmen had beamed through the glass doors at her while her husband's arms were wrapped around Carmen's voluptuous curves? Where was the big dramatic scene Carmen had intended to incite? Didn't this idiot know who Carmen was? That Carmen had at one time explored every inch of her man's body, and that there wasn't an inch of Carmen's creamy skin that Randall's tongue had not tasted? Didn't this fool for one moment suspect that her man might be getting a little extra attention on the old office couch while his wife wasn't around? Apparently not. Michelle didn't give Randall so much as a hint of a suspicious look or sarcastic question. She barely even paid attention to her husband once she took in Carmen's disheveled appearance.

Michelle had looked at Carmen's torn dress and the circles of mascara framing her puffy, red eyes and immediately made it all about Carmen. "Are you okay?" She glanced quickly at Randall with a look of curiosity, but didn't wait for him to explain his ex's presence, or her appearance. Instead she focused all her attention and her sympathy on Carmen.

Carmen had been so shocked by Michelle's absolute absence of jealousy, she couldn't do anything but stand there and stare at the woman in disbelief. She stood silently as Randall explained to his wife why Carmen had come to see him in the middle of the night. Carmen noticed something odd about Randall's behavior then too—he didn't seem the least bit nervous or uncomfortable to be caught there with his ex-girlfriend. That kind of thing only happened in the movies; at least that was what Carmen had always believed. But the two apparently had something Carmen had never really thought was possible. They apparently *trusted* each other, and Michelle's behavior toward Carmen proved it beyond a shadow of a doubt.

After hearing Carmen's story in all its graphic detail, Michelle insisted on driving Carmen to the police station in Encino, where Carmen lived—where the crime had been committed. Michelle, it turned out, was a volunteer rape crisis counselor for LA County, so, she insisted, it made sense for them to ride together. That way she could help Carmen prepare for the questions the police would ask, and tell her what to expect during the examination. It was also Michelle's suggestion that Randall follow them—in Carmen's car. Carmen had been so dumbstruck by the surreal scene, she didn't have the presence of mind to object to Michelle's offer, so there she was, seated next to Mrs. Randall Winston while Mr. Winston trailed behind them in Carmen's Lexus.

Carmen looked back over her shoulder at the headlights a few car lengths away. Randall was following right behind them, like they were some kind of happy little caravan. She looked over at Michelle. *I am riding in the car with Randall Winston's wife.* She tried to wrap her mind around the idea, but it was way too preposterous. If anyone had told her that the possibility of this moment existed, Carmen would have suggested they find a damn good therapist—they would have to be certifiably insane to suggest something so ridiculous.

Michelle turned to Carmen, breaking the silence between

them. "I hope I wasn't too pushy back there, and"—she smiled—"and I hope I haven't made you uncomfortable."

"Oh. Not at all," Carmen lied. "Why would I be uncomfortable with someone so—" she smiled sweetly, showing too many teeth—"so . . . *nice*."

Michelle laughed. "I'm not that nice."

"Yes, you are. You are one of those people who can't help it. You volunteer to help abused women you don't even know, for God's sake."

"I was raped when I was nineteen," Michelle responded solemnly.

Carmen kept her mouth shut.

"I went to a clinic, and an absolute stranger was there to hold my hand. To tell me how to deal with the police. To tell me what to expect during the medical examination." She shot Carmen a serious look. "I owe."

Carmen swallowed hard. She tried to find a voice to tell Michelle she was sorry that happened to her, but her throat wouldn't cooperate.

"I know from experience how frustrating it can be to go to the police. They may not treat you with respect, so it helps to know what kind of questions to expect. The more prepared you are, the less likely you will be made to feel like you've done something to deserve being attacked."

"I didn't do a thing to that dirty old bastard," Carmen spouted angrily.

Michelle glanced over at her. "If you can, try to avoid cursing during the questioning. It doesn't make sense, I know. After being violated, you want to scream curses from the mountaintops, but don't. It tends to make the police stereo-type you." She explained to Carmen what she should be pre-pared for at the police station. Avoid sweeping arm movements. Keep your hands in your lap. Sit up straight with your knees together, and look the officer in the eye when you speak. Speak softly. No cursing. Don't embellish. Answer the questions with short, succinct sentences. Avoid harsh words. If you feel like crying—do. Carmen was attentive. She needed every bit of advice Michelle had to give her, and she knew it. She didn't want to do or say anything that might compromise her intended lawsuit against Browning.

"They're going to ask you, repeatedly, whether you had a prior relationship with the perpetrator, and whether there was any previous physical contact of any kind."

Carmen thought about the ear bath Browning had given her at their first meeting, but she didn't want to talk about it. Why make herself look like she asked for that kind of attention?

"I met George Browning for a lunch meeting *once*," Car-men stated matter-of-factly. "We met at McCormick's on Rodeo, and he was a perfect gentleman. He asked me about my qualifications for the promotion. He told me I had been suggested to him as an excellent candidate. He said he had gone to school with my father, and that he knew and admired both of my parents. When he asked me to meet with him again before making his final selection for the job, I was ecstatic."

She looked out into the darkness along the roadside and took a dramatic breath before continuing her story.

"My *relationship* with George Browning, if that's what it can be called, was strictly professional." She liked the way she sounded. She could picture herself on the stand before a judge and jury making that creep look like the pervert he really was.

"They will ask you to tell your story more than once. Just to make sure you don't have more than one version. Be prepared for them to send in more than one officer to ask the same questions. When they realize who your perpetrator is, they will not cut any corners."

"Will they arrest him?"

"They will bring him in for questioning. But he won't stay in custody long. You can believe his lawyers will have him out within a couple of hours—if not minutes. Now, about the exam—"

"Exam?"

"You'll need a physical exam."

"I don't think I need an exam."

Michelle looked at Carmen's torn dress, then back at the road. "You'll need an exam."

"I mean he didn't—"

"They'll photograph any bruises you have, and any . . . any semen he left will be collected as evidence."

"S-semen?"

"You did say he ejaculated?"

"Yes. But I-I washed it off."

Michelle was visibly upset by Carmen's words. She looked at Carmen, looked ahead at the road. Looked at Carmen. "Unfortunately, that is often the first thing an assault victim will do."

"When he left my house I ran straight to the bathroom and grabbed a washcloth. I had to. I couldn't stand it."

Michelle was quiet.

"That wasn't too smart, was it?" She looked down at the torn Versace—at the crusty, dried-up stain that still remained on it. Pinching a section above the stain between her thumb and forefinger, she held it out away from her exposed thigh with disgust. "It is still on my dress, though."

Michelle glanced at a crusty spot on Carmen's dress, then shifted her eyes back to the road. Carmen expected a comment from her, but Michelle didn't utter a sound. She wondered where Michelle had suddenly disappeared to—what had her mind so preoccupied? Perhaps in glancing over at Carmen's dress, she got a good eyeful of the incredible body Carmen was packing. Maybe she was so quiet because she was sitting over there thinking about what her man was no doubt comparing his dumpy wife to every time he saw her without her clothes on. What a blow to her self-esteem that must be, Carmen thought. *Oh well. That's what happens when you take up with another woman's leftovers before they even have a chance to cool. Especially when that woman is a hundred times better looking than you.*

"Sorry I disappeared on you like that," Michelle suddenly said. "I was thinking about what we should do about your dress."

"My dress?"

"I'm thinking you might want to go home first and change your clothes. I wonder if it might be better if that dress were not introduced into this yet."

Carmen got an instant attitude. She knew where Michelle was going with that comment. So what if the dress was a bit sexy. That didn't mean she *asked for it*. George Browning had no right to attack her, regardless of what she was wearing, and this puffy little bitch had a lot of nerve to suggest he did. A sour attitude came pouring out all over Carmen's next words.

"There is *nothing* wrong with this dress. I paid a lot of damn money for this damn dress, and I think it looks *nice* on me. I can't help it if . . ." Carmen let out an angry little breath and looked Michelle up and down. "Pssh. It doesn't really matter what I put on, you know. I'm going to look *attractive* regardless." She glared at Michelle. "You have no idea—" Carmen stopped talking suddenly and turned to look out the window. "*You* just don't have a clue what it's like to be—" She stopped herself before she said something she couldn't take back.

In the long silence following her outburst Carmen stared sullenly out the window, wondering why the idiot didn't at least try to defend herself. She had basically just told the pudgy little woman she didn't know what it was like to be attractive.

Without a word to Carmen, Michelle suddenly reached forward and pushed a button on the car's console, instantly filling the interior with the sounds of a gospel choir harmonizing soulfully.

Michelle sang along quietly, her voice a near whisper, then rising slightly as the song progressed; it was a song about how when things aren't going right in your life you ought to think about whether God is trying to tell you something.

Michelle's voice rose into a soulful current that flowed in through Carmen's ears and radiated in her chest. Carmen vaguely recognized the song, but she couldn't remember where she'd heard it. She hadn't stepped foot in a church since her father's funeral, and she wasn't one to buy gospel music; but the tune and the lyrics tugged at a memory she couldn't quite place.

After a few minutes Michelle reached to turn down the volume, then cleared her throat with a quiet little cough. She looked solemnly at Carmen's dress, then into her eyes. "Um. Carmen. Let me apologize for what I was saying about your dress. It didn't come out the way I intended. I wasn't referring to the way the dress *looks* on you. I actually think it's very beautiful. I just think it is a key element in your case against George Browning."

Carmen wasn't following.

"I have a feeling Browning might try to deny he was ever in your apartment. He'll say he was never alone with you. If he is the creep you described, he will probably try to get away with that. He knows it's your word against his. So if he denies he was ever alone with you, you've got him. With the DNA evidence, not only can you prove he was with you, you can prove he lied about it, and the court will have to recognize that the only reason he would lie about it—"

"Is because he *does* have something to hide," Carmen interjected matter-of-factly.

"That's right," Michelle responded. "And once it's been established that he's a liar, your word against his takes on a whole new meaning."

A smile dawned slowly across Carmen's face. She suddenly felt an overwhelming urge to reach across the seat and hug Michelle. Instead she just looked at her for a long moment. As much as she really wished she could despise her, Carmen had to admit that Michelle was just plain impossible to ha— *Unh unh.* Carmen closed her eyes and took in a soft, quick breath. She felt a wave of sickness in the pit of her stomach. In the darkness behind her eyes, the face of her friend Yvette loomed— the wide smile and sparkling brown eyes of a friend Carmen had known since the seventh grade. *Impossible to hate.* Those were the exact words Yvette had used to describe Randall's new wife after she and Evan had run into Randall and Michelle on the golf course. Words that prompted Carmen to call Yvette a two-faced bitch and accuse her of betrayal. She had not spoken a word to her best friend since that argument, and Carmen had been walking around for nearly a year convincing herself that she had every right to dismiss Vette for her unforgivable disloyalty.

Now here Carmen was, kicking it in the passenger side of the enemy's vehicle, thinking how if the circumstance weren't so strange, she'd probably be trying to hug her. The woman really was impossible to hate, and Yvette would have been lying to say otherwise. Carmen gazed out the window and fought to keep the tears behind her eyes from falling. *I'm sorry, Yvette.* It seemed crying was all she did lately, and every time she turned around, someone was telling her something about herself she really didn't want to hear.

As Michelle's Land Cruiser slowed and headed down the off ramp toward Ventura, the sound of her singing underscored what Carmen already was beginning to believe. *Maybe God is trying to tell you something.*

⇒ 18 ⇐

We Meet Again

Carmen told her story to the detective for the third time, and for the third time she found herself fighting back tears as she described the terror and helplessness she'd felt when Browning overpowered her.

"He forced his tongue in my mouth. He pushed me to the floor and he—" She stopped to wipe a tear from her cheek. "He would have raped me if he could have, but—"

"But he didn't," the detective interjected blandly. The tone in his voice said he wasn't sure Carmen was telling the whole truth. He leaned back in his chair to study her thoughtfully, then scribbled a note on the yellow pad in front of him. When the phone on his desk rang suddenly the bulky, soft-spoken officer answered it quickly, half whispered into the receiver, then rose abruptly from his seat. He ran one hand across the top of his balding blond head and rested the other on the revolver at his waistband.

"If you're sure there's nothing else, miss . . ." He eyed Carmen carefully, then leaned across the desk to offer her a business card. "After I've questioned the alleged perpetrator my report will go to the district attorney. If he feels there is ample evidence that a crime has been committed, you'll be informed. If not . . . you'll be informed."

Carmen stood up hesitantly. When the detective turned and walked away from the desk without another word to her, she limped along behind him. She followed him toward the lobby, stopping at the low bench where Randall was waiting for her.

"I can go home now." Carmen tried to smile at him. "Tell your wife . . ." It hurt Carmen's heart to say the word "wife" to him, but it was a pain she knew she had to deal with. "I appreciate what she did for me tonight." Michelle had insisted that Randall accompany Carmen inside the police station, while she waited outside in the car.

"I'll tell her." He nodded his head, acknowledging what he knew was a difficult thing for her to say.

Goodbye, Randall. It wasn't easy for her to admit it, but he was forever gone, and Carmen knew it. She looked into his eyes and tried again to smile, but her bottom lip was quivering uncontrollably. "Your wife's very nice."

Before he could respond, the door to the police station suddenly flung open, and someone was walking through it, shouting angrily.

"This is preposterous! Do you have any idea who I am?"

The door had opened wide to let in two uniformed officers

accompanied by George Browning dressed in a blue pin-striped business suit, his crimson tie neatly knotted at his fat triple chin. Two middle-aged white men, also wearing suits, followed close behind him.

Carmen moved closer to Randall, a look of panic spreading like a dark cloud across her face. The sight of Browning made her heart race, and she felt her knees weaken beneath her. She remembered Browning's hot breath on her face, his tongue prying its way into her mouth. She looked at Randall with a desperate expression that said she wasn't going to be okay. In an instant Randall moved in front of Carmen, placing himself between her and her attacker.

"This is preposterous," Browning was sputtering loudly to the officers who had led him into the station. When he spotted his accuser standing less than twenty feet from him, he shook his head and glared at Carmen with an expression that resembled paternal disgust—as though she were a bad little girl who had done something she should be ashamed of.

Carmen took note of how powerful Browning looked. She hadn't paid much attention to his stature before—that stocky build of an ex-football player. He looked as if he might have been quite athletic in his younger days. The shoulder pads in his expensive suit jacket accentuated his athletic appearance, and the wire-rimmed glasses and costly hairpiece added an air of well-groomed authority to his already eminent demeanor. Looking at him in these brightly lit surroundings, flanked by two important-looking lawyer types, Carmen wondered how she could have been stupid enough to assume he was just some old geezer she needn't fear. The realization that the man could easily have raped her wrapped itself around her rib cage like a boa constrictor, making it difficult for her to breathe.

Without warning a hot tear made its way down Carmen's cheek. "That's him," she announced angrily. "He's the man that attacked me."

Browning glared at her and pointed a rigid index finger in her direction. "That woman has been stalking me for weeks, officers," he bellowed. "For God's sake, if anyone is a victim here"—Browning pressed both palms dramatically to his chest and roared at the policemen—"it's *me*."

"You're a liar," Carmen shouted venomously. She felt Randall's hand grasp hers and squeeze tightly. She instantly lowered the intensity in her voice. "You attacked me in my apartment," she stated matter-of-factly, staring Browning in the eye. "You tried to rape me."

"I attacked you?" The incredulous look on George's face was Oscar worthy. He addressed the detective in a calm, sincere tone. "I'll admit I had a business lunch with this woman in a restaurant a few weeks ago, but I only agreed to that because the deputy superintendent asked me if I'd interview her for a job. I could see right away she wasn't qualified for the position she wanted, and I told her so that very day." Browning shot an evil look at Carmen. "This woman has been hounding me mercilessly ever since. I had to change my phone number, for God's sake, just to get a little peace of mind. I don't know what this lunatic is trying to pull here, but I have certainly never been to her apartment. I don't have any idea where she lives." George placed a hand on the shoulder of one of the two men who'd accompanied him and announced firmly, "This is my driver. He has been with me the entire evening. Neither of us has been anywhere near that woman."

"You'll get a chance to tell your story," the detective responded abruptly. He pointed to the empty desk behind the counter where Carmen had just been questioned. "Have a seat at that desk on the far wall, and we'll take your statement."

Browning stared solemnly into the detective's face. "I'm not going to walk past her. She's obviously mentally ill. "Who knows what she is capable of?"

The police officers looked Carmen up and down, trying to stifle grins. She was dressed in a pale yellow sweat suit and fuzzy pink slippers with her hair pulled up in a neat bun. She looked about as threatening as Tweety Bird. All three of the policeman laughed at Browning.

"You're laughing? Why don't you run a criminal check on her? You'll see why I have every reason to be afraid of her." Browning glanced at one of the Secret Service look-alikes standing close beside him. "My attorney will tell you. Tell them, Davis. I'm not the first man she's threatened."

Davis eyed Carmen with a slight arch in his brow and a faint little grin across his lips. "The woman's got a history of stalking successful men. She's got a criminal record."

Browning jumped in. "She's been charged with stalking, harassment, assault, and God knows what else."

Browning's smug little grin sent a wave of terror through Carmen. He'd already won. She could see it all over his face. George had covered all the bases. He'd arrived at Carmen's apartment armed with her past, knowing full well he could get away with assaulting her. Everyone in the city knew how politically connected the man was. He probably had the mayor or even the chief of police himself in his pocket. She couldn't believe how horribly it all had backfired. Not only would she never get the TAG counseling position she had been maneuvering for, she would lose her job at Overland as well. Browning would certainly have no problem making that happen.

"Perhaps your attorney should have done his homework a little more thoroughly," Randall interjected suddenly. Carmen heard a growl of anger behind his calm words.

Homework. What homework? she thought. Everything Browning said about Carmen was true. Randall had pressed charges against her for assault after she ambushed him one night in his driveway. Then there was the stalking charge. The restraining order was a result of all the harassing Carmen had done in the first month following their breakup, and the judge didn't hesitate to grant it. Why was Randall standing there acting as if none of the ugly past with Carmen had ever happened? "Miss DuPrè has no criminal record whatsoever, and you ought to be ashamed of yourself for suggesting it," Randall said with believable conviction.

"I don't believe I was speaking to you, young man," Browning scolded.

Randall pointed a rigid finger in Browning's face. "Well, I'm speaking to you. And I'm telling you it is a low-down trick to try to intimidate this woman because you somehow found out about some charges that were filed against her a long time ago—charges that were subsequently dropped." Randall turned to give Carmen a comforting look. A look that said *Don't you worry about this; I've got it handled.* When he spoke to Browning again, his voice had a menacing tone to it. "If you want to play that game, Mr. Browning, then let's play. Perhaps you'd like to suggest that the detectives check out your criminal history while they're at it." Randall knew something he wasn't telling. He had some kind of juicy information about George Browning, and Carmen wanted to know what it was. She shot a curious look at him.

Browning's lawyer cupped a hand to his client's ear and whispered in it. Whatever he said, it shut Browning's mouth. He didn't utter another word.

"You're going to have to come back here with us and answer some questions, sir." The detective gestured to Browning to follow him.

Randall stood directly in front of Carmen, moving to block Browning's view of her as he sauntered past, flanked by his lawyer and driver. When the lawyer passed, Randall held a business card out to him, raising his eyebrow with a demeanor that bordered on cocky. "We'll be needing to talk."

The lawyer studied the card for a moment, then closed his eyes painfully.

Randall grinned. "That's right, Mr. Davis. We meet again."

≋ 19 ≋

Who Are You, and What Have You Done with My Sister?

The beads at the ends of Lindsey's cornrows jangled noisily as she shook her head in disbelief. "I knew it, Car," she scolded Carmen from across the table in the crowded restaurant. "I knew that old man was up to no good." She lifted the bun from her grilled portabello mushroom sandwich and spread a thin layer of herb mayo on it, then pointed the knife in her hand at Carmen. "You are so lucky he didn't . . . I mean. I hate to say I told you so, sis, but . . ."

"Don't lie." Carmen scowled at Lindsey. Lindsey had been ranting and raving about George Browning for the last ten minutes, and Carmen hadn't bothered to try to stop her. She knew she deserved every word of the lecture she was getting. "The truth is, you *love* to say you told me so, and you're right, you did try to warn me."

Lindsey's head shook with more emphatic disbelief, and the tiny brass and silver beads made little clinking noises at her every movement, which was irking Carmen no end. She hated braids—and hated beaded braids even more. It wasn't that braids weren't attractive—she'd actually seen a few styles that she'd found tolerable—it was just that she never understood why any woman would ever consider wearing a hairstyle that gave even a hint that she had the need for a hair weave. Carmen would never be caught dead with cornrows, and certainly would never walk around with all that paraphernalia hanging off her head. To hear Lindsey tell it, all that clinking and clanging was some kind of symbol of African pride. As if Lindsey had any idea what it meant to be an African. *For somebody so smart and well paid,* Carmen thought, *my sister can act so ridiculous at times.*

"Well, I *did* tell you so," Lindsey muttered. "I told you that old man was up to no good. Need to listen to me more often, hardhead." She sent a playful smirk Carmen's way.

Carmen leaned an elbow on the table. "Well, I didn't tell you the really unbelievable part yet," she whispered dramatically.

Lindsey took a bite of her sandwich and raised an eyebrow at Carmen. She chewed slowly, examining Carmen's grin like she was trying to figure out what on earth her sister could be referring to. "You mean it gets more unbelievable than being assaulted by a man old enough to be your father, going to the police station in the middle of the night, catching the old geezer in a bold-faced lie, and having his lawyer call you two days later to try to offer you ten thousand dollars? Damn,

Carmen, what could possibly be more unbelievable than that?"

"You will never in a million years guess who drove me to the police station."

"Not Della."

"Hell no."

"Mama?"

Carmen looked at Lindsey like she'd lost her mind. She didn't bother to shake her head no.

"A man?"

Carmen smiled. "Nope. Didn't I say you will never guess?"

"Yvette?" Lindsey grinned excitedly. When Carmen shook her head at that suggestion, Lindsey took another bite of her sandwich and stopped trying to guess.

"Mrs. Randall Winston." Carmen picked up her wineglass and sipped nonchalantly from it.

Lindsey swallowed her bite of sandwich whole, nearly choking on it, and reached for her water glass. She took a huge swig before setting the glass down, her eyes carefully studying Carmen's face the entire time. After a few coughs, she finally managed to get the words out. "Randall's *wife* drove you to the police station?"

"You want to know what's crazier than that?"

Lindsey shook her head emphatically. "Nothing. Nothing is crazier than that, Car." She rolled her eyes to the ceiling and pretended to be contemplating the idea, "Let's see . . . I know . . . Tupac rode in the backseat?"

"Close. Randall followed behind us. He drove my car."

"Very funny." Lindsey's expression said she was sure it

was all a big joke. "You better quit lying, Car, it's not good for the soul."

"It gets even crazier." Carmen grinned mischievously. It was obvious Lindsey didn't believe any of it.

Lindsey just stared at her and waited.

"I like her."

"You *what?*"

"I know. I can't believe I'm saying this, Linn, but I like her. She really is impossible to hate."

"Didn't Yvette tell you that?"

"Those exact words."

"That's spooky."

"Yeah. Don't I feel stupid? I really need to talk to her."

"Mrs. Winston?"

"No, Yvette. I've got to call her and let her know I forgive her." Carmen was silent for a moment at the thought of how evil she had been to Yvette. If there was anyone needing forgiving, it was she. She'd called Yvette three times in the past two days, only to get an answering machine each time, and on the final attempt she decided to leave a message. She nervously muttered a weak comment about not being mad anymore, and would Yvette like to get together. So far she hadn't heard anything back from her, which she wasn't sure how to take. She thought about trying to call back and leave a better message, one that included a sincere apology, but Carmen was terrified that she might pour her heart out and instead of a warm "I still love you," she might get a cold shoulder in return. Not that she didn't deserve one. She just didn't think that on top of everything else she was going through, she could bear the thought of being cruelly rejected by Yvette. Not now. Carmen closed her eyes for a moment and banished that uncomfortable thought from her mind. When she opened them again, Lindsey was staring at her, waiting patiently for her to finish her story.

Carmen cleared her throat softly. "What I mean is, I need to call her and tell her how sorry I am."

Lindsey smiled.

"You want to know what else?" Her face and voice had turned solemn.

"*What else?* What the hell else could there be?"

"Randall and Michelle . . ." She disappeared for a long moment.

"Randall and Michelle, what?" Lindsey said softly.

"I realize he wasn't the one."

Lindsey stared at her sister in astonishment. "*What?*" She put her sandwich down and leaned in, searching her sister's eyes seriously. "Sis, I have never, *ever* heard you come even close to thinking Randall Winston was anything but the perfect man for you." She leaned back and stared hard at Carmen then picked up a French fry, dipped it in ketchup, and took a bite. She chewed slowly, staring Carmen down, as if trying to decide how much of the story was true.

"Randall was not perfect." Carmen announced plainly. "And neither was I."

Lindsey reached for her cell phone and flipped it open with a jerk of her wrist. "*Los Angeles Times?* Stop the presses. Carmen DuPrè announces she is not perfect. That's right. No. Yes, that is a direct quote." Linn stood up, leaned across the table, looked Carmen over closely as if she were inspecting a used car, then poked her a few times as if she was trying to make sure she was real flesh and blood. When she reached for a handful of Carmen's hair and tugged on it, Carmen smacked her hand away. Lindsey whispered into her cell phone, "Yes, my source is credible. I wouldn't believe it myself if it weren't coming straight from the horse's mouth."

"Very funny."

Lindsey sat back down in her seat, laughing at her sister playfully. "Seriously, Carmen, what brought you to that unlikely conclusion?"

"I never *said* I was perfect." Carmen rolled her eyes in mock offense. "I just thought I was perfect for Randall because we . . . we were so good together. I thought we loved each other so much. But you know what, Linn? I finally realize what folks mean when they say love is not enough."

Lindsey was frozen in amazement with a look somewhere between awe and disbelief etched on her face.

"I'm glad I saw them together. I'm glad I saw . . . I see what they have. Randall and I never came close to that." Carmen smiled a soft, resolved smile. "He called her his soul mate." She breathed in, then exhaled loudly, as if she were letting Randall out of her system right along with the air in her lungs. "And you know what, lil' sis? I believe him."

Lindsey's facial expression said she didn't believe a word of it. "The Carmen DuPrè I know isn't sure there is even such a thing as a *soul*, so I know she does not believe in soul *mates*. Who are you, and what have you done with my sister?"

194

Carmen laughed. "Sometimes the truth just comes and slaps you in the face, and there's nothing you can do but take it." She picked up her glass of zinfandel and took another tiny sip. "Randall was my first love, and I confused that for the first, last, one and only. But I was mistaken." She shrugged nonchalantly, her voice full of bland conviction, as though she were talking about having bought a pair of shoes that didn't quite match the outfit they were intended for, and there was nothing to do but shop for more suitable shoes. "Hmph. I worked so hard at being the perfect wife for that man, and it never occurred to me that I shouldn't have had to work to earn his love."

"Wow." Lindsey's eyes widened.

Carmen leaned into Lindsey and looked seriously into her eyes. "Not to change the subject, sweetie, but, speaking of 'the one,' how's *your* soul mate doing, and when do I get to meet this mystery man?"

Lindsey seemed instantly uncomfortable with the reference to her own love life. She cleared her throat quietly. "Kenny's fine. We're going to the Sparks game tonight." She glanced nervously at her watch.

"Sparks? You actually found a boyfriend to watch that damn women's basketball with you?" Carmen scowled playfully. "Hmph. Better hold on to that one."

Lindsey pursed her lips sarcastically, took a sip from her water glass, glanced at her watch again, then changed the subject. "So what are you going to do about Browning's settlement offer, Car? You going to take it?"

"Ten thousand? Not a chance. The district attorney's office indicted him on attempted rape charges. Browning swore to them he had never been near my house, but there were traces of his semen on my clothes and my carpet. My attorney thinks once we win the criminal case, the civil suit we filed against him will be open and shut, and that ought to be worth way more money in the long run."

"How are you managing at work? I mean, you do work in the school district that man runs."

"Oh, I'm not at Overland anymore, at least not now. The school district immediately put me on administrative leave. Until this thing is over, I don't have to show up for work *and* I still get a paycheck. So, the way I see it, there's no need for me to rush into any settlement. Besides, by the time I'm finished with that old fool, I'll be happy to take that counseling position I want at the Gifted Academy *and* about a quarter of a million dollars of George Browning's money."

"Two hundred and fifty thousand? Are you for real?"

"It is possible. Randall's law firm settled a suit against Browning a couple of years ago. It seems I am not the first district employee that old jerk tried to . . ." Carmen made a disgusted face. "You know."

"You mean there's *another* victim?"

"Try, *victims,* lil' sis. "Carmen held up two fingers.

Lindsey glanced at her watch nervously. "You've got to be kidding me."

Carmen shook her head no.

"What a pervert. I guess that tongue-in-the-ear thing should have told you something, huh?"

Carmen cleared her throat quietly. A flush warmed her cheeks, and her words came out coated with a tinge of shame.

"Yes, I should have known better. I'm lucky he didn't really hurt me."

Lindsey nodded in sympathetic agreement, then looked at her watch again.

"Damn, Linn. Are you in a hurry or something?"

"Huh?"

"Are you late for something?"

"I told you I'm meeting Kenny for the Sparks game."

"Do you need to leave?"

"Um. No. But you do."

"Excuse me?"

"Kenny's meeting me here at five-thirty. That's in, uh"—she looked at her watch again—"fifteen minutes."

"Great. I've been looking forward to meeting this mystery man of yours."

"Carmen, please don't stay. I'm not ready for that yet. I'm glad you dropped in on me at the office, and I'm really glad we took time to have a bite together, but . . ." Lindsey's face looked stricken, like all the blood had drained from it, leaving her usually flawless cinnamon complexion red and splotchy. "I'm glad we got to spend time together today, but—but . . . please understand, Car."

A wave of hurt feelings heated Carmen's face. "Fine. I'm out." She stood up abruptly and began gathering her belongings.

"Car, don't be like that. I just . . ."

"No problem." She slung her purse onto her shoulder and dug around angrily in it for her keys. She didn't make a move for the check. Lindsey was in a better position to take care of that anyway.

"Please don't be mad, Car. I'm just not ready to share Kenny yet."

The words had barely come out of Lindsey's mouth when the angry expression on Carmen's face melted away. It hit her suddenly. She finally heard what Lindsey was trying to tell her. This was her sister's first serious boyfriend. Lindsey's first chance at love. She didn't want her gorgeous older sister around her new man just yet. Carmen couldn't blame her for that. It wouldn't be the first time a woman's so-called true love had been distracted by Carmen's presence. Lindsey was smart to have considered it.

Carmen beamed a sympathetic smile. "It's okay, lil' sis. I understand."

"You sure?"

She stepped toward Lindsey, leaning over to plant a kiss on her cheek. "Positive. When you're ready to share him, why don't you bring him over to my place. I'll fix gumbo."

Lindsey smiled. "Gumbo, huh? No okra?"

"No okra, sweetie."

Carmen headed toward the double doors leading out of the restaurant, waving bye to Lindsey over her shoulder. She stepped outside into the blaring sunlight, stopping momentarily at the sidewalk to search her purse for her sunglasses. When she'd finally located the shades and lifted them to her face, an abrupt push from behind her sent her stumbling forward a couple of steps. She turned angrily to face a petite black woman wearing a midriff-baring halter top, a tiny diamond nose ring, and her hair shaved so close to her head, Carmen could see her chocolate brown scalp.

"Oh, I am so sorry," the woman gushed. She pointed at her feet. "I'm still learning how to walk in these things." They both looked down at the woman's platforms.

Carmen let out a little "mnh" before directing the woman's eyes to one of Carmen's own feet by placing one of them, toe pointed, directly in front of the woman's shoe. Their shoes were identical. They were both wearing the same Charles David platform sandals with one thin black strap across the toes, and another around the ankle. Carmen had had a hard time getting used to them herself. She smiled at the woman, in spite of her irritation.

"It takes a couple of wearings to get the hang of these. I nearly knocked over an old lady with a walker the first time I wore mine." Carmen laughed softly.

The woman winked at Carmen. "I guess that's what we get for trying to be cute."

Trying to be cute? Being cute would never be something Carmen had to try to do. She stared hard at the woman's closely shaven head and her repulsive nose ring. *Bald head. Skinny little no-breasted shape. You look like a chemotherapy patient.* Carmen's face was suddenly drained of color, and she felt as if all the air had been sucked out of her lungs. *Chemotherapy patient. Oh damn. Damn.* She instantly regretted her nasty attitude. *Damn. Why do I always go there?* This time she'd slapped her own face with her rotten attitude. *Chemotherapy is the last thing I want on my mind.* She had managed to avoid thinking about Dr. Lee's diagnosis for several days, and she would have made it to the end of this day without a reminder if she hadn't silently insulted a stranger who was simply trying to be polite.

You need an attitude adjustment, Carmen DuPrè, she scolded herself silently. Lindsey was wrong about Carmen not believing she had a soul. She knew she did. She just never was completely sure there was something or someone in the universe who cared what condition it was in. *Maybe God is trying to tell you something.* Carmen flashed a nervous smile at the bald woman who'd bumped into her. "Yes," she said softly, before turning to make her way toward her car. "That is what we get for trying to be cute."

≋ **20** ≋

Blessing the Watchman

A concrete walkway wended its way from the tenant parking
area to Carmen's latched wrought-iron fence, continued
straight ahead five feet to her front porch, then angled sharply
under her dining room window with an additional six or seven
feet of cement path that ended abruptly against the door to
her storage unit. The L-shaped path lined a small rectangular
lawn bordered by a row of oleander bushes crowded against a
tall, wooden fence that enclosed the private yard. Except for
Carmen's gorgeous white oleanders, which she had planted
herself a few months previous, and a potted palm she'd placed
near a low bench under the dining room window, all of the
apartments in Valley Gate Acres resembled one another. It
wasn't uncommon for a tenant's visitor to find himself at the
wrong unit, which is what Carmen first thought when she re-

turned home from the mall to find a man slumped, head between his knees, back pressed to Carmen's storage room door, apparently sound asleep.

After an initial jolt of apprehension, it took only a half second for her to realize who the sleeping man was. Even in the dim early evening light she recognized the shoes—beige and sable two-toned oxfords that hadn't been in style since the late 1950s. And that outfit. Plaid polyester slacks and a cream and tan striped sweater ribbed at the cuffs and waist. *Nobody in this millennium wears rib-cuffed acrylic sweaters,* Carmen thought. Though she couldn't see his face, there was no doubt who it was who had posted himself outside Carmen's front door. It could only be Eugene Timms.

Carmen closed the entry gate quietly. With a sly smile on her face she tiptoed over to Eugene and stood over him with her foot poised to give him a little kick. She intended to startle him—nudge him a little with the edge of her boot—but she couldn't do it. Looking down at him sleeping soundly, she felt an unexpected twinge of tenderness—a tiny hint of something behind her rib cage that glowed warm, and though she could hardly admit it to herself, she realized she had actually missed him.

Carmen bent down and leaned in until her lips were nearly touching Eugene's ear. "Eugene." She whispered playfully. "Euugeeene. Wake up, sweetheart."

Eugene raised his head. A childlike smile spread across his lips, but his eyes remained tightly shut. Carmen could see that he was awake, but he had not yet opened his eyes. "Eugene, what are you doing here?" she crooned in the same playful voice.

"I needed to see you," he announced calmly, his eyes still tightly closed.

"If you need to see me, it might help to open your eyes."

His smile widened, but his eyes remained shut.

"Why aren't you opening your eyes, Eugene?"

"I was just savoring the moment is all."

"What moment is that?"

"The moment when your sweet voice was the first thing I awakened to." His eyes opened then and he gazed serenely into Carmen's face. "I could get used to that," he added softly.

Carmen calmly ignored Eugene's fantasy of ever waking up next to her. "What are you doing here, Eugene?"

"I have something to tell you." Eugene's eyes were sparkling with intensity. "I've left you several messages, but you don't return my calls." He smiled confidently at Carmen. "I had to talk to you. I've been here for hours." He looked at his watch. "Four hours and twenty-two minutes to be exact."

Carmen crossed her arms defensively and studied Eugene with a guarded expression. "So tell me."

He stared at her thoughtfully. "Carmen . . ." He hesitated nervously, as if he was trying hard to be careful with whatever it was he had come to say. "Uh, Carmen, do you pray?"

"Excuse me?"

"Do you pray? I mean . . ." Eugene shook his head. "I'm sorry. You don't have to answer that if you don't want to. That's a pretty personal question, isn't it? I just . . . Well . . . As a matter of fact, never mind. Don't answer that."

Carmen's eyes became two wary slits.

Eugene began again. "What I'm trying to say is, *I* pray."

Carmen let out a sarcastic puff of breath. "You pray. All rightee. That's really nice, Eugene."

"What I mean is, every night before I go to sleep I meditate. I meditate and then I pray. I pray for the students at Overland. I pray for my mother and father who have passed on. I pray for—"

"Eugene, it's really not necessary for you to share your entire devotional list with me." She was getting impatient. What the hell was the man trying to tell her anyway?

"I pray for you every night also, Carmen." Eugene took a deep breath and gazed into her eyes. "And as I was meditating last night I . . . Well, I was thinking about what happened to you, and I was feeling so bad about having insisted you go with me to that dinner party. You met George Browning there and—"

"Stop, Eugene. Just stop right there." Carmen didn't need Eugene coming to her home to make her feel like a heathen for trying to get the job hookup from George. "What happened to me is personal, Eugene, and you are out of line for coming here to—" Carmen stopped midsentence. The painful look on Eugene's face prevented her from continuing her angry tirade. He'd closed his eyes tightly, and he looked as if he was in terrible pain.

"I didn't come here to upset you, Carmen." His voice was gritty with emotion. "I didn't come here to talk about George Browning either."

"What *did* you come here for?" She watched him open his eyes. He looked heavenward and sighed loudly.

"Last night as I was praying, I received a message I believe is for you."

What on earth is this fool talking about? Carmen raised a dubious brow and let out a sigh. "A message from whom, Eugene?" *Men. Always coming up with some new way to make their move on a woman. I disappear for a few weeks, and Eugene is hearing messages from God knows where about God knows what.* Carmen was sure she didn't want to hear another word of it.

"I can't say from whom . . ." Eugene hesitated. He realized he was beginning to sound insane. "I'm not crazy, Carmen. I don't hear voices or anything, if that's what you're afraid of."

"But you do hear messages?"

"Promise me you'll hear me out."

"Why would I promise that?"

"Please, Carmen. I've never asked anything of you, have I?"

Carmen thought hard about it. Even after the man had plunked down a few grand for the diamond bracelet he'd given her, he never made one demand of her in return. She couldn't think of anything Eugene had ever requested of her—other than her company. She shrugged her shoulders and sighed heavily. "No, Eugene. You have never asked me for anything."

"Please. Just promise me you'll listen to the entire message before you send me home."

She studied Eugene's face. Sincerity radiated from him. She decided to hear his so-called message. What harm could there be in listening to his little meditation experience anyway? "I'm all ears," she muttered softly.

"Is that a promise?"

"Don't get weird on me, Timms. I'll listen. What's the message?"

"Do you know the story of Layla and Majnun?"

"Never heard of it."

He smiled. "Layla and Majnun were lovers from ancient Persian literature. They were sort of the Romeo and Juliet of the twelfth century."

Carmen stared blankly at him. *Romeo and Juliet?* This crazy fool was asleep at her doorstep in near darkness, waiting to ambush her with a message about Romeo and Juliet? *Now I've heard everything.* She pursed her lips at him impatiently. "I'm listening," Carmen muttered, keeping her promise to hear him out.

"Majnun was a young man who was completely consumed by the love he had for Layla, and he spent every waking moment devising new ways to express to her the depth of his dedication."

Carmen laughed softly. "Well, now. That sounds like my kind of man."

"One morning Majnun woke to find that his beloved Layla had disappeared. He searched everywhere, but could find no trace of her. He sifted the dust hoping to find even a strand of her hair. He foraged through garbage to find some clue to her whereabouts. He went from shop to shop along the streets of the bazaar to listen for any message regarding her fate, all to no avail."

Carmen watched Eugene closely. The bumbling, nervous little man he so often was while in her presence was gone, and Carmen was more than a little impressed by the demeanor Eugene adopted as he told his story. His voice took on a deep, smooth tone, and there was not a trace of stuttering in his delivery.

"One evening," he continued, "as Majnun was searching frantically among the shops and alleys of the town, he attracted the attention of a night watchman. The watchman found Majnun's behavior suspicious, so he followed him through the streets." Eugene looked to Carmen for a sign that she was paying attention to his story. "Are you following me so far?" he asked anxiously.

Carmen rolled her eyes impatiently. Settling in for what was beginning to sound like more than a short story, she seated herself on the small bench nearby. Despite the odd circumstances, she had to admit she was feeling drawn into his little fable, and she actually found herself wanting to know what urgent message might be in it for her.

"Go on," she urged. "A security guard is chasing Majnun."

"Majnun was terrified. He could not risk being arrested by the watchman, since that would mean his search for Layla would be interrupted. So he ran as fast as he could, the whole time cursing his misfortune. He ran through the maze of streets and alleys trying desperately to shake the watchman from his trail, but it seemed the faster he ran, the faster the watchman gained on him." Eugene's face reflected a dramatic combination of sadness and despair. "Poor Majnun began to fear the worst. He might never set eyes on Layla again."

Carmen could see it coming. Something terrible was bound to happen to the man in the story, and the woman would spend the rest of her life alone and miserable, waiting to be found by a lover who would never show up. "Please tell me you did not come all the way over here to tell me some tragic love story, Eugene. I really don't need this tonight."

Eugene sent Carmen a look that said, *You promised to listen.* She sighed loudly. "Go on. Finish your damn tragedy."

Eugene continued, "Now, Majnun was running as fast as he could, but the watchman was too quick for him. As he fought desperately to stay a few steps ahead, Majnun cursed his terrible luck, and cursed the watchman who had appeared in the night to deter him from his search for Layla." Eugene put a hand to his heart dramatically. "Alas, just when Majnun thought his desperation could sink no deeper, tragedy struck."

Carmen sent Eugene an *I told you so* expression.

"Majnun had turned down an alley that ended fifty or so yards ahead at an impossibly high wall. The wall was the height of five men, and Majnun could see that there would be no escape for him."

Carmen actually felt her heart sink. *Great message, Eugene,* she thought. *This fool came all the way over here to tell me a pitiful little fable about unfulfilled love. Great.*

Eugene was really getting into his story. His voice rose energetically as he described the angst in Majnun's heart. "Imagine Majnun's absolute desperation as he raced toward the end of that alley. He had all but given up hope of ever being reunited with Layla when, in a sudden burst of will and courage, he somehow gathered every atom of the energy left in his limbs and threw himself over the impossibly high wall."

Eugene's eyes were glassy with emotion. He himself seemed to be Majnun declaring his unquenchable thirst for his own Layla. *Unquenchable thirst. Duh. Of course.* Carmen finally got the message. After all these months of playing it cool, Eugene was trying to let Carmen know that he had fallen in love with her, and this so-called message he had for her was his way of letting her know his feelings. He probably saw this story as a slick way to avoid rejection. *How weak can you get?* Carmen thought. She could give him a couple of points for creativity, but on the guts scale, he was *way* in the minus range.

"*That's* your message, Eugene?" Carmen let her voice express the disappointment she was feeling at having sat through Eugene's little farce.

"I haven't finished," he scolded, putting his index finger to his lips to remind Carmen of her promise.

She sighed impatiently and waited for the rest of the story.

"Majnun," Eugene continued, "had managed to clear the wall, and when he fell to the ground on the other side, imagine his surprise and exhilaration to find that he had fallen into a beautiful garden—at the feet of his beloved Layla."

"And they lived happily ever after," Carmen interrupted dryly. "You came all the way over here and waited four and a half hours to tell me that mess?"

"There's more." The corner of Eugene's mouth tilted up ever so slightly, as though he was about to drop some kind of secret bomb on Carmen. "As Majnun held Layla in his arms, he told her of the pursuit of the watchman, whom he had so heatedly cursed. When he had completely relayed his story to her, she tenderly stroked his hair, gazed into his eyes, and said to him, 'My love. It is not right that you should curse the watchman, for he is the angel of mercy who delivered my beloved to me.' " Eugene crossed his arms over his chest and gazed triumphantly into Carmen's eyes. "There. *That* is the message in its entirety."

"That's the message?"

Eugene nodded.

"All rightee, then." She raised an eyebrow at him. "So what are you trying to tell me, Eugene?" She blurted out a little laugh. "You're supposed to be Majnun, and I'm your beloved, Layla?"

"No," Eugene responded assertively. "Actually . . ." He raised his eyebrows and stated matter-of-factly, "In this metaphor, I would be Layla."

"You would be Layla?" Carmen burst out laughing. "I knew it. So that is your big secret. Is that what you were trying to tell me in your classroom that day we were interrupted? You're Layla? She stopped laughing suddenly. "Eugene, are you telling me you're gay?"

Eugene stared serenely into Carmen's eyes. "I am not gay, Carmen. Layla is a symbol. The beloved. The heart's desire." He cleared his throat softly. "What I was trying to tell you that day in my classroom is that you didn't have to worry about me trying to seduce you, or use you sexually. I am not . . . That is, I'm celibate."

"Celibate?" Carmen said it like she had no idea what the word meant, but she knew full well. She just didn't know personally any men who actually admitted to choosing not to have sex.

"I'm choosing to remain celibate until I marry. For spiritual reasons. That's a pretty personal thing to share, and that day we were interrupted, I was struggling with whether it was time to share it with you."

Carmen shrugged. She'd never intended to have sex with

the man anyway. "Okay, so you're celibate and you're Layla."
She smiled wryly. "That's your message?"

Eugene leaned his head back against the shed door and
gazed up at the sky, then back into Carmen's eyes. He opened
his eyes wide at her in exasperation, as if the gesture might
somehow help her see his point. "I am Layla *metaphorically*.
Layla is a symbol of the heart's desire. I am Layla, and
you . . ." He smiled knowingly. "You, my dear, are Majnun on
a desperate search for your beloved."

Carmen rolled her eyes, but she couldn't help but smile at
Eugene's bold announcement. "Desperate?" She twisted her
upper lip into a playful smirk. "Don't hold your breath waiting for me to sift through the dust to find a strand of your
hair, Eugene."

Eugene smiled broadly. "I *will* wait." His face held a look of
confidence Carmen had never seen. Not even cocky old Gordon Iverson had an expression like this one. Eugene was acting like he was privy to some kind of truth Carmen didn't
have access to—and the confidence it gave him was oozing
out all over the place.

Carmen suddenly felt extremely uncomfortable. Vulnerable. She stood up quickly, crossing her arms over her chest defensively. She spouted uneasily, "Uh, if you're finished," She
glanced nervously at her watch. "I have plans this evening."

Carmen's plan was to find Yvette and apologize to her. It
had been weeks since she'd left the message on Yvette's voice-
mail, with no response, and she'd decided it was time to try to
apologize to her in person instead.

"I've got to go, Eugene." She took a couple of backward

steps toward her front door. "I have something important to do and . . . I . . . It's time for you to leave."

"No problem." Eugene stood up. He didn't look offended in the least at being asked to go. "I just came to deliver the message. Mission accomplished." Eugene walked toward Carmen slowly, the whole time looking directly in her eyes. "You might be facing some very difficult times, Carmen DuPrè. But no matter how impossible your struggles appear to be, just recognize them for what they are."

"Which is?"

"The watchman is not the enemy. You should bless the watchman. He is adversity chasing you to your destiny."

"My destiny?"

Eugene smiled as he leaned in and planted a kiss on Carmen's cheek. "Me, sweetheart." Without another word, he turned and walked his Old Spice–smelling, polyester and acrylic–wearing self out of the gate.

≋ 21 ≋

A Two-faced Bitch for a Friend

There were only a couple of places Yvette London was likely to be found at seven o'clock on a Thursday evening—Star Coffee House on La Cienega, or that popular little black-owned bookstore over on La Brea. Carmen decided it would be best to attempt her reunion with Yvette at the coffee house.

Easing her car into an empty stall in the busy parking lot near the Star, she looked for Yvette's car. When she spotted the familiar black Camry parked several spaces away, her heart dropped like a stone behind her rib cage and began beating wildly. Yvette was there all right. Probably sitting in one of the overstuffed armchairs near the window where she and Carmen used to sit for hours talking and laughing and catching up on whatever needed catching up on. Thursday evenings at the Star had been like a ritual for the two friends, and over the years they had become known to the regulars as "The Watchers," because while most of the patrons would come to the Star dressed to impress and armed with a pocketful of business cards, Yvette and Carmen would show up every Thursday in some jeans or sweats just to sip on lattes and people watch. The two women considered their time together at the Star like a sacred friendship ritual, a weekly bonding session that offered them an opportunity to enjoy the relationship they had spent twenty years building. It was a sad irony that it was in those overstuffed armchairs near the window that their friendship came to an abrupt end on a warm summer evening so many months before. Carmen sat in her car trying to work up the nerve to go inside and find Yvette as the last conversation they'd had replayed itself painfully in Carmen's memory.

"Carmen, you are blowing this out of proportion, girlfriend. *All* I said was that she was nice." Yvette sipped her latte nonchalantly.

"Oh, is that *all* you said, Vette?" Carmen's angry sarcasm rang loud and clear. Several people sitting nearby had stopped their conversations to eavesdrop. Carmen didn't care—her voice got louder. "Is that *all* you said—that the bitch was nice?"

"I didn't say she was a bitch." Yvette let her voice rise too. She put her latte down firmly on the windowsill near her. "I believe I said the *sister* was nice."

"Oh. Well, I could've sworn I heard you say a whole lot more about her than that." Carmen scowled at Yvette, her neck twisting to the side for added emphasis. "If I *heard* you correctly you also said she had a *greeeat* sense of humor." Carmen's tone mocked Yvette's dramatically, and her face contorted with an expression of angry disgust. "Hmph. You're *supposed* to be my best friend."

Yvette lowered her voice to a forced whisper. "Damn, Carmen. I spent the day at the golf course with Evan and we accidentally got the same tee time as Randall and his wife. If you didn't want to know what I really thought of her, why did you ask me to be honest?" Yvette's tone said she was trying to mellow the conversation out—but her words were having the opposite effect. She softened the expression on her face and made another attempt at deescalating the argument. "Look, Carmen, I know you and Randall have some bad blood between you, but trust me, *even you* would've liked Michelle. She's just one of those sisters that's impossible to hate."

Yvette's words struck a wounded place deep inside Carmen and she found herself choking back tears that burned in her throat. She couldn't believe what she was hearing coming out of Yvette's mouth. Carmen smoldered in her rage while an irrational voice of hurt whispered silently in her head. *Even you would have liked Michelle? Even you? What the hell kind of thing is that to say to your supposed best friend? What am I, some kind of demon?* Carmen's insecurities boiled to the surface, and she conjured up imagined conversations between Yvette and Randall's wife. *"Did you know Randall had to get a restraining order against her?" "Yes. Poor Randall. I was there to help Carmen get over him, you know." "Oh thank God. You did my husband a great favor by straightening that crazy woman out."*

The idea of being betrayed by Yvette made Carmen's eyes burn and her throat began to constrict. If she hadn't pushed her next words out, they might have stayed stuck in her throat where they belonged.

"Since she's apparently *all that,* why don't you just give Randall's wife a call and see if she's looking for a two-faced bitch for a friend?"

"Two-faced bitch?" Yvette was on her feet in an instant. Every head in the Star was turned in their direction, but Yvette didn't seem to notice. "I know you didn't just call me a two-faced bitch."

Carmen was too devastated by what she could only perceive as Yvette's betrayal to take the words back or apologize for using them. Instead she jumped to her feet too and growled at Yvette angrily, "What kind of friend would kiss up to the enemy like that?"

Yvette didn't answer. She very calmly picked up her purse and her jacket and turned her back on Carmen. She walked slowly to the exit, and when she got to the door she just stood there for a moment—with her back to Carmen and her palm against the door, waiting for her friend to come to her senses and take back what she better not have meant. Carmen didn't make a sound or a move, and Yvette just walked right on through the door and out of Carmen's life.

The scene at the Star was the last time Carmen had seen or spoken to Yvette, and now here she was so many months later, about to walk in through the same door Yvette had walked out of, hoping she'd somehow be able to find the word to fix what she had shattered.

The moment Carmen pushed the darkly tinted glass door open, it seemed as if every head in the place turned to catch her entrance. She stuffed her hands into the pockets of her Old Navy sweats and slowly scanned the room, seeing a few familiar faces and nodding an unenthusiastic hello to a couple of them. Everything was as Carmen remembered it. A sweet, heavy odor of variously flavored coffee drinks perfumed the air. The sound of jazz mingled softly with the hum of chatter coming from every corner of the large coffee house. A group of chess players was camped out at the last three tables along the back wall. In the middle of the room college students, bent over laptops, sat at tables littered with stacks of textbooks. A couple of overdressed mack daddies nursing espressos stood near the newspaper racks in their designer suits, and there in one of the burgundy velour armchairs near the window sat Yvette, dressed in a navy and gray Nike jogging suit, sipping from her coffee cup and chatting away with a woman Carmen vaguely recognized.

Carmen's heart was instantly warmed at the sight of Yvette. *She looks really good.* Yvette was still wearing her hair in that super-short natural style not every woman could pull off—it made Yvette look chic and mysterious. An attractive woman whose smooth mocha complexion and stunning smile took ten years off her thirty-something face, Yvette had an uncanny way of exuding happiness, no matter what might be going on in her life. With the drama and misery Carmen was holding inside, that look of happiness on Yvette's face made her absence from Carmen's life that much more painful.

Fighting the urge to just run up on her old friend, haul her up out of that chair, and give her a dramatic bear hug, Carmen stayed put near the entrance, glaring at all the nosy patrons who seemed to be staring right at her. When she realized Yvette's eyes too were fixed on her, she smiled nervously and headed slowly in her friend's direction. Before Carmen could make her way across the room, Yvette turned in her chair so that her back faced her ex-friend.

She's still mad at me. Carmen's heart began beating wildly as a red-hot wave of hurt and embarrassment rushed into her face. She had hoped it would be easy—that Yvette would leap to her feet at the mere sight of her old friend and wrap her in a damn-I-missed-you-girl embrace. Carmen stopped short of her destination and just stood there, not knowing what to do next. She saw that the chair across from Vette—the one that used to be Carmen's—wasn't empty, and the person seated in it was someone she recognized. It was a face she hadn't seen in a while, but one she knew well. Francine Dominguez, that mouthy little history teacher from Overland who always managed to get on Carmen's nerves. What the hell was Francine doing here sitting in Carmen's old seat, talking and laughing with Carmen's old friend?

Francine smiled wide and gestured for Carmen to come over and join them, but Yvette didn't so much as glance in Carmen's direction.

"Well, what a coincidence," Francine announced loudly.

Carmen moved slowly toward them, pressing her lips together in a thin, straight line. When she was within a few feet of Yvette's chair, she opened her mouth to say hello, but Yvette rose suddenly, standing with her back turned to Carmen.

"I'm really glad you contacted me, Francine," Yvette muttered, picking up her purse. "I'm sorry to rush off, but I've got another appointment. I'll be at the hos—" She stopped abruptly, then began her sentence again, without looking at Carmen. "I will definitely be there all night on Sunday, and I will call you first thing Monday morning." Without a word to Carmen, Yvette rushed toward the exit.

"Yvette, wait," Carmen called out meekly after her.

Yvette paused momentarily at the door, then shoved the door open harshly and hurried out of the Star. A wave of nausea rushed over Carmen, and tears threatened to spill from her eyes.

"Wow. I thought you two were best friends."

Carmen blinked back her tears and turned to Francine. "Excuse me?"

"Well, just before you came through the door, we were talking about you. I would have thought from the things she said that you two were pretty good friends."

Carmen glowered suspiciously at her. "You were talking about me?" She eyed the chair Yvette had left empty. "Why would you be talking about me?"

"I mentioned that I teach at Overland, and she asked me if I knew you. I told her I didn't think *anyone* at Overland knew you because you are not an easy person to get to know." Francine smiled at Carmen, but she didn't get a smile in return. "I said you seemed kind of mean."

Carmen glanced in the direction of the door Yvette had just excited. "Hmm" was Carmen's agitated response.

"She said you have a hard exterior because underneath it is a really soft heart."

Carmen suddenly needed to sit down. She really didn't care to get too cozy with Francine, but with the way she was feeling, she didn't have much choice—if she didn't sit down, she would fall down. She stepped over Francine's purse and collapsed against the soft upholstered chair.

"I just met Yvette recently, but I understand you two go way back." Francine sipped from her coffee cup nonchalantly.

Carmen didn't respond right away. After a few quiet moments she finally said, "What else did she say?"

"She said you've been friends since middle school. She also said she thinks people don't see the real you because they're usually too busy looking at—" Francine didn't finish the sentence.

Carmen didn't need for her to finish. She knew what Yvette would have said. Yvette thought being so beautiful wasn't good for Carmen. She'd suggested many times over the years that Carmen should try toning down her looks—cut her hair shorter and wear less makeup. Carmen always thought the suggestion was ridiculous—that it would be plain ludicrous to hide what she had been given to flaunt.

"You really are beautiful." Francine said it like Carmen hadn't heard it a million times.

Carmen smiled uncomfortably. "So is that all Yvette said?"

"I got the impression she thought quite highly of you. Which makes it seem a little harsh for her to have rushed out like that."

Carmen thought it pretty harsh herself. Yes, she had been evil to Yvette all those months ago, but she did try to apologize. She called, didn't she? She came to the Star looking for her. Wasn't it obvious to Vette that she was sorry for what she'd said—for what she'd done to their friendship? *I'm sorry Vette. I really am sorry.* Carmen wished she could feel angry at Yvette's rejection, but all she wanted to do was cry her heart out.

Francine seemed to sense the pain Carmen was in and stopped talking. The two sat in awkward silence as Carmen distracted herself from her pain by studying a darkened mole a couple of inches to the right of Francine's upturned nose. The mole had obviously been augmented with eyebrow pencil, which was quite necessary if it had a chance of being seen underneath her thick layers of foundation and face powder. *She could be quite pretty if she didn't put on so much makeup,* Carmen found herself thinking. Francine had high maroon-rouged cheekbones and a heart-shaped mouth that was painted with wine-colored lipstick surrounded by a thin, dark pencil outline. Carmen tried to imagine a makeover for the woman. *Replace that ponytail with a nice hairdo. Scrape a layer or two of that foundation off and give her some rust, or maybe coral, lipstick.*

"Um, Carmen . . ." Francine interrupted Carmen's thoughts. "Can I talk to you about something personal?"

Carmen didn't answer. She didn't know if the something personal was Francine's something personal or her own, and she wasn't about to ask. She just stared at Francine blankly.

"I know you haven't been on campus for a couple of months, and—"

"I cannot talk about the lawsuit, Francine, so please don't ask." That had to have been where Francine was headed.

Everyone on campus knew about the sexual harassment lawsuit, and some had already taken sides.

"I wasn't referring to your lawsuit. I . . . Actually I have something else I want to speak to you about."

Carmen frowned suspiciously and waited.

"You know how your mailbox at Overland is right next to mine?"

Carmen raised an eyebrow. "Yes."

"And every once in a while we get each other's mail by mistake?"

Carmen crossed her arms over her chest and murmured a guarded "Mmm hmnh."

Francine seemed to be searching for the right words to say. Carmen prodded her impatiently. "So what is it? You have some mail for me?"

"It was in my box. I didn't realize it was for you until I had already opened it. Francine's eyes squinted into a painful apology. "It was from the Westside Oncology Center. They scheduled an appointment for your lumpectomy. February seventeenth. I hope you didn't miss it."

Carmen's eyes closed involuntarily. She didn't need this. She didn't need one more human being having this information. Until now Dr. Lee had been the only person on earth who knew about Carmen's defective breast, and that was the way Carmen needed it to stay. She knew she couldn't put it off forever, but what she needed now was time. Everything was falling into place for her now. The lawsuit. The new counseling position. Soon she'd be financially secure and ready to find someone to settle down with, then she'd worry about Dr.

Lee's diagnosis. *Damn, why does this woman have to be in my business?*

"I—I put it in your box right away, but it's been bothering me. I assume Rosa sends your mail home, but I still tried calling you, but no one ever answers and I thought maybe your number had been changed so I tried asking Eugene—"

Carmen let out an angry breath. "You told Eugene Timms about this?" That's all she needed. Eugene hanging around telling ancient love stories and offering to take her in to get her breast mutilated.

"Oh no. Of course not. I wouldn't share anything so personal with anyone. Of course not. I just asked Eugene for your phone number, but he said he couldn't give it to me without asking you first." Francine scooted to the end of her chair and stared into Carmen's eyes. In a tone of genuine concern she half whispered, "I'm so glad I ran into you here today. I have actually lost sleep thinking about that letter and whether or not you ever got it."

"Well, don't lose any more sleep over it," Carmen replied firmly. "I'm just fine." She forced a smile at Francine, and quickly changed the subject. "Since we're getting so personal, can I ask you a question."

"Sure."

Carmen tried her best to look nonchalant. "When Yvette left she said something about calling you on Monday. For what?" She hoped the jealousy she was feeling wasn't showing on her face. She didn't like it one bit that Yvette and Francine had a reason to call each other.

Francine's smile faded. A serious expression took its place. "We're forming an eldercare co-op."

"A what?"

"A support system for the care of our parents."

Carmen stared blankly at Francine.

"Yvette and I met at Pine Haven Hospital."

Carmen wasn't getting whatever it was Francine was trying to explain. She furrowed her brow and sent Francine a look that said *What are you talking about?*

"Pine Haven. Convalescent hospital. Our mothers are roommates."

Carmen tried to wrap her mind around Francine's last comment. Yvette's mother, Barbara, was not anywhere close to needing convalescing. The woman had run in the L.A. marathon the past three years in a row. At fifty-nine she was in better shape than Carmen and Yvette put together; she certainly wouldn't be in a convalescent home. *She must mean Vette's mother-in-law, Evan's mother.*

"Evan's mother is in a convalescent hospital?"

"I believe it is Yvette's mother. Yvette's mother is Barbara, right?

Carmen couldn't speak. She managed to nod her head yes.

"Barbara is my mom's roommate. Yvette and I met here this evening to discuss the possibility of setting up a co-op schedule for hospital visits. That way when she's there visiting her mother, she can check on mine, and vice versa. Alzheimer's takes such a huge toll on the family, you know."

"Alzheimer's?" Carmen's eyes widened. "Barbara has Alzheimer's?"

"Oh no, no. My mother has Alzheimer's. Yvette's mother had an awful stroke several months ago. She's been at Pine Haven since before Christmas."

"God, I had no idea." *I can't believe Yvette didn't tell me this,* Carmen thought. She pressed a palm to her forehead and held it there, closing her eyes tightly. In the darkness behind her eyes Carmen thought of Yvette's mother—the kind of mother Carmen had always wished Mavis could be. The kind of mother who attends your dance recitals and measures you for your prom gown. The kind who cares, really cares, what's going on in your life. *I can't believe Yvette didn't tell me this.*

Francine gazed compassionately at her and responded as if Carmen had whispered her thoughts aloud. "Maybe Yvette just didn't want to give you anything more to worry about . . . I mean . . ." Her eyes traveled from Carmen's face down to her bosom and rested there for a silent moment.

Carmen wanted to leap from her chair and clasp both hands over Francine's mouth before it was too late. She was going to say it out loud, wasn't she? She was going to make it real after Carmen had worked so hard to deny it. Carmen watched helplessly as Francine's mouth moved to form the words that would seal the coffin on Carmen's denial.

Francine lowered her voice to just above a whisper. "I'm sure getting through your breast cancer treatment is more than enough for you to worry about right now."

22

An Immaculately Polished Black Casket

Carmen could not remember how she arrived at the church, or why she had come; but there she was in the shadowy, candlelit cathedral, on her knees, behind the last pew—and she wasn't alone. Accompanying the sound of her own panicked breathing was an eerie chorus of voices echoing around her from the shadows. Voices that moaned soft, ghostly prayers in a language Carmen did not recognize. And, as if the scene and the sounds around her were not disturbing enough, reverberating loudly above the chorus of moans was the bone-chilling sound of a woman sobbing—ponderous, grief-stricken sobbing that invaded Carmen's chest, pressing her lungs so tight she could hardly choke in a breath.

As if compelled by some force outside herself, Carmen peered out from her hiding place to locate the source of the

227

sobbing. She quickly shrank back, suppressing a scream she was too terrified to let go of. At the frontmost section of the huge church she had seen an immaculately polished black casket perched atop a clear glass pedestal raised six or so feet from the floor. Above the casket a chandelier of dimly glowing candles hovered, floating in the darkness as if held by the wavering hand of something or someone unseen.

Please, God. Carmen closed her eyes tight and prayed silently. *Please get me out of here.* She tried to remember the Lord's Prayer, *Our Father, Who art in Heaven.* But the words came to her jumbled and out of order. *Forgive us our sins. Our daily bread. As it is in heaven.* She couldn't fit the pieces of the prayer together, so she went back to *Oh God. Please. Help me.* The harder Carmen prayed, the louder the sobbing seemed to grow, until it echoed from every corner of the spacious cathedral.

I'm dreaming. God, I must be dreaming. Carmen repeated it over and over in her head. *Oh God, let me be dreaming. Oh God.* Suddenly she felt herself sliding involuntarily away from her hiding place as if she were being pulled by some unseen force that sent her sliding inch by inch along the polished wood floor toward the candlelit altar. She tried in vain to resist the force by reaching out frantically as she slithered along, grasping at each of the wooden benches along her path. In a final lunge of desperation, she clutched at the corner of the frontmost pew and held on. She was determined to stay put there, to avoid moving any closer to the source of that horrible sobbing, but she could only watch in breathless terror as each of her fingers slid from the edge of the pew and her body continued sliding toward the pulpit. The sobbing seemed to be growing louder and more frantic. Carmen was suddenly standing straight up on her feet. beneath the looming glass pedestal with her hands pressed tightly to her ears. She watched in terrified awe as the casket above her began to shrink. It grew smaller and smaller, until the coffin had become a small rectangle no bigger than a narrow shoebox—a box that was now perched precariously at the pedestal's edge.

It occurred to Carmen that the sobbing was coming from inside the tiny casket, and she thought that if she could somehow close the lid, she could make it stop. Standing on her tiptoes, she reached with her fingertips, stretching to push the tiny lid closed. The lid didn't budge; instead the box slid toward her, and, as if in slow motion, it slid off the edge of the pedestal and fell, still open, into Carmen's hands.

She stared down into the miniature, satin-lined casket in terror, her breath lodging itself in her chest at the sight of what the casket contained. Lying stiff among the satiny pink folds lay a beautiful doll. A naked doll that was the size and shape of a Barbie, only with one very striking difference. This Barbie had only one breast. And in the space where the other breast should have been, a tiny fire was raging—a fire with hot angry flames licking hungrily at the air. It was then that Carmen realized that the doll was not Barbie at all. The tiny plastic face was an exact replica of her own face. Carmen dropped the casket in terror, but instead of falling to the floor, it hovered in the air in front of her, close enough for her to watch as a tongue of flames licked hungrily at the doll's auburn curls, instantly consuming every inch of her hair until all that remained was a smoldering bald head.

Carmen awoke to the darkness of her bedroom and to the realization that the unbearable sobbing she had been trying so desperately to silence was her own.

It wasn't until she found herself sitting in her car wearing a raggedy gray sweat suit, no makeup, and a sloppy knot of hair on top of her head that Carmen realized she had decided to spend Sunday morning visiting her father's grave. She had no idea why she was going—she didn't believe in all that spirit-of-the-beloved-can-hear-your-prayers craziness. Her daddy was gone. Long gone. Carmen visited his gravesite once a year with her family out of respect, but she had always believed people who visited cemeteries regularly to converse with dead people were idiots. The only reason Carmen could find for actually being on the highway headed in the direction of the cemetery was that she had awakened from her nightmare weeping uncontrollably, rocking herself pitifully, and desperately missing her father. She needed to be near him. Even if what was left of him was buried six feet underground.

When she arrived at the entrance to the Mountain View Cemetery, Carmen drove in through the open gates, eased her car into a parking space, and headed in the direction of her father's gravesite. She had no trouble finding his headstone among the dozens of mostly indistinguishable grave markers. Amid the lawn-embedded cement rectangles surrounding it, the DuPrès' impossible-to-miss four-by-five-foot shimmering marble headstone shone in the cloudless morning sunshine like a Vegas marquee. Mavis had selected the stone herself, no doubt drawn to its magnitude and brilliance.

Mavis wasn't one to cut corners when it came to maintaining appearances. Though she too only visited the gravesite each year on the anniversary of her husband's death, she paid a hefty monthly charge for weekly maintenance and fresh flowers for Wilfred's resting place. Carmen believed her mother's real purpose for putting out all that dough on behalf of her dead husband was so that her kids would keep up the practice after she was in the ground with him. Not if it was up to Carmen. She *might* visit her mom's grave once a year, but she wouldn't be paying for a weekly supply of flowers for a dead Mavis; of that she was damn sure.

A fresh bouquet of white chrysanthemums lay against the base of the headstone, and Carmen bent to reach for it as she sat cross-legged in the freshly mown grass. She'd heard somewhere that you weren't supposed to stand or sit on a person's grave, but she sat directly above where her father's body lay. She wanted to feel as close to her daddy as possible today.

She tore a thin white petal from one of the flowers and rolled it between her thumb and forefinger nervously. "Okay, Daddy, I'm here," Carmen announced expectantly, as though he was scheduled to meet her there. "Don't ask me what I'm doing here, 'cause I don't have a clue." She scanned the rolling hills surrounding her, catching sight of a visitor on the far side of the cemetery. She wondered if the person over there was talking out loud to the dead like an idiot too.

"I need help, Daddy." Carmen's voice trembled. Her stomach clenched back an erupting sob, trapping the urge to cry in her chest, where it lodged itself painfully behind her heart. She wiped a lone tear from her cheek, plucked another flower petal, and let it fall to the grass at her feet. "I know I need help, but I don't have anyone to—" She gazed up at the gravestone and read the epitaph Mavis had prematurely engraved next to her husband's. *Loving Wife and Mother.*

Carmen plucked angrily at another petal and dropped it on top of the first. "She doesn't care what happens to me." She wiped another tear. Scanned the cemetery another time. Went back to plucking at the flower.

A pile of the tiny white slivers was forming at Carmen's feet as she pulled petal after petal from the defenseless chrysanthemums. "I wish you were here, Daddy. I know you wouldn't let me do this al—" Without warning the sob she had suppressed before made its way back up into her throat. *Alone. Say it, Carmen. Alone.* Carmen's eyes burned with salty tears and her breaths came out in short little puffs that ached to become loud weeping. Not saying it out loud couldn't make it not be true. She was alone, and from the looks of things, there wasn't much she could do to change it. The person she really needed was Yvette, but that was out of the question now. *Lindsey cares.* Lindsey would be more than willing to be there for her, but Lindsey would surely tell Della and Della would tell Mavis, and having Mavis know would be far worse for Carmen than facing this on her own. *There's nobody.* It seemed suddenly pitiful to Carmen that she couldn't think of anyone else in the world she trusted enough to ask for help.

Stifling another sob, she lifted a flower from the diminishing bouquet and hurriedly pulled a dozen or so petals from it, watching as they fell one-by-one onto the growing hill of white slivers at her feet. "I'm keeping a secret, Daddy, and I don't know who to tell." Carmen's chin dropped to her chest, and she closed her eyes as if closing them might blot the thought from her mind. *Cancer. Say it, Carmen.* "Daddy, I have cancer." Tears dripped down her cheeks. "I have cancer . . . and they want to mutilate me . . . and I'm scared, and . . . and I don't have anyone . . ." Her shoulders collapsed suddenly and she planted her elbows in the grass, rested her forehead on her crossed arms, and sobbed mournfully. Slumped over in that position of surrender, with a soft pillow of chrysanthemum petals under her face, Carmen let go of all the dread and terror she'd been holding onto since she'd sped away from Dr. Lee's office months before. She sobbed loudly until the need to cry suddenly disappeared, and when the last shudder left her motionless and exhausted, she whispered aloud, "I need help, Daddy. I can't do this *alone*."

≡ **23** ≡

The Most Powerful Force in the Universe

"*I usually visit* my son on Thursdays," he explained to Carmen while he shook a dusting of pepper onto his scrambled eggs. "But I missed this Thursday, so I decided to make up for it today."

She sipped her coffee and silently watched Pedro Camacho over the rim of her cup.

"I was on my way out of the cemetery, but I recognized your Lexus in the parking lot. I came over to see if you could use a shoulder to cry on." He reached across the table and motioned for Carmen to lean toward him, which she did. He picked a thin white petal from her cheek and held it up in front of her face, smiling teasingly at her. "But you seemed to have found something else to cry on."

Carmen half smiled. Averted her eyes. Sipped nonchalantly

from her coffee cup. She was embarrassed. She knew he'd heard her sobbing her heart out, but she wasn't sure if he'd caught the conversation she'd had with her father. It was so unlike her to do something as ridiculous as talking aloud to the dead, and it bothered her to think she'd been caught at it. To make matters worse, the man probably heard what she was crying about. She shifted uncomfortably in her seat, and without looking at Pedro, she asked nervously, "How long were you standing there?"

He stared hard at Carmen, then picked up his fork, stabbed at his eggs, and lifted the fork to his mouth. Before taking a bite he stated matter-of-factly, "Cancer is not the most powerful force in the universe, you know." The way his words sounded—the conviction in his voice and his eyes—Carmen could almost believe him.

He raised a hand to get the waitress's attention, then waited patiently while she returned with a bottle of Tabasco for him. Carmen sat quietly, intently studying the man's every move. She watched him smother his eggs in hot sauce before putting another forkful of them in his mouth. She watched the smooth caramel skin at his temples tensing and relaxing as he chewed. There wasn't an adjective in the English language Carmen would choose to describe him. *Gorgeous? No, too pretty sounding. Handsome? Not close. Stunning. That's it. Stunning.* Perfectly straight, gleaming white teeth. Flawless cinnamon brown skin. That high, regal forehead and a square jaw lined with an immaculately groomed beard. The old Carmen would never consent to having breakfast with a man so drop-dead stunning. And she certainly wouldn't have sat there so comfortably knowing she looked like something the cat dragged in. But, for some inexplicable reason, in his company she didn't care a bit about her scraggly appearance, and she got the impression Pedro wasn't paying much attention to the way she looked anyway.

She stared at him curiously, pondering his bold but obviously flawed announcement about the power of cancer. "You say cancer's not the most powerful force in the universe? That's quite a statement coming from a man who lost his son to it."

"Who says I lost him?" There was that teasing smile again.

"You visit him in a cemetery once a week, and that's not a loss?"

"If I believed he was dead, I would be completely devastated, but I am convinced otherwise."

Carmen put her coffee cup down abruptly and stared blankly at Pedro. "The day I met you, you told me your son died of cancer. You are really confusing me."

Pedro closed his eyes and held them closed for a few seconds. When he opened them again, she was staring at him expectantly. "Closer than your life vein," he whispered. He raised an eyebrow at Carmen and pointed at his throat. "That is how close they are to us."

Carmen thought hard about that one. She wasn't sure she wanted to be that close to dead people. "Says who?"

He put his fork down and stared solemnly into Carmen's eyes. "Do you think this was a coincidence? Me being at the cemetery the same time as you? Us having breakfast together at this restaurant?"

Carmen shrugged. "Maybe." She shook her head no. "I don't know."

"You should pay close attention to the coincidences in your life, Carmen. It is said that through coincidence the angels leave their mark on the world."

Angels? Carmen stared at him curiously. He seemed sincere enough, but he wasn't making much sense to her. *There's no such thing as angels.* Of course it was an odd coincidence to find the man standing near her father's grave watching her cry her heart out—and even more odd that just as she was begging her father for help, here was this tall, beautiful, broadchested man right there to pull her to her feet and wrap her in a desperately needed hug. *Coincidence?* If the word ever fit a situation, this was it. But Carmen couldn't think of any real coincidences in her life other than this one. They just didn't happen to her. They seemed to happen to Lindsey all the time. And Yvette. She could even recall Mavis talking about having been in the right place at the right time by "sheer coincidence." But Carmen apparently wasn't worthy of the angel's efforts.

"When it comes to coincidences in my life, this is a first," she said in a tired voice. "They don't really happen to me."

"Hmm. I sincerely doubt that. Maybe you just aren't aware of them when they do."

Carmen shrugged again. Pedro gazed into her eyes for an uncomfortably long moment, and she stared right back at him, wondering what on earth he was looking for. She couldn't imagine what was going on in his head. Every time the man opened his mouth to speak, something came out that seemed just out of Carmen's grasp—just a little bit over her head.

"Close your eyes for a minute, Carmen."

For a split second she flashed him a look that said she had no intention of doing such a thing, but the serene expression on his face made her quickly do exactly what he'd asked. She closed her eyes and waited for him to explain why.

"I want you to try this. Try focusing on recent events in your life that you could never have predicted. If you meditate on it for a moment, I bet a few will come to mind."

Carmen did try. She kept her eyes tightly closed and pondered the last few months of her life, searching for evidence that angels might have visited her "coincidentally." She tried hard to remember even the tiniest possible miracle, but all she could focus on was the misery she'd been through. She'd lost her best friend. Got diagnosed with breast cancer. Almost had sex with a man she didn't love. Nearly got raped. *Nope. No evidence of angels in any of that.* She was just about to open her mouth to say so when her recent attempt to meet Yvette at the Star came to mind. Maybe it *was* a coincidence that Francine was sitting there in Carmen's chair. And *maybe* it was Francine's mention of Carmen's having cancer that led to her dream about the burning Barbie. If she hadn't had that awful nightmare she certainly never would have visited her father's grave, or run into the man she was now seated across from. The longer she considered the idea of coincidence occurring in her life, the more she realized that she really hadn't been paying attention. If her terrible encounter with Browning hadn't happened, she wouldn't have gone to see Randall—

she'd still be whining about how Randall had single-handedly ruined her life, *and* she would never have met Michelle. And if she never met Michelle, she would never have realized how very wrong she had been to Yvette. And then there was Eugene. *Bless the watchman.* Eugene had come to her home with a message about how blessings are hidden in adversity, and now here was a man she barely knew trying to get her to see the same thing.

Bless the watchman. Carmen, obviously stunned, opened her eyes wide and gazed at Pedro solemnly. "Adversity is chasing me," she said matter-of-factly, repeating Eugene's words.

Pedro's dark eyes sparkled knowingly at her. "Tu no eres solo, Carmen."

When the words came out of Pedro's mouth, a wave of peace washed over her—the same feeling of utter peace she'd experienced at their first meeting. Her eyes began to glisten with the hint of tears.

"What did you say?" It didn't bother her one bit that he'd spoken to her in Spanish—his words penetrated somewhere deep in her chest, even though she had no idea what they meant. "What did you say to me?"

"I said you are not alone. Someone is working hard to get your attention. Someone who loves you is trying to take care of you."

Carmen didn't even try to suppress the hopeful expression that dawned across her face. She knew instinctively that Pedro wasn't referring to himself as the one working to get her attention. *I begged my daddy for help, and he heard me.* The thought that her father might be able to show up in her life, even after all these years of being gone, made her feel warm all over. She smiled. A genuine smile with just a tiny twist of disbelief at one end of it. "Oh, so you think my father sent you?"

"I think you need a friend. I'm volunteering for the job."

Carmen laughed. "You are a brave soul."

Pedro's expression turned serious, his voice deep and sincere. "A brave soul is exactly what you need on your team right now."

She felt a twinge of irritation at his use of the word "need." Who was he to tell her what she needed? And what on earth did he think he was going to get out of a "friendship" with her anyway? The old Carmen, the defensive, distrustful Carmen, responded sarcastically. "So what are you, the Salvation Army?"

He smiled broadly, his dimples becoming two deep crevices. "Okay."

Okay? She didn't expect that response. "*Okay?* What's that supposed to mean?"

"You are facing a battle. You are in need of salvation. If it's going to take an army to save you, then, okay, I will enlist."

Carmen sat in stunned silence. When she finally responded, her words were harsh and honest. "You couldn't save your own son. What makes you think you can do anything for me?"

He placed his elbows gently on the table and leaned into Carmen. "My son never needed saving. It was I who was in a battle for my life. It might not make sense to you at this moment, but trust me, one day you will understand perfectly what I mean."

Carmen picked up a slice of toast from her plate. She tore a tiny piece from one corner of it and put it in her mouth. She didn't speak to Pedro for a few moments, but chewed slowly on the bread crust and studied his face thoughtfully. She watched him as he picked up his fork and took the last bite of his scrambled eggs, then reached for his glass of orange juice. She watched him swallow his food. Watched him empty the glass. When the silence got too heavy, she tore another corner from her toast and pointed it at him weaponlike.

"What do you get out of being my friend? What do you want from me?"

"Ahh. Now you are asking good questions." He put his fork down and reached into the hip pocket of his jeans, pulling out a fat wallet and placing it on the table.

"The only real happiness in this life comes from helping others." He smiled. "Right now to you that might sound ridiculous, and maybe you just cannot allow yourself to believe it, but it really is the truth." He caught Carmen's expression of disbelief and shook his head softly. "I haven't always thought so either, you know. I wasted a lot of years chasing money, expensive things, beautiful women. Now I look for opportunities to help others. It's what makes me happy."

Carmen's eyebrow lifted involuntarily. She wasn't sure what to make of this man or of his sudden appearance in her life. *I asked for help,* she reminded herself silently. She had cried out to her father for help, sobbing and begging him not to let her face cancer alone. Was it crazy to think that this beautiful stranger might actually be that help she requested?

She wanted more than anything just to let her guard down, but she was having a hard time believing that a stranger-—a man—especially one as attractive as this one, had no ulterior motive.

As if he were reading her thoughts, Pedro suddenly slid his dishes off to one side. "Let me share with you some things about me." He put his wallet where his plate had been and began pulling items out of it one by one. With his left hand he slid Carmen's mostly uneaten meal off to the side also, then placed something on the table in front of her. A small photograph.

"This is my son Pedro Junior. He was eight in that picture."

Carmen studied the picture of a Hispanic-looking boy with tanned skin, wavy black hair, dark eyes, and a smile identical to Pedro's. Before she could comment on how handsome the little boy was, Pedro was already placing another item next to the photo.

"This is my wife, Ariselle. She's in Juarez, Mexico, with her family."

Carmen's eyes went immediately to his left hand. There it was as clear as day. A thin silver wedding band she hadn't noticed before. Hadn't she looked for it? She thought of the day they'd met in the Overland parking lot. *Were his hands in his pockets?* She struggled to remember their brief encounter, but could not remember seeing a ring.

Sensing Carmen's confusion regarding his marital status, Pedro instantly added, "My wife has decided to volunteer for a few months at an orphanage in the town where she was born. It is one of the ways she's chosen to deal with the death of our son. She'll be back home before school starts in September. She teaches eighth grade."

Carmen stared at the photograph of the pretty Mexican woman smiling up at her. She was still trying to absorb the idea that this married man was offering to be her friend when Pedro placed another item next to the photograph of his wife.

"This is my father. He's a retired auto mechanic." He tapped the photo with his index finger. "In El Salvador he was a dentist. That was before he came to live in America."

An aging Hispanic man with tired eyes smiled at Carmen from the tattered photograph. Despite the fact that Pedro's father had the skin color of a white man, Carmen found the resemblance to Pedro striking. *El Salvador?* With Pedro's dark caramel skin, Carmen had assumed he was a black man who just happened to have learned Spanish.

"This is my mother." He picked up the picture of a mahogany-skinned black woman with graying hair and an amazing smile. "Born and raised in Watts." He kissed the photo, smiled at Carmen, then put the picture back down next to the others and reached for another item from his wallet.

"I think you've seen this." He took out a business card and laid it on the stack of photos.

Carmen immediately recognized the At Your Service logo she had seen on the side of Pedro's truck.

"This is my Red Cross blood donor card." He pointed at some tiny print, and added teasingly, "Type O Positive, if you *must* know."

Carmen was too overwhelmed by it all to laugh.

244

"This is my ID card for the Eastside Math Project where I am a math tutor—"

"Okay." She interrupted what was obviously meant as an exhibition of Pedro's humanity credentials—his attempt at proving that he was worthy of her trust. She smiled in defeat. "Okay, so you're a good guy. I get the point."

He winked at Carmen and piled more cards onto the stack. "I shop at Ralph's and Price Club, *and . . .*" He placed the last card on top of the stack with a flick of his wrist. "Bam," he announced dramatically. "I am an eleven-year member of Triple A."

Carmen allowed a slight smile to light her face. She studied the stack of cards and photos for a long moment, sorting through the pictures of Pedro's loved ones, stopping to look at each one thoughtfully. Finally she stared into his face seriously. "Why do you want to be my friend? You don't even know me."

His eyes became two black pools Carmen couldn't save herself from falling into "I *am* you," he whispered softly.

When the words came out of his mouth, the sincerity with which he said them made them the truest words she'd ever heard. *I am you.* For the life of her, Carmen had no idea what he meant, though her heart told her it was something very real and very deep. All of the man's words seemed to be. She remembered the words he'd left her with the last time she saw him.

When I get up in the morning, I sit on the edge of my bed and ask myself, "Pedro Camacho, what is the most important thing for you to accomplish today?"

She had agonized for weeks over the answer to that question, wishing she hadn't let him get away without telling her what it was, and now that he was sitting right in front of her, she wasn't sure she really wanted to know.

I used to answer that question from some ridiculously long list . . .

Somehow Carmen knew that the answer to Pedro's daily question would do something permanent to her life that she wasn't sure she was ready for.

But now . . . I have only one answer.

Carmen opened her mouth to ask him. "Pedro," she began cautiously. She stayed quiet for a long moment.

"Ask. I will tell you." His smile was so sincere, his voice so caring, it sent a shiver of fear down Carmen's spine.

She quickly swallowed the question she'd intended to ask and replaced it with a less frightening one. She met Pedro's gaze with a determined glint in her eyes. "So, if you are the Salvation Army, exactly when does the battle begin?"

≋ 24 ≋

Somebody's Guardian Angel

Carmen did everything Pedro had told her to in preparation for the evening. *Absolutely no artificial light. Wear clothing made from natural materials, preferably cotton, preferably either a light shade of blue or white. Sprinkle rose oil along the baseboards in the living room, and heat three pints of water—making sure the water is at a brisk boil when the clock strikes eight.*

At exactly seven forty-five she stood in the middle of her living room admiring how beautiful Eve and her sisters looked in the glow of the candlelight that softly illuminated them. Carmen had searched every cabinet in her home and managed to come up with twenty-two variously sized and scented candles, which were lending a warm radiance to every corner of the room. Mingled with the subtle scents of the vanilla and hibiscus candles, the rose oil mist she had lightly sprayed along the baseboards graced her apartment with a gentle aroma that made Carmen want to just kick back on the sofa with a glass of wine, close her eyes, and free her mind of every thought that didn't make her feel peaceful or warm or safe.

When she heard the sound of the latch on her gate opening and closing, she felt her heart begin to speed a little. Before Pedro could ring her doorbell, Carmen was already at the door, turning the deadbolt with one hand and grasping the doorknob with the other. But when she pulled the door open to let Pedro in, she immediately sensed something wasn't right.

He looked like he could be somebody's guardian angel, standing there with his hands behind his back, striking an exceptionally handsome pose. He was just as gorgeous as the first time she laid eyes on him. He was even wearing the same white velour jogging suit with blue trim he'd had on that day they'd met at Overland. He appeared to be the same man who'd coincidentally showed up out of nowhere in the deserted cemetery—a man who appeared just in time to convince her that he was the answer to her prayers for help, but something about the look in his eyes tonight made her a little uneasy. Carmen stood in the doorway, not ready to let him into her home.

"Beautiful," he said earnestly. "I see you are dressed for the occasion."

Carmen had followed his directions by wearing a loose-fitting white gauze pantsuit she'd picked up a few years earlier in Jamaica and hadn't put on since. Her hair was swept up into a baby blue silk headwrap with a few tiny auburn ringlets hanging loosely around her face. Pedro's instructions hadn't included whether she should wear makeup for their "appointment," so Carmen had opted to put on only a little moisturizer and some clear lip gloss. It wasn't as if she was trying to impress the man—he had already seen her at her worst at the cemetery, and seeing as how he was, in his own words, "happily committed" to his twelve-year marriage, he wasn't interested in her beauty anyway; at least, if he was, he deserved an Academy Award for the role he'd played so far. From day one not so much as a hint of flirtation had escaped Pedro's lips or his eyes. Even now he was standing calmly in the dark, waiting for Carmen to let him in her apartment, and his eyes were fixed firmly on hers—seemingly uninterested in Carmen's curves hidden just beneath the soft gauze fabric that draped them.

"May I come in?"

Carmen didn't move. "I don't know." Her voice was tinged with apprehension.

Pedro raised an eyebrow. "You don't know if I can come in?"

She shook her head slowly. "Something doesn't feel right."

A soft smile lit Pedro's face. "You've been praying." It wasn't a question. He said it as though he'd actually been in her apartment with her all week watching her get on her knees every morning and evening.

"Twice a day," Carmen confirmed. "For guidance and clear intuition—as instructed."

"And that intuition you prayed for tells you I cannot come in?"

"You're hiding something," Carmen announced with a certainty she didn't know she was feeling until the words came out of her mouth.

"Hmm. Perhaps." He said it with absolutely no emotion.

She tossed his word back at him. "Perhaps?"

"Perhaps I *am* hiding something. Or perhaps you are simply *afraid* I'm hiding something."

Carmen felt a hint of irritation at the wordplay. "What difference does it make? Either way, I'm not sure I want to let you in."

"Carmen. Let's be clear. He leaned toward her. "You should *not* trust me." Pedro's face gave no sign that he was joking.

She pulled the door closed a little, shrinking the space in her doorway.

His lips formed just the hint of a smile. "You should trust *you*."

"What?" Carmen wasn't following. She could only interpret Pedro's statement as some kind of word game meant to confuse her—which was exactly what it was doing.

"Do you know why I suggested you spend this week praying for only two things, guidance and clear intuition?"

She didn't have an answer.

"When you have clear intuition, you don't have to ever worry about trusting another human being. Once you trust yourself—trust the voice within—you will always know what the best decision is for you. You become your own best guide."

Carmen turned the words over in her head for a moment, then studied Pedro's eyes. "Well, my intuition tells me you are hiding something."

Two deep dimples formed at the ends of Pedro's smile.

"Well, then, your prayers are working." He pulled a white chrysanthemum out from behind his back and held it up to her.

She reached out and took the flower, holding it briefly under her nose. She let a tiny smile show on her lips, but she didn't open the door any wider, and she didn't give him any indication that she intended to.

"Always trust your intuition, Carmen." Pedro took a step back. He gazed silently into her eyes. "Your own voice will tell you if you should let me into your home."

Carmen stared into Pedro's eyes while she made her decision. She knew. She knew from the very first day they'd met that Pedro Camacho did not wish her any harm. The only doubts she had about his intentions were not coming from her intuition, they were coming from her past. From every bad decision she'd ever made when she didn't listen to her inner voice—a voice that had quieted down to a faint whisper over the last few years. She had been ignoring her own guidance for so long—usually because it was trying to guide her away from pursuing something she didn't need, but wanted really badly—something she was sure she couldn't live without, like moving in with Randall, or going after a promotion she hadn't earned.

How does he know? she thought. A clear picture of Pedro entered her mind. A picture of him on his knees, his hands and face lifted heavenward in prayer. The thought came to her so lucidly, it could have been a memory. It occurred to Carmen then that Pedro had been praying for her all week. The entire time she had been working hard to follow his instructions, nervously speaking to a God she hadn't said "boo" to in years—each and every day she'd been dropping to her knees in prayer to ask for guidance, Pedro had been talking to God about her too. She didn't need to ask him if it was true. She just knew that it was.

Carmen let a tiny smile break through the stony expression on her face. "My *inner voice* tells me you are here to do good." She backed into her living room and swung the door wide to welcome Pedro into her home, and as he crossed the threshold she added, "But it also tells me you are hiding something from me, and before this evening is over, you *are* going to tell me what it is."

She led him into the living room and offered him a seat on the sofa facing the Eve photographs. "I have water to boil," she announced, pointing to the glowing numbers displayed on her nearby CD system. "It's almost eight." She set the white chrysanthemum down on the glass coffee table and quickly headed for the kitchen.

By the light of a single candle she'd left burning in the kitchen, Carmen turned on the gas flame under her tea kettle, then quickly returned to the living room. Pedro was on his feet, standing in the glow of candlelight in front of Eve and her sisters, with his head cocked slightly to the side and his hand slowly stroking his goatee. He studied the photographs quietly for a few moments, then motioned for Carmen to come over and stand near him. Looking into her eyes with serious concern, he asked, "Why are they here?"

She didn't expect that question. *Who are they?* or perhaps *Who is the artist?* But not *Why are they here?* Carmen wasn't sure how to answer it.

"Oh. I . . ."

She started to tell Pedro about how she'd kidnapped the artwork from Randall the day he put her out. About how she only took them out of spite—simply because she didn't want Randall to have them—but something told her that story wouldn't come close to answering the man's question. *He wants to know why these women are on my wall,* she thought. *He is asking my why* these *women.* Carmen smiled softly at the inner monologue going on in her head. It was not like her to think deeply about a statement before letting it come out of her mouth. She was far more likely to say something off the top of her head that she thought sounded cute or smart—not caring if it was what she really meant or felt.

Pedro was still staring thoughtfully at the prints. "These women are very sad," he whispered. "They're sad, and they're lost."

"They're miserable," Carmen affirmed. She certainly wasn't going to argue with Pedro's conclusion. The sisters were sad. Actually, it was what she'd always loved about the photos. Their sadness had always given Carmen a strange kind of comfort. And, pitifully, it was a comfort she had grown quite accustomed to.

She half smiled when she finally said, "Misery loves company," but she wasn't trying to be flippant. She chose the words carefully, knowing in her heart it was the truest response to his comment she could have given.

The high-pitched whistle of Carmen's tea kettle sent her hurrying to the kitchen to turn off the flame. When she returned to the living room, she found that Pedro had seated himself on the sofa and was pulling a small brown paper bag out of the pocket of his sweat jacket. He reached into the bag and pulled out a small plastic envelope full of something that looked like tea bags, which he placed in front of him on the coffee table.

The man brought his own tea? She wondered if he planned to read her tea leaves. She wouldn't be surprised if he suggested it. Especially with all the strange instructions he'd given her. Though none of the things he'd asked of her so far were harmful to her in any way, she couldn't help but think of them as extremely odd. Rose oil? Water boiling at exactly eight o'clock? She'd asked him on the phone to explain the purpose of his requests, but all she got in return was "*I will explain it all to you in person.*" She decided not to wait another minute to ask.

"I see you followed all of my suggestions, Carmen," Pedro began before she could open her mouth to question him. He breathed deeply of the scents enveloping him, his chest expanding, then relaxing slowly. He smiled mysteriously. "I know you must be very curious about the purpose of all of this."

Carmen let one of her eyebrows lift slightly in affirmation. She barely knew the man, and he already seemed to be able to read her mind.

"There is no strange mumbo-jumbo attached to any of this, though I know you must have been thinking there might be."

Carmen nodded.

"And, honestly, I purposely made the instructions sound somewhat mysterious, hoping it would influence you to treat our meeting tonight ceremoniously."

Carmen wasn't sure why he would want a simple meeting between the two of them to feel like a ceremony, but she kept the thought to herself.

"I asked that you not use artificial light simply to set a mood for contemplation and serenity—nothing more. Candlelight is soothing—it creates a kind of peacefulness that I thought might serve us well this evening."

She silently accepted the explanation.

"The rose oil I suggested for much the same reason. I recommended a scent that is a pleasant one to most people. The rose symbolizes love and purity, two things we will definitely want present in the room this evening. I'm not deep into aromatherapy or anything, but I do think certain scents can be quite calming."

Still no comment from Carmen. His explanation was making sense so far, and she had even begun to jump ahead of him. If peace and comfort were the intended outcomes of his list of instructions, she could definitely get with the suggestion that she wear natural fiber clothing. That suggestion really wasn't necessary, though, since polyester and acrylic were already at the top of Carmen's list of fabric no-nos anyway. But what about the request that she wear only shades of blue or white? And what about the boiling water? What would hot water have to do with whatever it was he had come to her home to help her accomplish, and why did it have to reach a boil at exactly eight P.M.?

Pedro continued. "Of course, the suggestion that you wear natural fibers was simply a comfort thing." He patted his chest. "And blue and white are our team colors. Unless of course you decide to change that." A mischievous glint appeared in his eyes then. It was the same glint she'd noticed when she first opened her front door. It was an *I'm hiding something* glint.

"Team colors?" Carmen asked.

"Mm hmm. Our team." He chuckled. "I think you referred to it the other day as the Salvation *Army,* but really we're not going to be about fighting, we're going to be about healing. I'm thinking 'team' might have a more positive ring to it."

Pedro reached forward to pick up the tea bags from the coffee table, and cradled them in the palms of both hands.

"So . . ." Carmen prompted him. "Why did you ask me to make sure the water would be boiling at eight."

"So we could serve tea to our guests when they arrive." He held the tea bags out to Carmen, but she didn't reach for them. "One of them is due any minute now."

"Our guests?" Carmen could not believe her ears. *I knew he was hiding something,* she thought angrily. "You invited strangers to my home?" Just as the words were out of her mouth, Carmen heard the sound of the metal latch on her gate opening, then clanging shut.

"I would never invite strangers to your home without your permission," Pedro said calmly. He stood up then, and just as the doorbell rang, he was at the front door, turning the deadbolt with one hand and pulling the door open with the other.

≋ 25 ≋

You Gotta Trust Somebody Sometime

Carmen watched as Pedro wrapped Lindsey in a warm hug and exchanged "nice to finally meet you" greetings with her.

He had no right, she thought. She waited to feel the wave of angry heat that usually warmed her face in situations like this one, but her cheeks remained cool. She could not find the well of rage she was so used to dipping into whenever she felt it was the least bit justified. Instead of spraying Pedro with an angry onslaught of curses, she just stared blankly at the embrace taking place before her eyes.

When Lindsey was released from Pedro's hug, she stood frozen near Carmen's doorway for a moment, staring soberly at her sister. Her eyes stayed on Carmen's face, but her words were directed at Pedro.

"I don't know how to thank you for calling me. I could

never even come close to repaying you"—she glanced briefly at him, then glued her eyes once again on Carmen's face— "for including me on Carmen's team."

It was then that Carmen realized Lindsey was dressed in blue and white. She had chosen a pair of white denim jeans and a powder blue baby tee with the words "be yourself" air-brushed in a faded pastel rainbow across her chest. The beads she'd worn the last time Carmen saw her were gone, and her mass of tiny black braids had been swept up underneath a white fur Kangol. On her feet were a pair of white-on-white Adidas basketball shoes. Lindsey had obviously been drafted into Pedro's army.

He told her everything, Carmen realized. It was clear from the look on her sister's face that she knew all the unbearable little details about Carmen's diagnosis. Lindsey was trying hard to hide her emotions—trying to look as if she had no idea that her sister was standing in front of her with a cancerous breast. Pedro had no doubt warned her not to look too scared or sad, because she had a way too sweet smile planted firmly across her face. Lindsey was giving the stoic look a mighty effort, but she really wasn't too good at it. The words "Please don't die, Carmen" could have been written across her face in Magic Marker.

Lindsey stepped to Carmen, wrapping her arms around her older sister in a too tight hug, but Carmen did not hug her back—she just let her arms hang limp at her sides. Over Lindsey's shoulder Carmen glared accusingly at Pedro, but he smiled at her serenely and headed toward the kitchen. Lindsey was holding on so tightly, Carmen could feel her sister's heart beating hard against her own breast. *She's scared,* Carmen thought. She felt sorry for her then. Sorry that she hadn't confided in her own sister, and even a little ashamed that Lindsey had to get the news from a complete stranger. She tried to imagine how Pedro had managed such a feat—and over the phone no less? *Poor baby. She must be scared to death.* Sensing Lindsey's emotional distress, Carmen finally lifted her arms and held them limply around her sister's waist.

"Dammit, Car," Lindsey whispered into her ear, "you gotta trust somebody sometime."

The word "trust" jolted her. The realization of why she hadn't told Lindsey in the first place instantly flooded Carmen's thoughts. Lindsey surely couldn't be trusted with this kind of information. There was no way she could know something so important without sharing it with Della or Max or Mavis. *She better not have told Mavis.* The thought of Mavis knowing about her condition sent a wave of terror through Carmen. She shrugged her way forcefully out of her sister's arms. She needed to see Lindsey's face.

"Who have you told, Lindsey?" It was supposed to be a question, but with the tone Carmen used, it came out sounding more like an accusation. Carmen knew her sister. She knew there was no way she could hold on to this kind of news.

Lindsey looked toward the kitchen as if seeking help from Pedro. "I haven't, Carmen." Her eyes were glassy, and the corners of her mouth were struggling to stay upturned, but Carmen didn't see an ounce of betrayal in Lindsey's face. "He insisted I couldn't tell a soul. Not even Della. He made me promise." Lindsey's voice wavered as she spoke; she clearly wanted to cry, but was trying her best to be a good soldier. "He convinced me not to call or come over here until tonight. It's the hardest thing I've ever done, Carmen. I've been dealing with this by myself for four days now, and it's been . . ." She looked toward the kitchen again, then back at Carmen. "I really had to struggle to keep that promise—to not rush right over here to talk to you about this."

A wave of relief washed over Carmen, and she managed a soft smile for Lindsey. She couldn't imagine what Pedro must have said to her to get her to trust him, to get her to accept that whatever he had planned was worth Lindsey's suffering in silence for a few days, but whatever it was, in that moment Carmen was grateful for it. She grasped her sister's hand and squeezed it gently.

The tiny muscles around Lindsey's mouth began to twitch. "I can't believe you didn't tell me, Car." Tears threatened to spill from Lindsey's eyes, but she managed to hold them back. "I can't believe you've been walking around with this by yourself for months."

"Let's all come in here and have a seat," Pedro interrupted suddenly, returning from the kitchen holding a steaming mug in each hand. He placed the cups on the coffee table, then motioned for Carmen and Lindsey to join him on the sofa.

When they were both seated, he picked up the mugs and held them out to the women. "Black tea. No sugar. No cream."

They both made faces that said there was no way they would be drinking that.

"It's a powerful antioxidant."

Lindsey smiled politely, but neither of them reached for a cup.

"There is a compound in black tea which is believed to be one of nature's most powerful anticancer agents. In lab experiments this compound left healthy cells alone, but caused cancer cells to commit suicide. And it is believed to help prevent normal cells from ever becoming cancerous."

Lindsey reached for the cup Pedro held out to her, but Carmen looked at the remaining one with obvious reservation.

Pedro smiled knowingly at her. "I did put a little honey in it."

Carmen finally reached for the mug, cupping it in her hands but not drinking from it.

"The studies also suggest that the polyphenols are strongest without any additives, but a little honey might not hurt too much."

Carmen took a tiny sip. "Okay, Dr. Camacho," she teased. "I didn't know you were such an expert on polyphee— whatever the hell you said." She took another small sip from her cup and winked at Lindsey. "He takes a little getting used to, doesn't he?"

"You never mentioned on the phone that you were a doctor," Lindsey said to Pedro.

Pedro laughed softly. "I'm not a doctor." He turned to Carmen. "But speaking of doctors, I did talk with Dr. Lee a couple of days ago."

"Why doesn't that surprise me, *Sherlock*?" Carmen muttered. In the two or three conversations she'd had on the phone with him during the week, Pedro had asked a million and one questions about family and friends—no doubt the reason he was able to find and contact Lindsey, but Carmen couldn't remember telling him where to find her doctor. She might have mentioned Dr. Lee's name to him once or twice, but that was about it.

"I suppose Dr. Lee told you all about how I stormed out of her office at my last visit?"

"Of course not," Pedro replied. "She didn't tell me anything about you, specifically." He made a motion toward Carmen's cup that suggested she should be drinking from it, so she took another sip. "Doctor-patient privilege won't let her reveal anything about your medical condition to me without your consent. But I got the impression she was extremely happy to hear from me. She was relieved to know that you are choosing to deal with this. She happened to mention to me the kinds of treatments a person with a condition *similar* to yours should be receiving. I called this meeting tonight so we can plan our strategy.

"Strategy?" Carmen asked.

"To make sure your medical needs are met. Getting you to the doctor. Making sure you take all your medications. And we want to see that your spiritual and emotional needs are met as well. Your teammates will play a part in attending to at least one of those areas."

"You're scaring me," Carmen muttered.

"No room for fear. That's commitment number one. Teammates have to leave fear outside when they come in." He turned to Lindsey. "Right, Lindsey?"

She answered as though she had been coached. "No fear

allowed." She smiled softly at Carmen. "We're going to win, sis."

"Win?"

"We cannot waste any more time getting you ready for this tournament.

"Tournament?"

"Yeah. Healthy cells versus cancer cells. You already have a hell of a team." With this kind of line-up behind you, it oughta be a shutout. Pedro held an imaginary bat in his hands. Just as he wound up for the swing, they all heard the distinct sound of the latch on Carmen's gate clanging shut outside.

Pedro was on his way to the door before either of the women could move. Lindsey and Carmen looked at each other curiously, but it was apparent that neither knew who was approaching her door.

When it suddenly occurred to Carmen who it might be, she was instantly on her feet. "Don't open that door," she commanded in a frantic whisper. She wasn't smiling.

Pedro's hand held the doorknob, but the bell hadn't rung yet.

Carmen's voice had a desperate, pleading tone to it. "Please tell me you didn't invite my mother here tonight, Pedro."

The words were barely out of her mouth when the sound of the doorbell echoed around them. Pedro didn't open the door; instead he turned to Carmen and asked, "Do you remember that conversation we had on Sunday?"

Carmen sent him a look that said she didn't have a clue what he was referring to. *That better not be Mavis out there,* was all she could think.

"You agreed that actions, not words, are the best way to decide who to trust, didn't you?"

She rushed to the door without answering him. She was not about to let the man open that door and let Mavis DuPrè in her living room to revel in her doom. Carmen had made it very clear to him that her mother was the last person on earth she wanted knowing about her cancer. She pressed her palm firmly against the door, whispering harshly in Pedro's face. "*Don't* let that woman in here."

"What did I ask you that morning?" Pedro responded calmly.

"What?" Another hoarse whisper from Carmen. She jerked a stiff index finger to her lips— demanding that Pedro whisper too.

He complied. "Sunday morning," he whispered. "I asked you to tell me the people in your life who had given to you without expecting to receive anything in return. I asked you to list them for me."

"And?" The word barely came out of Carmen's mouth when the doorbell rang again.

"Was your mother on that list?"

"No," she said softly, forgetting to whisper. She left her hand planted firmly against the door.

"Then she's not on your team."

Carmen let her hand fall to her side and took a step backward. *Of course he wouldn't have invited her.* If there was one thing Pedro excelled at, it was intuition. He certainly would know better than to call Mavis.

"The person standing on the other side of that door is *sup-*

posed to be here," Pedro announced confidently. "He belongs on your team, Carmen. And that's why I invited him."

A feeling of utter confusion came over Carmen. *He belongs on your team?* She remembered the list. *Lindsey. My daddy . . .*

When Pedro pulled the door open and his invited guest stepped into Carmen's living room, it took her a moment to realize who he was. He resembled Eugene Timms, but the handsome stylishly dressed man standing in her doorway looked as if polyester and Old Spice had never come close to his skin.

"Eugene?" Carmen heard herself say incredulously.

Apparently Eugene had been coached on what to wear, because he was dressed in a straight-hemmed white linen summer shirt that buttoned up the front and was meant to be worn untucked——and against all possible odds, Eugene had actually left it untucked over a pair of loose-fitting blue jeans. Carmen could have fainted in disbelief. It was the first time she'd ever seen the man with a shirt made of fabric that wasn't likely to melt at high temperatures, that wasn't buttoned clear up to the neck, and wasn't tightly tucked in. She couldn't help but smile.

Eugene interpreted Carmen's smile as a sign that she was happy he had been invited. He stepped forward to hug her, smiling broadly, but before he could get his arms around her, she backed away from him.

"What are you doing here?" she asked bluntly.

Eugene's smile disappeared. "Am I not welcome?"

Carmen had to think about that for a moment. She wasn't really sure how to answer that question. She was the one who had included Eugene on her list—the people in her life who had given to her without any expectation of receiving anything in return. She had no idea Pedro was going to use the list to decide who to put on her "team"—she didn't even know there was going to be a team—but since it was *her* list, technically she had helped to invite him.

"Well," Carmen quipped, looking Eugene up and down. "You have on the uniform, so I guess you must be on the team." She turned to look at Pedro. "Coach over there says you're supposed to be here." Carmen said it with just enough nonchalance to insinuate that it wasn't really her decision to invite him.

Eugene didn't accept her response. He repeated his question, this time with added emphasis. "Am I *not* welcome?"

Carmen could see from his expression and the tone in his voice that he was not there simply because of Pedro's invitation. He was there because he genuinely cared about Carmen and because he knew full well what she was facing and wanted to be there to support her. The only thing Eugene wanted from Carmen was to know that she actually wanted him there.

Carmen turned to Pedro, but he stared back at her expressionless. His eyes seemed to be telling her she was on her own—that it really was up to her whether Eugene was welcome.

She decided to listen to her inner voice. *Eugene really cares what happens to you. He is not here because he wants something from you; he's here because he believes he has something to give.* Carmen smiled. She took a step toward Eugene, opening her arms to offer him a hug. "I don't really know what's going to happen here tonight, Eugene. But you *are* welcome."

Carmen let Eugene's arms envelop her in an embrace that had a familiar warmth to it she didn't know she missed until that moment. She breathed in a soft, subtle hint of cocoa butter. His enthusiastic hug, the genuine spirit of concern he had for her, and his sweet, clean smell bathed Carmen in a warm glow she wanted to linger in for just a few seconds longer. She even pressed her face gently to his chest. "Thank you for coming, Eugene." She surprised herself with the sincerity in her tone. She really was glad to see him.

When Eugene released Carmen from his embrace, Pedro immediately grasped his hand in a firm handshake, pulling him forward so he could pat Eugene affectionately on the back. "Thanks, Gene."

"No thanks required, P. I told you on the phone there's nothing I wouldn't do for this woman." Eugene looked at Carmen. "I have always been on your team," he said to her softly before turning back to face Pedro. "I don't believe she knows how very sincerely I mean that."

Carmen didn't respond to Eugene's comment. She was too busy trying to figure out how the two men were referring to each other as "Gene" and "P."

"You two know each other?"

Both men grinned. They each held up a hand making a strange sign consisting of what Carmen could only interpret as a tangle of fingers twisted awkwardly around each other.

"Eastsiiiide," they said simultaneously, laughing out loud.

Former gang members? Carmen nearly laughed out loud herself at the thought of it. *Maybe Pedro—in his younger days—but Eugene? Out of the question.*

"Eastside Math Project," Pedro explained. "We're both tutors there on evenings and weekends. I've known Gene, for . . ." He looked to Eugene for help.

"Since '98." Eugene said matter-of-factly. "I believe I recommended his auto repair business to you, Carmen."

Carmen smiled.

"It was you that put the At Your Service business card in my box at Overland?"

Eugene nodded. "Guilty as charged."

Pedro pushed the front door closed and motioned Eugene toward the living room. "You've already met Carmen's sister Lindsey, right?"

Lindsey and Eugene exchanged hellos.

Pedro stood alone near the front door glancing at his watch.

"Expecting someone else?" Carmen asked. She mentally recalled the names she had given Pedro. It was a short list. *Lindsey. Daddy. Eugene. Yvette.* Carmen prayed silently, *Please, God, let there be one more guest.*

The sound of the gate outside clanging shut made it impossible to keep the tears from welling up in Carmen's eyes. *Yvette.* Just as a tear found its way out onto her cheek, she whispered the words softly at Pedro. "You are an angel."

≼ 26 ≽

Beyond a Shadow of a Doubt

Seated comfortably in their favorite burgundy velour armchairs in a dimly lit corner of the Star Coffee House, Yvette and Carmen stood out like two angels against a velvety Christmas scene. Dressed in white, and sipping honey-sweetened black tea, the two sat together in silence, each obviously lost in thought.

Carmen's head was filled with images of the evening's events. She felt an unbelievable sense of relief now that it was all out in the open. Her impending treatment wasn't nearly so unspeakable to her once Pedro persuaded her to face it head-on. As hard as it was for her to deal with something as terrifying as cancer, Carmen realized if it hadn't happened to her, she would never have known how much love she had in her life. She was overwhelmed by the support everyone was so willing to give her. *Especially Eugene. Bless the watchman.* Eugene had tried to tell her that adversity could be a blessing in disguise, but she didn't understand it then.

Eugene really is on my team. She smiled softly to herself. Pedro knew what he was talking about when he said that Eugene was *supposed* to be there. The man volunteered for just about everything Carmen might possibly need help with over the next few months. If she needed a ride to the doctor, Eugene wanted to be the one to take her. If she needed someone to make sure she was taking her medication, Eugene wanted to be the one to make her take it. He made it clear that there wasn't anything Carmen might need that he wouldn't volunteer for. Eugene even opened and closed the meeting with prayers that let everyone in the room know just how much he cared for Carmen.

". . . and Lord," he'd offered sincerely, "Thank you for letting us all be a part of Carmen's healing. And thank you, Lord, for this opportunity to show her how much we care for her."

Eugene cared deeply for Carmen, though she still wasn't sure why. She had never given him any reason to hold her in such high esteem. Actually, she wished she'd treated him better, because he was turning out to be one of the only true friends she had. Eugene, and Yvette. *Another name to add to the list of those you wish you'd treated better,* she thought.

Carmen sat across from Yvette as they sipped their tea in the dim light of the Star, each lost in her own quiet thoughts. She listened to the soulful music piping softly throughout the coffee house. *Don't take for granted the love that's in your life . . .*

Carmen recognized the song, but couldn't place it. *Every day brings a change . . . but it's love that will remain and memories that survive . . . EnTrance?* It was that artist Eugene had taken her to see in a small blues club on their very first date. *That's from that EnTrance CD Eugene gave me,* she thought. *Don't take for granted the love that's in your life. . .* Carmen smiled at the message. *Coincidence?* She listened intently to the song, just in case an angel somewhere was trying to tell her something.

Nobody knows how many more sunsets and rainbows
No way to make them last, as this day fades in the past
Nobody knows how many more sunsets and rainbows
So I'm gonna say I love you now
The best way I know how.

Carmen stared solemnly at her friend sitting across from her, lost in her own world of thoughts. She could have burst out in tears from the pure joy of knowing that though their friendship was a little battered, it had weathered the storm and managed to stay afloat. She wished she had some words to let Yvette know how much she'd been missed, and that Carmen would never take their friendship for granted again. She wanted her friend to know how much she was beginning to appreciate things she hadn't paid much attention to before— like the incredible patience Yvette must have had to have stayed friends with someone like Carmen for so long. Just as Carmen was about to put her feelings into words, Yvette broke the silence first.

"I have some things I need to say to you, Carmen." Yvette was staring down into her teacup when she spoke; her eyes seemed a little reluctant to meet Carmen's. "I know we have both already made peace with what happened between us, and I hope you believe me when I say that I've missed our friendship, and—"

Carmen interrupted her. "If you're going to try to apologize for something you didn't do"— Carmen sent Yvette a fierce look—"don't even try it." She put her teacup down on the nearby windowsill. "You have nothing to do with what happened between us, Vette. I didn't know that then, but believe me, I know it now." She shook her head softly. "It was no coincidence that I spent those few minutes with Randall's wife. Nothing else would have made me see so clearly what a horrible brat I had been to you."

Yvette studied Carmen's face, her eyes glistening with emotion. "Carmen, I need you to make me a promise."

"Okay." Whatever Yvette was about to ask her to commit to, Carmen knew it was the least she could do.

"I'm going to say some things that are going to be really hard. Hard for me to say, and"—she paused—"and hard for you to hear."

"Okay."

"And you have to promise me that you won't apologize anymore."

"Okay."

"I don't want you to tell me you're sorry anymore, because that's not what I'm trying to do. I'm not trying to make you feel sorry. I just want you to hear me, okay?"

Carmen wasn't sure what Yvette meant, but she promised anyway. "I promise. No 'S' word." She smiled softly.

Yvette placed her teacup on the window ledge and let her eyes rest on Carmen's face. She cleared her throat softly. "Do you remember that time we went to see *Miss Saigon* at the Ahmanson?"

Carmen nodded. "I loved that play."

"You caused a little scene that night; do you remember it?"

Carmen's happy expression suddenly faded, and was replaced by a look of utter shame. She shifted uncomfortably in her seat. "Yeah," she muttered sheepishly. "I wish I didn't."

"What do you remember about it?"

Carmen let out an exasperated breath. "I was so angry. That white woman would not stand up and let us get to our seats. Remember that marvelous mink stole wrapped around her shoulders? She was on the aisle and our seats were right next to hers, but we had to walk all the way around to come in through the other aisle. I was so mad at that ol' rich white woman I could've spit on her."

"You must've called her every name in the book."

"She never said a word to defend herself."

"You probably scared her half to death."

"When that attendant came at intermission to *lift* the poor woman into her wheelchair, I could have died." Carmen shuddered just thinking about how horrible she'd felt that night. "I didn't even bother trying to apologize to her. I just kept my mouth shut for the rest of the evening."

Yvette smiled softly. "That wasn't the worst part," she reminded Carmen.

"No, it wasn't." Carmen agreed. "The worst part was when the curtain came down and the houselights came up and she leaned forward and looked right past you to talk to me."

"Am I remembering it wrong, or did the woman have tears in her eyes?" Yvette asked.

"She did," Carmen confirmed. "I thought she was going to burst out crying when she said, *'Wasn't that just beautiful?'* And then *she* apologized to *us* for us having to walk all the way around to get to our seats . . ." Carmen's eyes filled with tears at the memory. Her voice quivered as she continued the story. "Then she told us about how much she enjoyed coming to the theater, and how, since her husband died, it was one of the few things in her life that brought her joy."

Yvette stared solemnly at Carmen.

Carmen looked down at her hands. "I saw that old lady and her expensive mink and immediately assumed she was just some old snooty white woman with too much money who didn't *have* to stand up for a couple of black women trying to get to their seats."

Yvette nodded.

"Turns out she was just a lonely old lady trying to find some joy in life." Carmen's voice trembled with emotion. "A lady who couldn't have gotten up out of her seat if the theater was on fire."

"You know, Carmen," Yvette said, "My reason for mentioning that incident is just"—she leaned forward to hand Carmen a napkin—"is just to say that I learned something that day that's stayed with me ever since."

Carmen used the napkin to wipe a tear from her cheek.

"You never know what someone else is dealing with. You never know if the reason your waitress can't get your breakfast order right is because she was up all night with a sick child."

Carmen nodded.

"You never know if the young woman behind the counter at the coffee shop is so quiet because she just lost both her parents in a car accident." Yvette's eyes directed Carmen to the Star's cashier.

Carmen instantly glanced over her shoulder at the young woman who'd sold them their tea.

"You never know if the friend you lost your temper with had come to meet you for coffee to tell you some really good news that she never got to share."

"Good news?"

"I came here that day to tell you Evan and I were expecting a baby." She frowned sadly at Carmen, her eyes filling with tears. "I wanted you to be the first to know."

Carmen's face lit up with an excited smile. "Oh my God, *Yvette*, that's *wonderful*. You and Evan have been trying to—" Carmen stopped herself. *That was nearly a year ago.* She looked down at her friend's flat belly. "You have a baby?"

Yvette shook her head no. "I miscarried a few weeks after our argument."

"Yvette, I'm so sor—" Carmen remembered her promise and stopped herself. "I mean . . . Why didn't you . . ." She buried her face in her hands shamefully and stopped talking. When she raised her head again to look at Yvette, she could see that her friend was trying desperately not to cry. Carmen didn't know what to say.

"I was still trying to recover from losing the baby when I got a call from the gym where my mother works out." Yvette's eyes dripped a single tear. "She went into the sauna and didn't come out, so somebody went in to check on her and . . ." She swiped at the tear that was threatening to slide off her face. "She had the stroke in December and has been in the hospital ever since."

"Oh God," was all Carmen could manage to say. "Oh my God, Yvette." She'd already told Yvette how sorry she was to hear about Barbara's stroke. The second Yvette walked in her apartment door wearing white capris and a "Just Do It" T-shirt with a powder blue swoosh, Carmen had instantly thrown her arms around her friend and whispered every "I'm sorry" she could think of. Now all she wanted to do was say, *I am so so so sorry* as loud and as many times as she could. *Yvette was smart to make me promise,* Carmen thought. *I'd be spouting I'm sorrys all over her right now.*

"I'm telling you all this because I want you to know why I didn't try harder to fix our friendship. I want you to know why I rushed out of here that day when you tried to apologize. I just didn't—"

"Don't, Yvette. Don't you apologize to me for something I'm responsible for."

"I could have tried, though. I just . . . After the miscarriage . . . trying to make arrangements for my mother's care, I just didn't have it in me to give to you, Carmen."

It occurred to Carmen then how truly lucky she was. She had done nothing she could remember to deserve the love Yvette had for her. Carmen sat in silence wiping tears from her face with her already tear-soaked napkin and trying to think of ways she could give something back to her friend.

"I'd like to go see Barbara," she finally said.

"She'd like that."

After another lengthy silence Yvette added, "There's one more thing, Carmen."

Carmen waited.

"At the meeting tonight. I'm sure you noticed that I didn't speak up much when Pedro asked for volunteers to get you to and from your medical appointments. I mean, I was all over the daily prayer thing, but . . ."

"That's okay, Vette. Lindsey and Eugene will have my radiation treatments covered. I'm just glad you're on my team."

"I just want you to know that I have so much on my plate right now. Evan got laid off last month, so I can't take any time off from work. And I'll be spending four evenings a week with my mom, so—"

"Stop it, Vette." Carmen interjected forcefully.

"I just want you to know that if you don't see me as much as the other teammates, it's not because I don't love you."

Carmen smiled. She scooted to the end of her chair and motioned for Yvette to lean forward so she could hug her. "I love you too, Vette." She held on to her friend for a few moments longer, her heart filled with joy at how fortunate she was to have her back in her life.

Suddenly Carmen felt Yvette's spine stiffen. She whispered in Carmen's ear, "Carmen, do you know this man?"

Carmen released Yvette from the hug and sat back in her chair. Standing not more than two feet away, staring down at Carmen with a huge grin on his face, was Gordon Iverson.

"Wow, what a surprise." He seemed genuinely happy to see her. "Hello, Carmen. Wow, what a surprise to run into you here."

"Hi, Gordon." Carmen managed to say it with a measure of civility. She remembered their last phone conversation and wondered if he'd ever gotten around to washing his sweat suit. She hadn't talked to him since that day she hung the phone up in his face. "*I love you, Carmen,*" were the last words Gordon had spoken to her. She looked up at Gordon's beaming face and couldn't help wondering if it was at all true.

Carmen turned to Yvette. "Yvette, this is Gordon. Gordon, Yvette."

They nodded politely at each other.

"What a surprise to run into you here," Gordon repeated for the third time. He looked at his watch. "It's almost midnight. I didn't realize this place stayed open so late." He was obviously struggling to make conversation. "You're as beautiful as ever."

Carmen smiled uncomfortably. "They stay open till two A.M. on the weekends," she stated matter-of-factly.

Gordon shifted his weight nervously. Carmen knew he was trying to figure out whether her demand to stay away from her was still in effect.

"You two ladies coming from that Badu concert?" More small talk.

Carmen smiled wide at him. A thought occurred to her suddenly that made her scoot to the edge of her seat and motion with her index finger for Gordon to come closer. He knelt on one knee near her chair.

"Yvette and I were just sitting here discussing my treatment," she whispered.

"Oh." Gordon nodded his head yes like he understood what she was talking about. "Treatment?" He seemed to relax a little—happy that Carmen hadn't instantly ordered him out of her presence. "You're writing a screenplay?"

Carmen chuckled softly. "No, Gordon." She leaned in until her face was less than a foot from his. "My *cancer* treatment."

Gordon just stared at her. The words she'd said to him didn't seem to register at all. She knew it was a little mean to just spring something so serious on Gordon in such a casual situation, but she also knew it would settle once and for all how the man truly felt about her.

Carmen remembered the desperation in his voice the last time she'd spoken to him. *I wish I could live that night all over again, and wake up next to you, baby. I miss you. Carmen, I—I love you.*

Since Gordon still hadn't responded to Carmen's announcement, she waved a hand in front of his dumbstruck face and whispered at him, "What's the matter, Gordon? Didn't you hear me?"

Gordon's Adam's apple did a somersault. "I, uh, I'm sorry to hear that, Carmen. Is . . . uh . . . is there anything I can do?"

She let an overly dramatic expression of gratitude fall across her face and whispered, "Actually, I could use another good friend to help me when I begin my radiation treatments. I don't think I'll be able to drive to them myself, and with the nausea and vomiting that sometimes occurs . . ."

She wasn't being intentionally cruel, she was just double checking what her intuition was already telling her. *Gordon Iverson does not love anyone but Gordon Iverson.*

"I'm crossing my fingers that there won't be any hair loss." Carmen was pouring it on a little thick now, but she knew exactly how Gordon would react. "And if they have to actually take my *entire* breast . . ." Carmen choked on her last words, and abruptly stopped talking; pretending to be so unemotional about what really could be in her future had stretched the limit of her acting ability. Gordon was suddenly on his feet. She could see he'd had enough.

"Yeah," he muttered nervously. "Well, whatever I can do, Carmen, you just let me know, okay?"

He'll be out of here in less than a minute, Carmen thought. She caught him glancing around at the exits, trying to plan his escape.

"Well, I gotta get going. Just . . . just give me a call anytime, okay?"

Carmen watched as Gordon backed his way across the room and out the door.

Yvette was sitting like a statue, staring at her friend in disbelief. "What was that about?"

"Somebody from my past life," Carmen answered.

She heard Eugene's voice in her head then. *I have always been on your team, Carmen.* And she knew beyond a shadow of a doubt that it was true.

⋚ 27 ⋛

What Could You Possibly Love?

Eugene pulled back the drapes on Carmen's bedroom window with a loud, dramatic whoosh that startled her out of her lethargic stupor and sent her beneath the covers to avoid the bright sun pouring into the room.

"Enough of this darkness, young lady," he growled in a fatherly tone. "You're getting out of this bed today. You're going on a field trip."

Carmen peeked her head out from under her bedcovers, wincing at the bright sunlight. "Close the drapes, Eugene." Her voice sounded as cracked and dry as her lips felt. She ran her tongue across her bottom lip, but there was no moisture to be found.

In an instant he was at her bedside, pouring water from a pitcher on the nightstand into a glass. "Have you done any of the things I asked, Carmen?" He looked down at her pitifully, then gently ordered her to sit up. "Sit up, now. Come on. Drink some of this. I asked you to drink at least two glasses of water this morning, and this pitcher is still completely full."

Carmen listlessly obeyed, sitting up against the pillows Eugene propped up behind her and sipping from the glass he held to her lips. After a couple of tiny swallows, she tried to lie back down.

"Oh no, you don't." He held the glass out to her sternly. "All of it."

Scowling in irritation, she sat up again and reached obediently for the glass of water. "If this makes me vomit, I'm going to make *you* clean it up." She managed to lift the corners of her mouth into a tired smile. They both knew the risk of her vomiting wasn't much of a threat to Eugene. He had had plenty of practice cleaning up after Carmen's bouts of nausea over the past few weeks.

"I'm up for the challenge," he teased.

As she held the glass to her lips and forced the water down in tiny sips, he began rifling through her dresser drawers, pulling out items of clothing and laying them at the foot of the bed next to her crumpled bathrobe.

"I'm not going to tell you what to put on." He tossed a baby blue V-neck T-shirt and a pair of white Adidas sweatpants atop the lavender bedspread. "But I am going to tell you to get up out of that bed and get dressed." He reached into another drawer and pulled out a white lace bra, letting the bra dangle in the air for a moment. "This one will do just fine." He tossed it in her direction. "Now I'm going to run you some bathwater." He headed for the door, stopping at it long enough to scowl threateningly at her. "I expect you to be out of that bed, out of your pajamas, and into that bathrobe before I come back in here. He stepped out the door, then turned and stepped back in, replacing his pretend scowl with the smile Carmen had come to look forward to over the last few weeks. It was a smile that had gotten her through more suffering than she thought she was capable of enduring.

Despite her irritation with his Gestapo tactics, she smiled back at him—but she didn't agree to get dressed. The moment he backed out of the room and pulled the door closed behind him, Carmen pulled the covers up over her head again. Getting dressed meant getting out of the bed, and she had no intention of doing that. She'd just have to eat lunch on a tray in her bedroom as she'd been doing for the past month and a half. It would put her closer to the bathroom anyway. And it was likely she'd need to stay close, since keeping food in her stomach had become a constant battle—a battle she seemed to lose more than win.

Eugene popped his head back in the door. "Do I have to bathe you myself?" He didn't sound like he was bluffing.

Carmen peeked out from under the covers long enough to note the look of determination on Eugene's face. *What happened to that man who could barely say the word "panties" in my presence a few months ago?* Eugene had made a lot of noticeable changes over the last few weeks, actually. She didn't know what possessed him to lose the Old Spice cologne, though she suspected Pedro might have suggested it. Ever since the team meeting, Eugene smelled only of vanilla soap and cocoa butter lotion. And he must have spent a fortune on new clothes, because he had shown up at Carmen's apartment every day for the last month and a half wearing various shades of blue and white clothing. Today he had on a pair of denim jeans, topped with a white football jersey with powder blue trim, and a pair of white Nikes.

"You've been dressing like a fashion model lately, Eugene," Carmen teased. "You got a girlfriend shopping for you?" She was just teasing, but after the words came out of her mouth, a picture of him walking through the mall hand-in-hand with another woman entered her mind, and she realized she didn't like the thought one bit.

He didn't take the bait. He calmly repeated his threat. "Do I have to bathe you myself?"

She could see he wasn't playing around. She could picture him actually carrying her bony self to the bathroom and putting her in the tub himself. She decided to give in before it came to that.

"Fine, Eugene. I'm getting up." She heaved the bedcovers off and swung her legs over the edge of the bed. Surprisingly, she didn't feel the wave of nausea that usually greeted her at the beginning of each new day.

"You received the last of your chemo series on Monday. And we added that new prescription to your medications day before yesterday," Eugene reminded her. "Your doctor thinks it will work well for you. A lot more energy, and no more nausea." He crossed his fingers, raised both eyebrows in a hopeful expression, and then left the room.

Carmen stood up slowly. She felt a little light-headed, but

the usual urge to gag was gone. *Thank God for whatever drug is responsible for this,* she thought. She attempted to pull her nightgown over her head, but it required too much energy for her arms to cooperate, so she unbuttoned the gown down the front and let it fall to the floor at her feet. She made her way slowly to where her bathrobe lay and sat down on the edge of the bed, donning the robe one arm at a time, then wrapping the belt around her thin torso. She closed her eyes and let out a long, tired breath. *I'll be glad when I don't feel so exhausted all the time,* she thought.

It had been over a month since Carmen's chemotherapy series had begun. Although Dr. Lee had previously assured her chemo wouldn't be required, in the months Carmen had spent avoiding reality, the cancerous cells had spread; at least that was the way it was explained to her by the specialists Dr. Lee referred her to. Carmen's oncologist and her surgeon insisted the chemo was necessary before surgery, and both tried to prepare her for the possibility of losing her entire breast, warning her that they couldn't be completely sure whether the breast could be saved until they "got in there to have a look around."

Wrapping her arms around her frail rib cage, Carmen let the memory of Dr. Lee watching her speed angrily away from her office materialize behind her closed eyes. *Breast cancers in very young women typically spread much more quickly, but yours is localized at this point. It is not too late for a simple lumpectomy,* she had warned. Carmen wished she had listened. *I'm lucky,* she quickly reminded herself. *I'm lucky I didn't wait any longer than I did. I'm lucky Francine got my mail by mistake. I'm lucky I went to the cemetery to talk to my daddy. I'm lucky Pedro found me.* She opened her eyes and looked around the room at the collection of cards, stuffed animals, and flowers Eugene had brought to her bedside each day. *And I'm lucky Eugene is my friend.*

She heard a soft knock on the door, but didn't move. Though she knew she'd better be heading toward the bathtub or risk having Eugene come back in to threaten her some more, all she really wanted to do was get back in the bed.

Eugene opened the door slowly and peeked in. "I know you don't want to get dressed, but I am under strict orders to get you out of the house today."

"Coach is back from Mexico?" Carmen asked, referring to Pedro, who had gone to visit his wife and her family.

Eugene nodded. "Last night. He was going to come by on his way home from the airport, but I told him you and I had a field trip planned today, so he decided to let you get your beauty rest."

Carmen closed her eyes. "I don't want to go anywhere, Eugene."

"I know, sweetheart, but your oncologist says you can't stay in the house for so many days at a time. It drags your spirit down to be in bed all the time. And when your spirit drags, your healing drags."

"I don't want anyone to see me." Carmen gazed pitifully at Eugene. "I can't handle the staring."

"People have been staring at you all your life, Carmen." He said it so matter-of-factly, it struck Carmen as hilarious. She laughed.

Eugene walked over to where she sat, taking her hands in

his and pulling her to her feet. "Come over here." He gently pulled her over to her mirrored closet door, turning her around to face her reflection. He wanted her to look at herself, but she closed her eyes tightly.

"Open your eyes." He stood behind her, his hands holding her firmly by each shoulder. "Look."

Carmen opened her eyes and looked in the mirror for a split second, then quickly shut them again. "Let's do this next year, Eugene," she said weakly. "Maybe by then my hair will have grown back, and I will have some meat back on my bones, and my clothes will fit better, and—" Carmen stopped talking. Without warning, tears began to drip from her closed eyes. Eugene tightened his grip on her shoulders and pressed his face gently against her cheek.

"And what?" Eugene prodded her to finish her sentence. He wanted her to say aloud what they were both thinking.

She opened her eyes and looked into the mirror, but she couldn't look at herself; she stared unblinkingly into Eugene's eyes instead. "*And* when I have one less *breast*." She said it like it was a challenge. Like it was some kind of scary voodoo curse that would send Eugene running from the room in terror.

He stared back at her calmly. "It's a breast, Carmen." He smiled reassuringly. "If the doctors decide it's best to take it, we will live without it."

"That's easy for you to say."

"Yes. It *is* easy for me to say." He turned her around to face him, but Carmen refused to look him in the eye.

"I don't know how you can stand this, Eugene. I don't know how you can come in here and look at this every day."

She fixed her eyes on a spot on the wall behind Eugene to avoid the intensity of his gaze.

"You do know."

"I really don't. Really." She meant it.

"I love you, Carmen." He lifted her chin gently, until her eyes settled on his. "That's how."

Eugene's words should have soothed her, but they burned like acid in her heart instead. Fresh tears fell from her eyes, and she didn't try to stop them. "What could you possibly find to love?" she whispered painfully. "I mean, I know what you saw in me before, but now . . ."

"You haven't a clue what I saw in you, Carmen."

What else could you have seen? she thought, but didn't say. *What did any man ever see in me that didn't fit in a size 34D?* Carmen exhaled a long, tired sigh. "Want to know what's really sad, Eugene?"

Eugene shrugged his shoulders and frowned with mock impatience. He was obviously trying to bring a light-hearted end to Carmen's pity party. "Me, if you don't get in that bath-tub and get dressed?" He smiled warmly.

Carmen didn't smile back. She had something important to say that she wanted to make sure Eugene heard. "What's really sad is that it never *once* occurred to me. *Never*." Carmen glanced down at her worn, weary body shrouded in her over-sized bathrobe. "That you could possibly have been attracted to anything other than my looks."

"That is sad." He pulled her to his chest and wrapped his arms around her, holding her close for a long, silent moment. He was still holding her tight when he finally spoke in a hushed tone in her ear. "Carmen, the first time I ever laid eyes on you, I was stunned."

She pounded her forehead softly against his chest in frustration. "See?" she complained.

"You were hollering at a group of boys outside the girls' gym. Do you remember it?"

Carmen stayed put in Eugene's embrace, but shook her head no to his question. She had met Eugene in an Overland staff meeting. She had no idea what he was talking about.

"You were so angry, I was afraid you might hurt one of those boys."

Carmen shrugged weakly. How many boys had she fussed at while working at Overland? *Hundreds*.

"I thought they must have done something terrible to you. Maybe cursed you, or disrespected you in some way." Eugene chuckled. "Turns out they were just late to class." He chuckled again, then planted a kiss on Carmen's peach fuzz–covered head. "You told them if they couldn't get to something as easy to find as *class* on time, how in the hell were they ever going to find their way anywhere in life?"

Carmen shrugged again. When *wasn't* she fussing at some Overland student to act like they cared about their education—like they cared about their lives? Not that the fussing seemed to do much good.

"I fell in love with you that day, and I've been waiting for you to love me back ever since." He leaned away from her so he could see her face.

I do love you, Eugene, Carmen's inner voice shouted. She couldn't dare say it aloud.

Eugene didn't wait to hear the words anyway. "Now," he said firmly, obviously changing the subject, "I am determined to get you out of this house today. Are you going to get in that bathtub voluntarily, or am I going to have to see you naked before it's my time?"

"Before your time?"

Eugene grinned. He didn't say anything but raised his eyebrows at Carmen suggestively. She knew he was referring to the idea that he might someday make love to her.

"You wish, *Layla,*" she teased.

"No." He winked at her confidently. "I know. I've always known." And before she could fire a comeback at him, he had already made his way out of her room and was on the other side of her closed bedroom door.

⋚ **28** ⋚

Not That Kind of Bad

Instead of hopping on the nearby entrance to the 91 freeway, Eugene took the scenic route to Marina del Rey, navigating through the Westchester hills until his Ford Explorer came to a stop on a small cul-de-sac overlooking the Pacific Ocean.

Carmen sat with him in silence, taking in the splendor of deep blue water set against a radiant, cloudless sky.

"You were right, Eugene," she conceded. "I did need to get out of that bed. I already feel better than I have in a long time." She sighed deeply, gazing out over the expanse of sea and sky. "It is gorgeous out here today."

Eugene studied Carmen's face thoughtfully. He didn't speak for a few moments, but just sat there behind the wheel watching Carmen watch the ocean. "Exceptionally gorgeous," he finally said, obviously referring to Carmen, not the scene before them.

She turned to face him, fluffing her curly auburn wig playfully. "Amazing what a little hair and makeup can do, huh?" It had been a long time since she felt like putting on makeup, and she hated wearing the wig, but since she didn't know where in the marina Eugene planned to take her for their "field trip," she decided she'd better be prepared for exposure to the public.

"You're gorgeous without it," Eugene stated matter-of-factly.

Carmen looked at him sideways at the ridiculousness of his statement. Anyone with eyes could see that without her wig and makeup, she looked like a bruised caramel apple on a stick. "You're full of it, Eugene," she answered with an equally matter-of-fact tone.

"I see what I see.

"Then you must be blind."

Eugene smiled knowingly. "Maybe," he admitted, nodding his head yes at Carmen. He reached to turn the ignition key, revving the engine as he stared solemnly into Carmen's eyes. "Or maybe my vision is perfectly clear."

He pulled away from the curb and began his descent down the winding hill that led to Vista del Mar and then to Culver Boulevard. As Eugene navigated through the sparse midmorning traffic along Culver, Carmen watched a flock of seagulls gliding around one another in wide circles high above the road.

"It's nice being out on a beautiful weekday like this," Eugene said, breaking the silence between them. "This is the first time in eleven years that I haven't taught summer school."

Carmen studied him thoughtfully. "You've made a lot of sacrifices for me, Eugene."

"That's what friends are for, sweetheart."

It occurred to Carmen in that moment that Eugene had been calling her "sweetheart" all morning. It used to grate on her last nerve when he called her that, but not today.

"You know what, Eugene?"

"What's that?"

"You are one of the best friends I've ever had."

Eugene smiled softly, keeping his eyes on the road ahead. Carmen turned to stare out the window at the passing scenery, and they spent the rest of the ride to the marina in comfortable silence.

When he pulled into the valet lane at the Cheesecake Factory, Eugene immediately hopped out and walked around to Carmen's side to open her door. He locked his arm in hers, helping her down out of her seat. After pocketing the ticket from the valet, he led her slowly toward the restaurant's entrance, keeping a watchful eye on her movements the entire time.

"Let me know if you need to stop and rest."

Carmen felt more energetic than she had in weeks. "I feel good, Eugene." She smiled at him. "Really good. I haven't felt this good in a long time. Thanks for being so hard on me this morning."

When they entered the restaurant, Eugene approached the

maitre d' podium and announced, "We're with the DuPrè party of five."

Carmen smiled happily. *Yvette, Lindsey, and Pedro must be here too.* Though Lindsey and Yvette had come by her apartment the evening before, she hadn't seen Pedro in two weeks. *I miss him.* She was looking forward to seeing her friend and hearing all about his trip to Mexico. He had been so excited before he left; Carmen had never seen the man so emotional. At the mere mention of how eager he was to see his wife, his eyes would get all wet and glassy. *That woman is really lucky to have a man like him,* she thought just as Eugene gently grasped her hand and led her past the maitre d' stand.

"Right this way," the hostess announced pleasantly. "Your party is waiting for you on the patio."

When they stepped through the glass door leading onto the wooden deck overlooking the sailboat-packed marina, Carmen scanned the tables searching for her team, but they weren't in sight. Her eyes settled instead on two familiar young faces at a table on the far side of the deck. *What are they doing here?* As Eugene pulled her gently toward the table, Jessie and Angel stood to great them, each wearing a beaming smile.

Angel stepped forward first, shaking Eugene's hand enthusiastically, then stepping past him to grasp Carmen's. If the boy noticed Carmen's obvious weight loss and the deep purple circles under her eyes, his face didn't let on. "We missed you, Miss D."

"Yeah," Jessie piped in, reaching around Angel for a chance to grab Carmen's hand. "We heard you was real sick."

Eugene commandeered both boys back to their seats. "Let's let Miss DuPrè sit down."

Carmen's eyes silently asked Eugene to explain what was going on, but he only smiled at her in return.

"We told Mr. Timms all about that promise you made us."

Carmen lifted her eyebrows questioningly.

"Yeah," Angel added. "Then we showed him our report cards."

"We both got A's in that class you helped us get into," Jessie announced proudly.

"You said if we got A's we was supposed to get a date, remember?" Angel added.

Carmen felt her throat tightening up, and her eyes began to fill with tears. "You two must have worked really hard," she managed to say without her voice shaking too much. It touched her that the two boys had been so inspired by something she said to them, and that they had not forgotten her.

Jessie and Angel grinned at each other.

"We're taking geometry next year. Then *trig*." Jessie looked and sounded as if the last thing he could possibly be talking about so excitedly was being admitted into some math classes. Anyone watching would have thought he'd won a trip to the Super Bowl.

Carmen reached for her napkin just as their waiter arrived to ask for their drink orders. She dabbed at the corners of her eyes, then asked for a cup of black tea with honey.

"I'll have the same," Eugene said.

"Can I have a Coke?" Angel asked Eugene.

Eugene nodded at the waiter. "He'd like a Coke."

"Me too," Jessie added.

Before the waiter left the table, Eugene reminded him there would be one more drink order. "Pedro brought the boys," he explained to Carmen. He turned his attention to the two boys. "Is he in the restroom?" he asked them. They both shrugged.

"He said he'd be right back," Jessie offered.

"Man, look what Paid gave us," Angel spouted to Eugene excitedly. He held out his arm, showing off a very good Rolex knockoff.

Jessie held his Rolex look-alike out too. "For getting good grades this year," he explained.

Carmen studied the boys' outstretched hands. "M-a-l-o," she read aloud from the tattoos across their knuckles. "That means 'bad.' " *Paid gave them Rolexes? They're still hanging around with that lowlife, I see.* "Boys, why do you two have tattoos that say you're *bad*?" She frowned at them. "It makes you look more like hoodlums than mathematicians."

"It's not that kind of bad, miss," Angel said.

"Yeah," Jessie added. "It stands for something. Mejicano Americanos de Libertad y Orgullo."

Carmen stared at him blankly.

"It means Mexican Americans striving for Independence and Pride," Angel explained. "It's like a club. We do community service and stuff."

"Ohh." Carmen nodded her head. She was glad they cleared that up, though she still didn't understand what pride had to do with accepting gifts from gangbangers.

"Guess what, Miss D? Me and Angel are taking a college class this summer," Jessie gushed excitedly.

"Angel and I . . ." Carmen corrected.

"Angel and I are taking an astronomy class at East LA Community College. We get to go to the Griffith Observatory and see the telescopes and stuff."

"Yeah. And it counts double credits for graduation," Angel confirmed proudly.

"Yes, I know it does." Carmen laughed softly. They seemed to have forgotten she was a college counselor. *It feels good to sit here with these kids,* Carmen thought. *I actually miss this.*

Angel and Jessie sent each other looks that said, *Duh.* Angel said, "Oh yeah. We almost forgot you was a counselor."

Jessie looked Carmen in the eye sadly. "You been gone a long time, Miss D." He shook his head. "They got some ol' gringa in there now."

Carmen knew that meant the sub they'd put in her office was a white woman. "You don't like her?" Carmen asked.

They both shrugged. "I ain't talked to her yet," Jessie added.

I ain't talked to her? Carmen decided to pass on the English correcting. She could be at it all afternoon if she took it too seriously. "Give her a chance, you two," Carmen said sternly. "She might be able to help you get in the right classes next year."

The boys nodded their heads. Jessie said, "I *guess*. She *could* be all right."

"You just make sure you get in geometry, and you have to take a lab science too if you want to be eligible for a university when you graduate."

The two boys looked at each other and fell silent. Carmen

locked eyes momentarily with Eugene before turning again to look at the boys.

"You two do plan to go on to college, right?" Eugene asked as if the answer to the question could only be yes.

"Uh," Angel said.

"Um, yeah," Jessie added uncomfortably. "I'm definitely going, but . . ."

Angel was visibly nervous. His cheeks flushed a subtle shade of pink. "I . . . uh . . . I'm illegal," he finally spit out. "I can't get no grants or loans or nothing, and my moms and pops don't have the money. So I doubt I'll be able to go to college."

"You're *not* illegal." Eugene's tone sounded angry, but his face was calm. "You might be undocumented, but *you* didn't do anything illegal. I don't know how your parents got to America, but I'm sure you didn't have any say in whether to come here, *or* whether to stay."

Before Angel could reply, a Hispanic man old enough to be the boys' father approached the table wearing an apron and carrying a tray of drinks. They all sat in silence as the man put the two Cokes in front of Angel and Jessie, and the tea in front of Carmen and Eugene.

"Thank you," Eugene said. The man nodded at him and promptly disappeared.

It was not lost on any of them that it was quite possible the man who served them might be undocumented as well. His job as a busboy was typical of the minimum wage jobs illegal immigrants held. The scene seemed to accentuate the reality that Angel didn't have much of a future to look forward to without a college education. They all sat in uncomfortable silence.

Carmen thought of the many times she'd angrily insisted "illegal aliens are soaking up all the money in California—money that ought to be spent on Americans." She'd been very vocal in her defense of those who'd voted yes on proposition 187. Randall had tried to get her to see that while she was suggesting that the children of undocumented immigrants didn't belong in public schools, she was condemning them to lives of ignorance and poverty. *Kids like Angel,* she now realized sheepishly. Kids forced to hang out in the streets all day? *Not a bright alternative.* She cringed. "Spend it on education or spend it on law enforcement," was what Randall had been trying to get her to see. *Angel didn't ask to come here,* Carmen thought, suddenly feeling much more open-minded. 187 seemed cruel and unfair to her now, now that someone she cared about was affected by it.

Carmen broke the silence at the table. "Angel, don't you worry about college. You just take all the classes you need, and you keep your grades up. If you're eligible when you graduate, you're going to college if I have to pay for it myself."

The boys stared at Carmen in disbelief.

Angel objected immediately. "I can't let you do that, Miss D," he said sadly. She could tell he meant it. "You got your own life to worry about. Besides, that's a long time from now anyways."

"Don't tell me what to do with my own money, young man," Carmen responded firmly. "There's no way someone who works as hard as you do should miss out on college." She could see that he was really affected by her offer. Behind his eyes was a light that warmed her heart from way across the table. She softened her tone when she added, "You have to be educated, Angel. For all we know, *you* could be the one to discover the cure for cancer."

Angel grinned at the thought. Suddenly his grin grew wider as he waved his hand over his head, obviously waving at someone he knew.

Carmen felt Pedro's lips press against her cheek in an affectionate smooch before she saw his face. "Missed you," he said into her ear. "Missed you too," he said to Eugene, reaching for a handshake. He looked at Carmen and whistled. "I can see this man's been taking great care of you. You look marvelous."

Carmen tried to smile.

"Sorry for leaving you guys," Pedro said to Jessie and Angel. "I had some important phone calls to make." After seating himself in a chair next to Jessie, Pedro reached down under the table and brought out a large, brightly colored gift bag bulging at the seams.

"I bring gifts from Juarez," he announced happily.

Carmen watched Pedro's movements carefully. She'd never seen Mr. Calm, Cool, and Collected act so bubbly. *Must have been the time he spent with his wife. If it makes him this happy, he ought to do it more often.*

"This," he began, extracting a gorgeous handmade leather attaché from the bag, "is for Mr. Timms." He handed the case to Eugene.

"You shouldn't have done that, P." Eugene said.

"That's where you're wrong," Pedro corrected him. "Didn't you read Gibran in college?"

Eugene stared blankly at him.

" 'Give now, while the season of giving is yours and not your inheritors.' " He flashed a knowing look. "In other words if you've got it, give it, 'cause after you're gone, it'll belong to somebody else anyway."

Eugene nodded. "Thanks, P."

Pedro reached into the bag again and pulled out a folded bundle of what looked like a very large knitted blanket. "This is for you from Ariselle," he said, holding the bundle up. "It's hand-woven. Made by a fourteen-year-old girl who lives in the Juarez orphanage."

Carmen tried to reach for it, but her arms wouldn't cooperate. She was beginning to lose the energy she had been feeling when they first arrived at the restaurant. She took a deep breath, then closed her eyes for a moment. Eugene immediately stood up and took the blanket from Pedro, setting it on the chair next to Carmen's. When she opened her eyes, Eugene was kneeling at her side, and they were all studying her closely.

"It's really good to see you up and out of the house and looking so beautiful," Pedro began, "But are you feeling up to this?"

Carmen didn't want to ruin the party, but she was beginning to fade. "I'm fine." She motioned to Eugene that he could sit back down. "I'm just a little tired is all." She reached her hand out to stroke the soft ivory blanket in the nearby chair. She studied the intricate weave pattern, fingering it gently. "It's beautiful," she said sincerely. "Tell Ariselle I love it."

Pedro turned his attention to the boys, then back to Carmen and Eugene. "How 'bout those math grades? Pretty impressive, yes?"

The boys turned their wrists over and back, modeling their watches for Pedro. "Thanks, Paid," Jessie said sincerely. "I never had nothing like this before, man."

"Paid?" Carmen looked back and forth between Pedro and the two boys. "You're Paid?"

"It's short for Pedro. You know. Pay-dro."

She shook her head slowly in astonishment. "You're the math tutor they raved about? All this time I thought they were talking about some filthy rich thug type, and they were talking about you?"

Pedro grinned. "I might be mistaken for a thug, but I'm definitely not filthy rich. That adjective would refer to my friend Eugene here, but not to myself. I'm nowhere near his tax bracket."

Eugene waved Pedro's comment away. "I'm just a lowly math teacher, P."

Pedro winked at Eugene. "I don't know anybody else personally who bought thousands of shares of AOL and Amazon way back when they were like twenty-five cents each, and then sold everything *just* before the bottom fell out of the tech market."

Carmen stared blankly at him. She had no idea what Pedro was talking about, but she thought he might be insinuating that Eugene had made a fortune in the stock market.

Eugene signaled to the waiter on the far side of the patio. "Are you all ready to order lunch yet?" He seemed happy to change the subject.

302

The mention of food turned Carmen's stomach. Pedro caught the sick look on her face and asked her again, "Are you sure you're feeling okay, Carmen?"

She smiled weakly. "This is my first time out of the house for this long of a stretch since . . ." She closed her eyes. She meant to open them back up, but they didn't seem to want to cooperate.

"You don't look so good, Miss D," Jessie said softly. "We didn't mean to make you feel bad." Carmen opened her eyes in time to catch the look of serious concern on Jessie and Angel's faces.

"Oh no. I'm really happy to see you two. I really am. I'm just not . . ." She swallowed. "I'm just a little tired, that's all. I promised you two lunch, didn't I?" She managed another tired smile. "So let's order lunch."

Eugene stood up. "The boys would be happy to take a raincheck, wouldn't you?"

"A what?" Angel asked.

"That's like when you gotta reschedule something," Jessie explained.

"Oh. Oh yeah, Miss D," Angel said. "No doubt. A raincheck. Definitely."

Eugene pulled his wallet out and placed a hundred-dollar bill on the table in front of Angel. "You guys go ahead and eat, okay?"

Angel reached for the money, grinning from ear to ear. He looked at Jessie excitedly, then back at Eugene. "Thanks."

"Split the change," Eugene added.

"Thanks," they sang in unison.

Carmen felt Eugene pulling her chair out a few inches from the table so she could stand up. When she was on her feet she turned, placed both palms on the table, and looked directly at the boys. With all the sincerity she believed she'd ever felt she said, "I'm really proud of you two."

"Just wait till we get to college, Miss D." Jessie beamed.

"Yeah, Miss D," Angel added. "You ain't seen nothin' yet."

≋ **29** ≋

Angry at the Wrong DuPrè

"*The best thing* about finally being done with the chemo is that I've been through the worst," Carmen explained to Lindsey on the phone. "It's all smooth sailing from here." She paused, remembering that she was due for surgery at the beginning of next week. "Well, compared to the last month and a half, that is."

Carmen was in high spirits. It had been three weeks since her chemo series ended, and she was finally beginning to get her energy back. Her skin didn't have that gray cast to it anymore, and she could even go without a wig if she wanted to— her previously bald head was now covered by a cap of baby-fine hair that was already close to an inch long.

"Do you think you'll feel up to going to the family Fourth?" Lindsey was referring to the annual Fourth of July event held at the DuPrè house every year. It was three days away.

"That's not on my list of things to do this summer," Carmen said matter-of-factly.

"I'm planning to introduce Kenny to Mama," Lindsey confided, "and I could really use your support."

'What? I assumed you two broke up. I haven't heard you mention the man in months. I've never even met him, Linn."

"I know, Carmen. I know you haven't met Kenny yet, and I'm sorry. I want to explain everything to you; just tell me that I've got your support on the Fourth."

"My support?" She laughed at the thought that anything she supported would have an ounce of impact on Mavis's opinion of it.

"I was asked by Eugene and Pedro to a party at the tutorial center that day, but I can miss that if I have to. Actually, if you don't mind going over to Mavis's a little late, I can ask Eugene to come too. I'm sure he'd love to meet us there. He still hasn't met Mavis."

"I'd really appreciate it, Carmen. I'm really going to need support on this because—"

Carmen cut her off. "Of course I will be there if it's important to you, Linn."

"I plan to be with Kenny forever. It's about time I—"

"Forever? Linn, I still haven't met your mystery boyfriend, and you're over there talking about forever." Carmen added teasingly, "I was beginning to believe he didn't really exist."

"I've been a little insecure about this, sis," Lindsey responded.

"It's okay if he's not super good-looking or anything. If you love him, I'm sure I'll love him."

"Um, Carmen. *She's* not a him."

"Hmm? What did you say, sweetie?"

"Kenny. Her name is Kendra."

Carmen closed her eyes tight and tried not to drop the phone.

"Don't hate me, Carmen. Please. I just wasn't ready. I mean . . . I know it's a big deal. I know everybody in the family is going to have a fit. I know I'll probably be in this on my own for the rest of my life, but . . ."

Carmen couldn't speak.

"I know I should have told you sooner, Car, but with everything you've been through, I just—"

"Lindsey, you *never* listen to me, do you?" Carmen interrupted forcefully.

Lindsey didn't respond.

"I believe I just *said*, if *you* love her, then I'm sure *I'll* love her."

Carmen heard a long silence, then soft sniffling on the other end of the phone.

"Lindsey?" she asked gently.

"Mm hmm." Lindsey was obviously trying not to cry.

"Why don't you and Kenny give me a ride to Mavis's house on the Fourth, okay?"

"Okay," Lindsey answered softly.

"What time?" Carmen asked.

"I love you, Carmen."

"I know, sweetie. That is one thing I definitely know."

"Four-thirty. Five?" Lindsey said softly.

"That's fine, sweetie."

"Carmen?"

"Mm hmm."

"How many times have I asked you not to call me sweetie?"

"About twelve million."

"Yeah. Well, never mind."

As Lindsey pulled her convertible Mustang into the fast lane on the 405 South, Carmen and Kendra were still laughing at the private joke they shared. Lindsey was getting a little irritated that they hadn't yet let her in on what was so funny.

"You would never believe two people who are so obviously different, would have the same taste in shoes," Kendra said for the third time. She had already uttered the words accompanied by a tone of utter disbelief twice since pulling away from the curb at Carmen's apartment.

From the backseat, Kendra had lifted one of her red-white-and-blue leather Converse All Stars onto the armrest between the two front seats. Carmen pulled her right foot up and onto her left thigh and let it just rest there conspicuously, just to give Lindsey another look at the evidence.

"Okay, so you two are wearing the same shoes." Lindsey stared back and forth between the two women with a clueless expression on her face. "Why is that so damn hilarious?"

Kendra began first. She extracted her sneaker from the armrest and leaned forward. "Linn, remember that evening we were going to the Sparks game, you asked me to meet you at Marie Callendar's at five-thirty?"

Carmen jumped in. "And you were rushing my ass out of

that same restaurant around five-fifteen? Trying to keep your love life a secret from me at the time, I believe."

Lindsey didn't say anything. She was obviously waiting to see where the explanation was headed.

"We literally bumped into one another outside," Kendra explained.

"Charles David," Carmen announced.

"Black platforms with the skinny straps," Kendra confirmed. "Cute as hell, but hard to break in."

Lindsey was finally beginning to get the gist of their conversation. "You two have already met?"

"Sort of," they both chimed.

"Your sister was giving me a little advice on breaking in a new pair of shoes," Kendra explained. "I just didn't know she was your sister."

Carmen remembered the day the thin, brown-skinned woman with the short natural hairstyle had bumped into her. She didn't mention the part about silently comparing the woman to a chemotherapy patient. She'd come a long way since then. Hell, she'd been a chemotherapy patient since then. Carmen reached her hand out to Kendra.

"Let's do this officially. Good to meet you, Kenny, I'm Lindsey's sister Carmen." She shook Kendra's hand. "I've heard nothing but . . . *nothing* about you." She smiled at her sister teasingly. "Just kidding. I've heard a lot of really good things about you, *Kenny*." Carmen emphasized the name when she said it. My sister has spoken very highly of you."

Kendra grinned. "It was getting a little cramped in that closet she was hiding me in."

Lindsey blew a teasing kiss to Kendra. When Lindsey pulled up to the curb in front of Mavis's house, they all got out of the car and stood near the curb talking quietly. Carmen knew Lindsey was trying to gather the courage to face Mavis. She heard Kendra whisper, "Listen, baby, if you're not ready for this, I'll understand."

Lindsey kissed Kendra right on the mouth. "I'm as ready as I'll ever be, Kenny. If I wasn't ready to share you with my family, I never would have invited you to spend this holiday with me."

Carmen caught a glimpse of Mavis peeking at them through the living room window. "Mavis has us in her radar," Carmen announced quietly. "Do you two have some kind of plan, or are you just going to hang out and let the chips fall where they may."

"My plan is to introduce Kenny as my girlfriend."

Carmen raised both eyebrows dramatically. "Uh. Della might pick up on that, but Mavis won't get it." Carmen shook her head no. "Maybe you should use the word 'partner' instead."

Lindsey shook her head. "No, she'll think I have a new business partner."

"Lover?" Kendra said, grinning. "That sounds good to me," she joked.

"Right," Lindsey said sarcastically. "Hi Mother, I'd like you to meet my lover, Kenny." She grinned too, then leaned over to plant another kiss on Kendra's lips. "Hey, I do like the way that sounds."

Carmen was a little uncomfortable with the public display of affection. She swallowed hard and suggested, "Maybe 'lover' is a bit . . . I don't know . . . personal."

"Hi, Mother, this is the love of my life, Kendra Gillis." Lindsey's face lit up with a beaming smile. "That's it," she announced confidently.

Carmen wasn't feeling quite as confident about it as Lindsey, but she was determined to support her sister—no matter what.

"I got your back, whatever happens, sis," Carmen assured her.

Lindsey took a deep breath and led Kendra toward the front walk leading to Mavis's door. "Let's just hope for the best," she said nervously as they approached the porch. She pushed the unlocked door open and entered the lioness's den.

Though she had obviously seen them standing outside in the front yard, Mavis had disappeared from the living room. The three women proceeded down the long hallway that led to the dining room. Mavis was camped out there near the food-laden table in one of her brocade-upholstered dining chairs.

"Mmm, smells wonderful in here," Kendra offered nervously.

To everyone's chagrin, Mavis had figured out the nature of Lindsey and Kendra's relationship before Lindsey got a chance to open her mouth. And she let Lindsey know immediately *and rudely* just how she felt about it. She eyed Kendra's hand clenched tightly in Lindsey's, and without hesitation made it quite clear what her position on their relationship would be. "What is this?" Mavis demanded to know. "What in the world is going on here?"

Lindsey tried out one of the lines she'd practiced by the car. "Mother, this is Kendra. She is the love—"

"How dare you." Mavis performed the sign of the cross over her ample bosom, looked Kendra up and down rudely, then turned her attention back to Lindsey. "I would have expected something like this from Carmen, but you? Lindsey Antoinette DuPrè, your father is certainly turning in his grave."

Lindsey stared hard at Mavis, the hurt showing plainly on her face. She responded calmly, "My father would be happy for me, Mama. My father would say if I'm happy he's happy."

"Bullshit," Mavis spat out. "That goes to show you how much you didn't know the man. He didn't have anything good to say about—" She looked Kendra directly in the eye. "He wouldn't approve, I can tell you that for sure."

"Mother—" Carmen began.

"You stay out of this," Mavis snapped.

Lindsey stared at Mavis for a silent moment, the painful expression on her face changing suddenly to anger. "Are you saying my guest is not welcome here?" Lindsey asked. She squeezed Kendra's hand tight. "Are you really that despicable, Mavis?"

Carmen raised her eyebrows in shock at Lindsey's statement. To this point, Carmen was the only DuPrè child who was detached enough from her mother to call her by her first name to her face. *Did she say the word "despicable" to Mavis?* This was getting ugly. Carmen decided it was time for her to try again to jump into the fray.

"Mother, really," Carmen interjected. "Times have changed, you know."

Mavis turned on Carmen and sputtered at her, too. "Times have *changed*? Times have changed all right. Naked people on prime-time television. Babies kidnapped out of their own front yards and found raped and dead days later. Pornography all out in public places." Carmen thought Mavis was finished with her list of deadly sins when she bellowed into Carmen's face, "Folks shacking up *instead of getting married.*" Carmen thought the woman was going to give herself a heart attack the way she was huffing and puffing. She decided not to try to say anything to defend herself against her mother's tirade. She'd learned a long time ago to just sit and listen when Mavis began behaving this way.

When she didn't get a fight from Carmen, Mavis turned her attention back to Lindsey. She looked at her daughter with an expression of harsh and absolute disgust. "Yes, times definitely have changed, now haven't they?"

"Bye, Mama," Lindsey said softly, pulling Kendra toward the living room. Carmen knew Mavis had no idea what Lindsey's "bye" really meant. Mavis thought she'd see Lindsey, without her new friend, at Thanksgiving dinner. Carmen knew better.

"Bye," Mavis retorted matter-of-factly. "*Good*bye," she added emphatically before she hoisted herself from her chair and shuffled angrily from the room.

Lindsey stopped at the entrance to the hallway, turning to face Carmen. Kendra reached up to brush a tear from Lindsey's cheek. "I'm sorry, baby," Kendra whispered.

"I'm not," Lindsey reassured her. "And don't you be either." She kissed Kendra on the lips again.

"If you two want to get out of here, Eugene will be here in a few minutes anyway. I can stand Mavis for a little while longer," Carmen assured them.

"Are you *sure,* Car?" Lindsey's face said she didn't want Carmen to end up getting more abuse from their mother. "I don't want her taking this out on you."

"Believe me, sweetie, I'm used to it." Carmen laughed. "You just got a small taste of what she usually reserves for me."

"Why do you put up with that?" Lindsey asked.

"She's my mother." Carmen shrugged. "I'm supposed to love her."

"Some people you gotta love from far away," Kendra interjected matter-of-factly.

Carmen smiled. "I like you," she said sincerely to Lindsey's girlfriend/partner/lover.

Kendra nodded. "I like you too."

"You sure you wanna hang out here, Car?" Lindsey asked.

Carmen looked at her watch. "Eugene will be here in about fifteen minutes."

Lindsey wrapped her arm around Kendra's waist. "I'll call you later, Car." They disappeared into the living room, leaving Carmen standing alone near the dining room table.

Carmen picked up a black olive from a nearby tray and popped it in her mouth. She could actually taste it. *Yes. My taste buds are coming back.* She'd be putting the meat back on her bones in no time now.

"You might want to eat a little more than that," a man's voice teased.

Carmen turned to see her brother, Maxwell, enter the room. "Hi Max." She leaned to give him a smooch on the cheek. "Haven't seen you in . . ." Carmen really didn't remember. "Since Christmas?"

"You've lost a lot of weight, Carmen." Maxwell took her by the arm and turned her around to inspect her. "I swear you've lost at least twenty pounds."

She huffed at her brother playfully. "Look who's talking." Max was six feet tall and as thin as Popeye's Olive Oyl. If it weren't for his round face and large, deep-set eyes, he would just be one tall straight line. "And you could use some sun, too," Carmen quipped. "I almost mistook you for that white man that lives across the street."

"Funny." Maxwell stopped the wordplay by gazing solemnly at Carmen and asking her, "Are you *okay*?"

Carmen thought he said the word "okay" with an odd accent on the last syllable. "What do you mean, am I *okay*?" She said the word the same way he had.

"I don't know. Folks are talking."

"You mean Mavis?"

"Carmen's on crack. Carmen's stalking a man again. Carmen has an eating disorder. Carmen's a heroin addict." He smiled nervously. "Which one is it?"

"None of the above," Carmen assured him.

A loud "harrumph" from the doorway startled them both. It was Mavis. "Rowena Matthews told my hairdresser that you were on some kind of sick leave, but I know you just started that rumor yourself so people would forget that you got fired from your job for trying to make money off of George Browning."

Mavis's attitude hadn't calmed one bit. She was obviously on a Fourth of July headhunt. Lindsey's head was safely on its way home, so Carmen prepared herself for the worst. Mavis settled her plump ass in a seat near the table.

"I didn't get fired, Mother. I've been on leave."

"Is that what you're calling it? I can't believe you set that nice old man up like that. It's just disgraceful."

"If you're referring to Dr. Browning, he pled guilty to a crime. He tried to rape me, Mother." She shook her head at Mavis in disbelief. "They bargained the charge down to sexual assault and he pled guilty to it. That man held me down and attacked me, whether you want to believe it or not."

Della entered the room just then and walked over to stand next to Mavis's chair, eyeing Carmen closely. "Hi, Carmen," Della said with more enthusiasm than Carmen expected. "You don't look well." She actually sounded concerned.

"It's good to see you," Carmen replied. It was easy to mean those words in the first five minutes. After that, there'd be no telling if seeing Della would still be good.

Mavis was still stuck on the George Browning conversation. "Well, if you hadn't accepted *money* from him, I might actually believe you. But, really, who settles out of court when they know they're telling the truth?"

Carmen didn't bother telling Mavis why she settled the lawsuit. Cynthia Bombeck, the attorney at Randall's firm who represented her, said the case could drag on for up to ten years, and since Browning had relocated to Washington D.C., Carmen was even less likely to end up with any kind of compensation. She settled for two hundred thousand dollars, though her inner voice had shouted to her loud and clear that she shouldn't spend a dime of it on herself. She decided she wanted to try to help somebody else—make a difference in someone's life the way Pedro had done for her.

Carmen had already sent a check for twenty-five thousand dollars to the orphanage in Juarez in memory of Pedro's little boy. Another thirty thousand dollars was being placed in a scholarship trust to help offset the cost of college for Angel. She'd offered another fifty thousand dollars to Eugene to help pay for his summer program—his plan to improve the math department at Overland, though Eugene was acting like he couldn't accept it. She hadn't decided yet what to do with the rest of the settlement.

"So what are you going to do to make a living for yourself now that you're out of a job?" Mavis asked.

"I'm not out of a job, Mother." Carmen smiled. "They actually offered me that Talented and Gifted Academy counseling position." Carmen could hardly believe it herself when the letter came in the mail

Dear Ms. DuPrè, the letter began. *We are pleased to inform you that you are being offered a position as head counselor at the District's Talented and Gifted Academy. Please call us at your earliest convenience to set up an orientation meeting with the hiring committee.*

"Well," Mavis replied. "I guess your little skirmish with Dr. Browning yielded some fruit then, didn't it?"

"I turned down the job offer," Carmen said happily. "I decided to stay at Overland." Carmen didn't add that she was learning to speak Spanish so she could communicate better with Overland parents. Mavis would surely ridicule her for wanting to learn their language.

"No one in their right mind would stay in that hellhole," Mavis snorted.

"I think Overland is where I'm really needed. I can do a lot of good there, and the kids there have taught me a lot about what it means to be a guidance counselor."

Mavis rolled her eyes but didn't say anything.

"You know, Mother, you really are too blessed to be so unhappy." Carmen said it in an absolutely calm tone.

The words had barely come out of Carmen's mouth when Mavis's cheeks turned bright red. "How dare you speak to me like that, Carmen Marie." She hoisted herself out of her chair. "What on earth would *I* have to be unhappy about? I have a beautiful home and a successful family. I have children and grandchildren who adore me." She wagged a stiff index finger in front of Carmen's nose. "Don't you blame me because your life is so miserable. I told you not to shack up with that no-good fellow. I warned you it would be the beginning of a long list of failures for you, but did you listen?" Mavis leaned in until her face was only a few inches from Carmen's. "It's what killed your daddy, you know. Your father called me that night to tell me he was on his way to your little love shack to try to talk you into coming home, and that's the last time—" Mavis's voice cracked just then, and she began to sob mournfully. Carmen just stood there, her mouth open in amazement. It was the first time she'd ever heard her mother blame her for her father's car accident.

A wave of peace swept over Carmen suddenly. *She blames me.* Carmen watched with an odd mixture of resentment and sympathy as splotches of beige makeup dripped down onto Mavis's American flag T-shirt. *He wasn't coming to see me,* she thought, but didn't say.

Della put an arm around Mavis's shoulder. "Don't cry, Mama."

Mavis was muttering something unintelligible along with her sobs. Carmen thought she heard her say, "Freeway at one A.M."

"Maybe you should go, Carmen," Della said firmly.

"I'm sorry you think I killed Daddy," Carmen said to her mother solemnly. "I'm sorry you think of me the way you do." She decided not to remind Mavis of the real truth. That Wilfred DuPrè's car crashed eastbound on the 60 freeway, not northbound on the 405. He hadn't been on his way to or from Carmen's that night. Maxwell knew it, and so did Della. Though they had discussed it in hushed whispers in the days following his death, none of the DuPrè children had ever been able to determine where their father had actually been headed.

"Just leave, Carmen," Della demanded. "Leave before this gets any uglier than it already is." Della was afraid Carmen might let Mavis know what they all suspected—that Wilfred DuPrè might have been out driving to get away from his wife that night.

"Why don't you stay out of this, Della?" Carmen responded. She had no intention of telling Mavis anyway.

"Why don't you go crawl back into whatever crackhouse you were in before you graced us with your presence?" Della growled.

"What?" Carmen felt a wave of heat in her cheeks. "What did you say?"

"Look at you. No meat on your bones. Your skin is a mess. Even your fingernails look like shit. We all know it, Carmen.

We all know where you've been these last few months, and we know what you've been doing. We've heard the rumors. You ought to be ashamed of yourself." Della moved in front of Mavis, blocking her from Carmen's view. She glared hatefully at Carmen then, narrowing her eyes into two slits. "Why don't you go back to the rock you crawled out from under."

Carmen couldn't understand why she had an uncontrollable urge to laugh. She was trying desperately not to let her face break, but it was a battle she was obviously losing. Within seconds Carmen was rolling with laughter—laughing so hard she had to hold the sides of her rib cage.

Della didn't appreciate Carmen's response to her anger. "You think this is funny?" She lunged for Carmen, grabbing a fistful of her hair. Carmen was still laughing when the wig came off in Della's clenched fist.

Carmen stopped laughing, but she had a hard time wiping the smile off her face. She managed to bring the corners of her mouth down into a straight, solemn line. "I just finished chemo a few weeks ago, Della. My hair is starting to grow back though." She put her palm to the back of her head and struck a model's pose. "What do you think of the look?"

An expression of absolute horror fell on Della's face. The mass of shiny auburn curls in her hand fell to the floor.

Carmen lifted her shirt and showed them a fresh scar on her torso. "This is where my chemo port was," she said matter-of-factly. "I still haven't had the surgery on my breast, though. It's scheduled for next Tuesday morning," She knew she was rubbing it in a little harshly, but she wanted Della to know just how stupid it had been to swallow Mavis's mixed-up version of the truth without tasting it first. She should have suspected it was poison.

Della began to cry. "Oh God, Carmen." She stood like a statue staring at Carmen's nearly bald head. Mavis shuffled calmly over to lower herself back into the dining chair she'd leaped out of.

"I'm over sixty years old and I've never had any problems with my breasts," she muttered. "You're not even thirty, Carmen. That's just not possible." She shook her head vigorously, obviously unwilling to admit she could have been so incredibly wrong.

"Mother, stop it," Della shouted at her. "I'm really sorry Carmen. I—" She stopped talking and stepped toward her sister, wrapping her arms around Carmen in a desperate hug. Carmen rubbed Della's back gently, comforting her sister while she sobbed.

Carmen looked over Della's shoulder at Mavis, who was calmly looking down at her hands, studying her fingernails. Mavis didn't look at anyone. Carmen opened her mouth to speak, then closed it again, deciding there really was nothing she could say. Mavis was . . . Mavis.

When Della finally released Carmen from her embrace, Carmen whispered, "Goodbye, Dell; goodbye, Mama." She waved bye to Max and left the dining room, moving slowly down the long hallway leading to the living room. The walls were lined with framed photos of herself and her siblings at various stages in their young lives. She stopped to look at a photo of herself wearing her high school cap and gown and standing between her parents. She stared at it, trying to remember if her mother had been happy that day. If she had ever been happy. Max and Della came down the hallway together, stopping beneath the photo with Carmen.

Maxwell spoke first. "I had no idea she blamed you," he said. "Mother needs to know the truth about that night." He rubbed Carmen's shoulder softly. "Do you want me to tell her?"

"What's that going to do?" Della asked fearfully. "When she realizes she'd been taking her anger out on the wrong DuPrè, it's going to kill her."

"She's already dead," Carmen replied sadly. "She just doesn't know it yet." Carmen said it like she knew exactly what it felt like to be Mavis.

Carmen, Della, and Maxwell sat together in the living room talking in hushed whispers, waiting for Eugene to arrive. Carmen had explained to her siblings in detail everything that had happened to her over the last few months. Neither of them could believe the part about Pedro—or Eugene either, for that matter.

"Who volunteers to help a complete stranger?" Maxwell said suspiciously. "That only happens in the movies."

Carmen smiled. "I gave up trying to understand that man a long time ago," she replied, referring to Pedro. "Sometimes I wonder if he's not from this planet. Eugene may not be one of us either," she joked.

Through the huge plate-glass window, Carmen watched as Eugene pulled up in his Explorer. She decided to circumvent any possibility of Mavis bringing her mean self out to the living room to torment him. She stood up, motioning for her siblings to follow her out to the curb to meet Eugene.

Maxwell extended a hand to him first. "Good to meet you. My sister has told us what a good friend you've been to her." Max's face held a pained expression. "We didn't know"—he couldn't bring himself to say the word—"about her condition. We're sorry we weren't there to help."

Della erupted into tears.

Eugene smiled softly and tilted his head slightly in a gesture that said he agreed—they should have been there. "Sometimes things happen the way they do for a reason, Max." He put his arm around Carmen protectively. "I consider myself lucky to be one of the friends she depends on."

Della wiped at her eyes, then exchanged looks with Max. "We can see the change in her. We've never seen her so"—she looked at Max again as if he might help her find the right word—"so peaceful," she finally added.

Carmen smiled. "I'm going into surgery on Tuesday," she reminded them. "Lindsey will be there. You two are welcome to come too, but don't bring Mavis. Please."

"What are we going to do about Mama?" Della complained sadly. She said it as if she believed something actually could be done.

"There is something you can do," Carmen announced confidently. "Pray." She saw a clear memory of herself sobbing her heart out at her father's grave and realized that prayer was exactly what Mavis needed. "Pray to God and then sic Daddy on her." *When it comes to sending help, Wilfred DuPrè does not play.*

⇒ 30 ⇐

A Faulty Distributor Hat

Carmen lay on her back in the darkness, drowning in a groggy soup of confusion. She ached to open her eyes, but her eyelids were lead weights she found impossible to lift. She wanted to cry out to someone to lift them for her, but could not remember where to find her voice. *I have no voice. I have no eyes. I have died,* she thought in a fog of panic. *I have died, and this dark nothingness is all there is.*

A tornado of jumbled thoughts whirled at the center of her semiconsciousness, competing to find a stable place to touch down in the confusion that was Carmen's murky memory. *Aggressive cancer cells. Should have come in sooner. Try to save as much of the breast as we can.* She sorted through the voices and images in her head, desperately trying to create from them a solid foundation upon which she might climb out of the terrifying darkness she had awakened to. In the black space behind her eyes she conjured up Eugene's comforting smile. Remembered him holding her hand tightly while the oncologist announced Carmen's treatment plan. *Tu no eres solo.* She heard Pedro's reassuring voice telling her that there were no coincidences in life—only miracles. And now, lying on her back on what had to be a hospital bed, Carmen slowly let the reality of what she had just been through sink in.

They've taken my breast.

It was then that the dull, aching weight that lay across her chest ballooned into searing pain—a block of hot cement that had suddenly plummeted onto her rib cage. She fought to open her eyes, but it was a useless battle. Instead she struggled to push a sound from her throat. She managed a raspy little "unh," hoping someone would be near enough to hear it. "Uhhhh," she repeated pitifully as the pain burned a crater into her chest.

Carmen heard the sound of approaching footsteps, then a woman's cheerful voice. "Miss DuPrè, are you back with us?" She felt the warmth of a hand gently squeezing her upper arm. "You've got to let me know if you're back, so I can get you something for that pain." The hand rubbed a few quick times against Carmen's arm. "Come on, Miss DuPrè, are you in there?"

This time Carmen's painful "unh" was met with a reassuring pat on her leg. "Okay, honey. I'm starting the IV drip now. Had to be sure you were up from the anesthesia, dear. Your vitals are excellent. You'll be feeling much better in five, four, three, two . . ."

Carmen conceded defeat in her struggle to regain con-
sciousness and welcomed the wave of numbness that rushed
in to wash away her pain.

There wasn't a space on the wall of Carmen's hospital room
that was not covered with a card or banner or poster saying
something about Carmen getting well. And this late in the
evening, almost twelve hours after Carmen's surgery, there
was little floor space in her private room that wasn't filled with
a person who had come to show her how much she was loved.
Lindsey, Pedro, Maxwell, Della, Yvette, and Eugene were all
crowded into the twelve-by-twelve space, anxious to let her
know that they were there for her—that they were pulling for
her to get better. Carmen could see in their eyes that they were
waiting for her to give them a sign. To let them all know that
she'd come through the surgery just fine. She motioned to Eugene that she wanted him to raise the head of her bed just a
little more.

"How's that?" Eugene hadn't moved it at all. He knew exactly what the doctor had said. Carmen wasn't allowed to sit
all the way upright until tomorrow.

Carmen scowled at Eugene and grunted, "Thanks." No
one in the room had spoken yet, so Carmen decided to end
their suspense. "What are you all looking at?" she growled in
mock anger. "Act like you've never seen a gorgeous woman
before." She felt anything but gorgeous, and God only knew
how she looked, but she wanted to give them something in return for all the love and support they had given her. The only
thing she had to offer at the moment was humor.

Pedro stepped forward first. He leaned over her bed and planted a kiss on her forehead. "How are you feeling?"

"How do I look?" she fired back.

"That good, huh?" He winked, then stepped back away from the bed.

Eugene promptly filled the open space.

"How long have you all been here?" Carmen asked.

"All day," Yvette offered, approaching Carmen's bed to kiss her cheek. She backed away to let Lindsey in. When everyone had taken turns planting a kiss on Carmen's face, Eugene smiled at Carmen mischievously. "I tried, but I couldn't get these people to leave."

"I think the man wants you all to himself, Carmen," Lindsey interjected. "He's been trying to talk us all into coming back tomorrow."

Carmen looked around the room, making eye contact with each of the loved ones who had come to support her. Everyone in the room had worn blue and white for the occasion.

"Eugene, have you been trying to bench my team?" she asked playfully.

Eugene glanced around the room nervously. "I . . ."

He pulled the only chair in the room over to Carmen's side and sat down on it.

"I just have something kind of personal I want to talk to you about, is all." Eugene looked nervous. "But there's no reason why I can't talk about it in this crowd."

He reached inside the pocket of his jacket and pulled out a small blue box. Carmen immediately recognized the Royalson's insignia. *Eugene and his gifts.* She scowled at him.

"Didn't you start enough drama with the last piece of jewelry you bought me, Eugene?"

He chuckled softly. "Carmen, I want you to know how much I've grown to love and cherish you over these last few months . . ."

"I love you too, Eugene." It came out of her mouth so effortlessly, no one listening could doubt it was true. *I love Eugene.* She marveled at how easy it had become to admit it to herself, and to him.

"I knew the first time I ever laid eyes on you that you were someone special." He smiled teasingly. "Maybe a little rough around the edges, but definitely special."

Carmen started putting two and two together. Jewelry box. Serious expression. Declarations of love. "What are you doing, Eugene?"

"The right thing, sweetheart." He opened the box to expose a shimmering solitaire—an outrageously huge diamond engagement ring. "I'm asking you to be my wife." He gazed at Carmen with absolute tenderness. "I'm asking you to be with me always."

Carmen couldn't breathe. Tears instantly flooded her eyes, but not for the reasons anyone in the room was likely to come up with. *Don't do this, Eugene,* she thought. She didn't want to hear what the man was saying. She did love him. She loved him enough to not do something as cruel to him as he was suggesting. She loved him enough not to burden him with the life he was blindly asking for. She wanted him to wait until he'd seen what the surgeons had done to her. She wanted him to understand what the chemo might have done to her

329

ovaries—to her hopes for having children. How could he possibly know what he was committing himself to?

"Will you, Carmen? Will you marry me?"

Carmen stopped fighting the tears, letting them drip slowly down her face. "I . . ." She tried to form the word "can't," but her mouth wouldn't cooperate. "I love you, Eugene," she said instead.

Eugene smiled broadly. He obviously misunderstood her. Before he could mistakenly interpret her proclamation of love as an answer to his question, she lifted her hand weakly and beckoned for Eugene to bend closer to her. He thought she wanted to kiss him, but she used her raised hand to turn his head to the side. "I can't," she whispered in his ear.

He leaned away from her and stared for a long, silent moment into her eyes. The hush in the room accentuated the low constant hum of the machine that monitored Carmen's heart.

"I know what you're doing, Carmen," Eugene accused her gently. "You think I don't know what I'm asking for." He looked around the room at the faces staring solemnly at him, then back at her. "I'm glad they took your breast, sweetheart."

Carmen's eyes widened in astonishment.

"I am, Carmen. If it means that you won't ever have to go through this again. If it means there's no chance of leaving a single cell of cancer to spread. If it means you'll be around to help me raise our kids . . ."

Fresh tears fell from Carmen's eyes.

"And I'm not saying they have to come from us," he added knowingly, addressing Carmen's fertility fears with the obvious solution—they could adopt children. "You know the surgeons are more than willing to put your breast back in whatever shape you want it to be in, sweetheart, but you don't need to do that for me." He gazed into her eyes with a look of tenderness she was sure no human being besides her had ever seen.

Carmen finally smiled.

Suddenly Eugene bent over her, kissing the area of her bedspread just above her missing breast.

"What are you doing, Eugene?"

"Without all that breast in the way, I can get that much closer to your heart."

Carmen laughed softly, then unexpectedly started to cry. "You are crazy, Eugene," she whispered tearfully.

"Crazy about you," he corrected her.

"I'd be a fool not to marry you, Layla." She glanced around the room at the happy but confused faces staring at her. She knew they had no idea what Carmen meant by calling Eugene by that name—that she was admitting that he was her destiny.

Eugene kissed Carmen's lips gently.

"Aren't you forgetting something?" Carmen whispered, nodding toward the Royalson's box and holding out her naked ring finger.

Eugene took the ring out of the box and slid it onto Carmen's finger. "I feel like the luckiest man in the world."

"You're lucky?" Carmen grinned. "I owe my entire life to a faulty distributor hat." She winked at Pedro. She knew the path toward happiness she was on began with Pedro. His decision to befriend a woman he had no reason to care about had saved her.

It was I who was in a battle for my life.

It occurred to her suddenly what Pedro had been trying to tell her that day he'd found her crying in the cemetery. *My son never needed saving. It was I who was in a battle for my life.* She knew now exactly what the words meant. Cancer wasn't the worst thing that could happen to her.

Pedro stepped toward the bed, placed a congratulatory hand on Eugene's shoulder, then bent over to kiss Carmen on her cheek. "Cap," he teased.

She looked at him questioningly.

"Distributor cap." He winked. "It was a faulty distributor *cap.*"

≷ 31 ≶

The Most Important Thing

Lindsey attached the last of the ivory glass beads to the ends of Carmen's braids and stood back to admire her handiwork. It was her suggestion that her sister consider cornrows, instead of a wig, to wear on her wedding day. Though Carmen's hair had grown to almost four inches in the six months that had passed, her hairstyle options were somewhat limited.

Carmen stared at her reflection in the mirror and marveled at the exquisite job her sister had done. "I look like royalty, sis," she whispered. Lindsey had created a finely tailored mass of tiny braided extensions that she'd swept into a French roll and accented with a few African cowrie shells and ivory glass beads. "Stunning," Carmen gushed. "Really, Linn. You've made me look like a queen." She added, "You know I never in a million years would have considered wearing my hair in braids before."

"Before what?" Lindsey asked.

"Before I got my distributor hat fixed," Carmen joked.

"I think it's time to get you in that dress," Lindsey suggested. "Yvette said she saw Pedro and Eugene out in the ballroom. The groom and his best man are already in their tuxes."

Where is my maid of honor? Yvette was supposed to be there to help Carmen into her gown. "Where is Vette?" Carmen asked nervously. Just as the question came out of her mouth, the knob on the locked dressing room door jiggled loudly. Lindsey let her in. Yvette rushed into the room, breathing heavily with a stricken expression on her face.

"Carmen," she huffed. "I think we have a problem." Her face said something terrible had happened.

Carmen's heart sank into the plush carpet beneath her feet. *Not on my wedding day.* She needed everything to be perfect. It was the only wedding she would ever have—of *that* she was absolutely sure—and she wanted it to be flawless. For her and for Eugene. He had gone to every possible extreme to make this day everything Carmen could dream of, and he'd spared no expense.

It was Eugene's idea to have the ceremony at Shutters on the Beach—a five-star hotel in Santa Monica with a huge ballroom overlooking the sea. Up until now, there hadn't been so much as a kernel of rice out of place. Even the January weather had decided to cooperate and grace them with a glorious day—the ocean sparkled deep blue under a sky of sparse, fluffy white clouds. Everything, at least everything up until this very moment, had fallen perfectly into place.

"What is it?" She held her breath, hoping she wasn't about to hear something terrible.

"Mavis is outside. She has an invitation in her hand. I don't know where she got one, but she is insisting on seeing you."

Lindsey grunted. "Where'd she get an invitation?"

Carmen smiled slyly. "I gave it to her."

Lindsey and Yvette traded bewildered looks. "When?" Lindsey asked. "And when were you going to tell me?"

"This morning." She apologized to Lindsey with her eyes. "I'm sorry I didn't tell you, Linn. I went over there this morning. It's hard to explain, but I had to see her."

"Well, whatever you said to her, I hope it was nice," Yvette warned. " 'Cause she's out in the foyer right now, demanding to be let in here with her daughters."

Lindsey looked angry. "I don't want her in here. I know she better not try to insult Kenny again." Lindsey scowled and pinned a couple of stray braids back into Carmen's twist. "That's all I have to say about it."

"She won't say a mean word to any of us," Carmen smiled knowingly. "Trust me."

Lindsey could see that Carmen had some information she needed to share. She stared her sister down and cocked an eyebrow. "What happened?"

"Mavis called me at six o'clock this morning," Carmen explained. "She said she'd had an awful dream about Daddy, and she needed to see me. She said she *had* to talk to me right away."

Lindsey and Yvette exchanged incredulous looks.

"Why didn't she call Della?" Lindsay asked.

Carmen shrugged. "All I know is when I got to the house she had been crying."

"Mavis is always crying about something," Lindsey said blandly. She was still angry at her mother, and hadn't set eyes on her in six months.

Carmen continued. "She said in the dream Daddy didn't speak to her at first, but she could tell he was really angry at her. She said she was so happy to see him and she tried to put her arms around him, but he disappeared and she was left clutching a pile of rotting clothes."

"Ouch," Yvette said. "That doesn't sound like a good dream."

"She said the next thing she knew, she was thrown like a sack of potatoes into an old wheelbarrow."

"Sounds like a good dream to me." Lindsey pursed her lips sarcastically.

"Daddy was pushing the wheelbarrow. She said he was pushing it so fast, she started to scream, and he suddenly let go."

"What happened?" Yvette asked, her eyes wide.

"Mavis tumbled out and fell in a heap against something hard."

"She told you all this?" Lindsey said doubtfully. "I cannot picture Mavis telling any kind of story where she didn't come out looking like a movie star and smelling like roses. Pitched out of a wheelbarrow on her ass?" Lindsey squinted suspiciously at Carmen. "Are you sure *you* didn't dream this?"

"Daddy was dumping dead flower petals on her head. She said there were thousands and thousands of decayed flower petals heaped all around her, and that's when she realized the hard thing she'd hit was Daddy's headstone. She said he was standing in front of it glaring at her. He never said a word, but just glared."

"No," Lindsey and Yvette said simultaneously.

"That's what she said. She said he had a crayon in his hand."

"A crayon?" Lindsey asked.

"Mm hmm. He used it to scratch her name off the headstone."

"No," Lindsey and Yvette said again, in unison.

"He exed out the word 'loving' first. He left 'wife and mother.' "

"And then he scratched her name out?" Yvette asked.

"Actually, he left 'Mavis' there. He scratched out the 'DuPrè.' "

"Ouch." Lindsey said it this time. "I would still be at home crying if I was her."

When the doorknob to Carmen's dressing room began turning slowly back and forth Lindsey flashed a doubtful look at Carmen, a look that said, *Are you sure you want to let that witch in here?* Carmen got up and walked over to the door. When she pulled it open, Mavis was standing there, dressed in a silver lamé gown, looking like she'd just come from the beauty parlor.

"Gorgeous dress," Carmen said matter-of-factly.

Mavis looked flustered. "I . . ." She spotted Lindsey across the room and settled her eyes on her for an uncomfortably silent few seconds. "I . . ." she began again. She reached into her handbag and pulled something out. She held what looked like a folded-up scarf out to Carmen without explanation.

Carmen took the bundle from Mavis, then slowly unfolded the edges of the scarf to reveal a pair of gorgeous sapphire earrings.

"Something blue," Mavis explained. "Della's begged me for them a hundred times, but I didn't ever want to part with them. They belonged to your great-grandmother. I wore them in my own wedding."

Carmen held the blue teardrops up to the light and watched them sparkle. "These are much too beautiful to part with, Mavis," she said softly. "Why don't we make this the something borrowed?"

Mavis turned and headed for the door. "They're just earrings, Carmen." She said it in that voice she used to use when they were kids. That two-plus-two-is-four voice. The one you didn't dare question. And then she was gone.

Carmen stood at the altar wearing a hand-beaded, curve-hugging, ivory silk and chiffon gown that fit so perfectly, it looked as if it had been sewn onto her. The fact that one of the breasts beneath the silken fabric was not her flesh but a form made of gel didn't detract from the gorgeousness of Carmen the slightest bit.

Eugene stood facing her, wearing a silk and satin tuxedo he'd had custom tailored to match her dress. *He looks like a prince,* she thought, taking in the sight of her man staring longingly at her. *My prince.* The depth of his love showed plainly in his eyes, and the look he sent her filled her heart like a mixture of helium and sunlight. She didn't try to suppress the broad smile that spread across her face.

For just the slightest of moments, Carmen felt as if she were in a dream, as if she were watching the minister perform the ceremony from somewhere up above the altar. When he asked her if she would take Eugene to be her husband, the sound of her own voice saying, "I do" rang in her ears like an angel's that seemed to echo in the rafters high above her head.

With the words "You may now kiss the bride," Eugene had taken her into his arms and pressed his lips softly against hers, and as she kissed him in return, Carmen began to cry. She held on to Eugene tightly, afraid to let go.

"Sweetheart, I think we're supposed to walk down that aisle and out the door now."

She didn't dare move. She needed to stay put in his arms. "Don't move," she whispered.

The room was filled with over three hundred guests, most of them Carmen and Eugene's students, all of whom were on their feet, applauding the kiss and waiting for the bride and groom to leave the altar.

"What is it, Carmen?" Eugene whispered into her ear. "What is it, sweetheart?"

Carmen couldn't tell Eugene the truth—that she suddenly felt paralyzed with fear. What if she couldn't do this? What if she turned out to be a terrible wife? What if she could only be a rotten mother as Mavis had been? Or what if she and Eugene loved and lost a child as Pedro and Ariselle had? What if her cancer came back and she got sick again, or Eugene died and left her alone as her father had? Carmen held on to Eugene tighter and cried harder.

"It's okay," he whispered calmly. "We can stand here as long as you want."

Carmen remembered the story Eugene had told her so many months before—about Majnun being chased by the watchman to his destiny. *It is not right that you should curse the watchman, for he is the angel of mercy who delivered my beloved to me.* She remembered Pedro's words to her in the Overland parking lot that first day, *Bad things sometimes happen to good people, but that's not always a bad thing. But what if the bad things just keep coming?* Carmen thought. *What if the adversity just never lets up? What do you do then?*

Pedro left his best man position beside Eugene and took a step toward Carmen. "Carmen," he whispered, "are you okay?"

She lifted her head from Eugene's chest just enough to shake her head no, then rested her face against him again. "Tell me something, Pedro," she muttered into Eugene's lapel, now damp with her tears.

"Yes?"

"You once told me that there was some important thing you do every day. One important thing."

Pedro's raised eyebrow said he thought Carmen had picked a fine time to reminisce. "Yes?"

"I need to know what it is," she whispered.

"You already know what it is, Carmen."

She raised her head and looked Pedro in the eye. "I *don't* know. I really don't have a clue."

Pedro smiled knowingly at Carmen. "Be happy."

"What?"

"That's it. That's the most important thing. No matter what happens, no matter what life sends your way, just try your best to be happy every day."

Carmen smiled serenely. She looked out over the crowd of expectant well-wishers, then turned to gaze into Eugene's eyes. "I can do that," she announced matter-of-factly, planting a soft kiss against Eugene's lips.

"*We* can do that, sweetheart," Eugene confirmed, dabbing gently at her tears with his handkerchief.

"Let's go, Layla," Carmen whispered playfully, grasping her husband's hand and turning toward the aisle leading to their future. "If that watchman is still behind me, I hope he's ready for one helluva race."